CW00351752

HOARD

Gary Clinton

MINERVA PRESS
ATLANTA LONDON SYDNEY

HOARD
Copyright © Gary Clinton 1999

ISBN 0 75410 896 1

First Published 1999 by
MINERVA PRESS
315–317 Regent Street
London W1R 7YB

Printed in Great Britain for Minerva Press

HOARD

*This book is dedicated, with all my love, to my father,
Samuel William Clinton, his wife, Basia,
my lovely Carol Jane, my twin brother, David,
Steve and Kay, Philip Carvey,
and to the memory of Duncan Crawford.*

What a piece of work is a man! How noble in reason! How infinite in faculties! In form and moving, how express and admirable! In action, how like an angel! In apprehension, how like a god! The beauty of the world! The paragon of animals! And yet, to me, what is this quintessence of dust? Man delights not me – no, nor woman neither, though by your smiling you seem to say so.

William Shakespeare

Chapter One

'You know, there are times, Harry, when I think you are a real tit.'

'Well, I reckon he's dead, and I think we should just leave him there. Look at his face: he's white as a ghost. Besides, it's none of our business.'

'His face isn't white, it's grey. He's always grey with a little bit of blue under the eyes – you know that. He's alive, I tell you.'

'Hollis, Hollis. For Christ's sake wake up, man, you're saturated. You're mad. You know you're mad. Everyone knows you're mad.'

Stan shook Hollis Woodhead furiously. Woodhead groaned and stirred in the long, wet grass that grew unattended in front of his shoddy twin-berth caravan home that he whimsically called 'The Womb'. Shading his eyes from the stark late afternoon light, he opened them to upside down faces murmuring above him.

'Ah, leave 'im where he is, Stan. I gotta go fishing.'

'Come on, let's try to lift him and get him into the caravan.'

The demise in the late seventies of his well-known, curiously named and moderately talented heavy metal band, had left lead vocalist, Hollis Woodhead, at something of a loose end. He had let the world of rock simply fall away from his life. He was happy to do so: it had sunk him into a breakdown that took over a year to struggle out of. But he was soon unable to rest on the withered laurels of his glorious ear-deafening, mind-blowing past, because the money he once had so much of had gone. Woodhead decided – in the throes of an extraordinary LSD flashback to embark upon a literary career and, after many years of damned hard work, dogged persistence and several million words, he had managed by middle age to carve out for himself in life practically nothing at all.

During those frustrating years, however, he had developed the burning urge to return to the high living of his earlier days, with its exotic travel, parties (the parties were something else) swimming pools and beaches, and the super women. He was inspired by his dream of fabulous wealth and a life of luxury as a tax exile. Up till now, though, he had survived on mainly liquid lunches, and anything he could scrounge or buy cheaply from the pub. The Womb had been his refuge, and place of work, for many of these last years, but now Woodhead saw deliverance from The Womb and squalid poverty.

'Is that you, Stan?'

Woodhead's face wrinkled under the strain of trying to focus his eyes.

'Stan, it's finished, it's finished! At last, it's finished!'

Woodhead's mind was hazy after privately celebrating for most of the day, and sleeping it off in the gentle warm rain that had fallen earlier. Woodhead felt no discomfort, though, because the reason for the celebration and the shining hope of his deliverance filled his mind.

'It's finished, Harry.'

'What's he talking about, Harry?'

'*Hoard*, Harry, *Hoard*!' broke in Woodhead loudly over Stan's bemused response. 'It's my book Harry. *Hoard* is my book, and it's going to make me rich.'

Although his lifestyle was shabby, and his mode of dress little better than a tramp's, Woodhead was university educated and bright. He had spent the last two years writing a book he was convinced would cajole a greedy public into 'shaking loose with the Shekels', as he always would say. A treasure hunt, but a special treasure hunt. *Hoard* was the means of the treasure hunt, but the special thing about it would be the prize. He had a plan about the prize. With these thoughts, Woodhead's mind suddenly sharpened.

'I gotta go.'

Without thanking his companions, Woodhead grabbed the coffee-stained draft of his completed *Hoard* from amongst the worthless junk that constituted one half of his worldly wealth, and leapt into his battered red Morgan, which constituted the other half of his worldly wealth, and departed.

★

Woodhead drove along the succession of narrow New Forest roads that led to his favourite watering hole, and the promise of a bath, The Green Boar at Stonebeggar. Ernest Clamp, Woodhead's only real friend, bought the pub with his pension from the Airforce, which he had left twenty-one years earlier as a grounded pilot. Since then, he had spent most of his time reading all the new stuff about military aeroplanes and flying, making model aeroplanes, drinking with the regulars and, of late, smoking a great variety of 'heavy stuff' with Woodhead. His special interest, though, was extraterrestrial life. Although he didn't believe in a God, a grand creator with life-rules and future promises for humankind, that life existed in myriad other forms – even invisible forms – was a given for Ernest Clamp. And why not UFOs? Why not? He had practised his own extrasensory communications, thought trans-missions into space at large. He would often stand on Moll

Hill, which rose up gently from the west side of the Green Boar, and speak to whoever in the Universe would listen.

Ernest saw all his pastimes as completely complementary: they were all a relaxing digression from the mundane world that Dora tried to create and sustain, and not, as she saw them a total waste of time. Occasionally, he was on 'special duties' that caused him to disappear for odd nights a few times a month. The talk in the pub was that he went to London to sample S and M and other extreme forms of sexual release, topics about which he delighted to expound vividly to his rustic patrons whom he said, knew only about what one could do to a sheep. He had no interest in running the pub – that was Dora's preserve – and she did it so well. It was her idea in the first place. She wanted to make it a trendy pub-restaurant, to serve an exclusive clientele, the town-and-country folk with whom she identified, the rich landowners who liked to hunt and shoot. Younger, she had had such a life and tried hard now to hold on to it. She still had her double-barrelled gun. This and a frequently foul temper were the two powers with which she occasionally reminded Ernest to stay in line. She had failed to realise at the outset that Stonebeggar was neither trendy nor exclusive, and that it and its environs were populated by only a couple of rich farmers and the salt-of-the-earth farmhands who worked for them.

Nevertheless, Dora ran The Green Boar with belief, energy and stark efficiency. She was in no way daunted by her incredible workload. Her dynamism was innate, a carry-over from her mother and grandmother before her who had, in turn, laboured similarly after marrying men of much the same calibre as Ernest. No doubt about it, with belief, energy, stark efficiency... and Mario. Dora was always pleased to have Mario around because he was 'so expert'.

Mario was from the city, had learned Italian cuisine in Milan, and English cooking and restaurant maintenance in London. He was so expert. Ernest resented Mario deeply. He was *so* expert. Ernest was never sure whether he should be jealous of Mario. He was not aware of any goings-on with Dora. Anyway, Dora was too old for him certainly. And what's more, his own relationship with Dora was so simple, it really didn't matter what Mario got up to. Dora was manager, chief cook, hostess and cleaning maid and probably had no time for other pursuits. Ernest was content: he lived with brow unfurrowed in the reassuring knowledge that Dora was competent. Moreover, The Green Boar had provided him with a veritable spring of liquid joy for over twenty-one years.

*

The Stonebeggar landsmen filled the pub early after a harvest day in the fields. Ernest did not do *real* work, so he liked to mix it socially with the these lads who laboured daily in heavy farming work.

He was attracted to the front window by the noise of spoked wheels crushing the pea-gravel on the drive.

'Ah, Hollis. Earlier than usual.'

'Hi, Ernest,' mouthed Woodhead silently to Ernest in the window. 'You're looking at a very happy man.'

'Have you been helping yourself to my home-grown again, Hollis?'

The police were not much in evidence in Stonebeggar, and Ernest found no difficulties in maintaining a veritable store of illegal substances. By now, both Ernest Clamp and Hollis Woodhead were expert users of all sorts of produce, and their private snorting, sniffing and pill-popping sessions, and long analytical discussions on the subject, had formed a lasting bond between them.

'Will you please take me seriously for a moment? I reckon I've got it made.'

'Got what made?'

'My future, Ernest.'

'Okay, tell me about it. It must be something bloody crooked if you've got anything to do with it, Hollis. Let's get a drink.'

★

'The culmination of two years work Ernie, baby.'

Woodhead beamed a smile through the raised glass of amber joy they affectionately called 'Dog's Tooth', a powerful beer brought in from the Midlands that was bread and butter to The Green Boar because of the way it attracted the farming machos.

'Two years in the darkness of The Womb. It's been a living hell, but I've finally got something that'll blow the lid off the market. Talking about blowing, have you got a roll, Ernest m'lad?'

When Woodhead outlined his story, it all sounded old-hat to Ernest.

'A treasure hunt story? I say, old chap, hasn't that been done before.'

Although he liked Woodhead, Ernest had little confidence that he could do anything creative that would be appreciated by the living masses.

'I can't tell you *all* about it yet,' said Woodhead, 'there are some details to go over in London, and I gotta get some agreements. And I gotta get cleaned up before I go. Any chance of a bath?'

'Of course, as always, Hollis, my dear chap. We're always pleased when you take a bath.'

★

'Off to London is he? Does that mean he might start paying us some money at last for all the Dog's Tooth he guzzles here?' snarled Dora.

'Don't start, sweetheart. He's in the bar. Say nothing that will upset him you know how sensitive he is.'

Ernest always thought of Woodhead as an insane crook, but his friendship for him was deep, and he protected him whenever he sensed the need, like now. Dora could never understand this close friendship, but Woodhead provided Ernest with intellectual stimulus in an intellectual desert. They also shared a thorough dislike of Dora.

*

'Okay, Hollis, your bath is ready. Dora has left the taps running so your bath should be pretty full by now. You look like you could do with a good scrub. I reckon they'll have to hose that headband off when you've popped your clogs.'

Woodhead wasn't normally concerned with physical cleanliness, but he had to impress real city people and they were always well-groomed and perfumed. Importantly, this very evening he would be in the company of a woman whose willing participation was essential to the success of all his careful planning.

*

'Oh God, I've drunk too much. I'd better get going. I keep forgetting, I've gotta drive to London this evening. Oh shit!'

With an act of self-control that astonished Ernest, Woodhead raised himself unsteadily to his feet and staggered upstairs where the horrific instruments of bodily hygiene awaited him. Visibility in the Clamp's bathroom was almost nil. He sunk himself gently into the hot water.

The joint he had shared with Ernest, the beer, the heavy atmosphere of the steam-filled bathroom, and the water so smooth from the washing-up liquid Dora had added to it, gave Woodhead a comfortable, swimming feeling. For Woodhead, a bath was an every-so-often event that needed to be done completely. Golden Girl Peachy Shine body shampoo not only had a float, which meant that he didn't need to search constantly under the water for it, but it didn't taste too bad either. He stood up in the bath totally covered in a superabundance of white foam.

'God, I smell like a Bordello,' he said.

Peering through the suds, he searched for hair conditioner.

'What the hell,' he mumbled, feeling about in the steam for a likely container.

He grabbed a bulky plastic tube, flicked back the lid and held it to his nose.

'Christ!'

Whatever it was he was sure it was not hair conditioner, so he dropped it to the floor and made another clumsy probe. His second attempt proved more promising and, after savouring the surprisingly pleasant aroma of the bottle's contents for a few moments, he coated his curly, long hair with it liberally. The agreeable bouquet Woodhead admired became immediately overpowering, and the once-smooth liquid became inseparable from his hair. He quickly ducked his head under the water in the certain knowledge that he had made a bad mistake. He feverishly rubbed at his scalp hoping to wash out the worst of the disaster but he made matters much worse, and to his horror the foul fluid started to congeal in his hair.

'Bugger, bugger!' he shouted.

He jumped out of the tub directly on to the full tube of liniment he had rejected earlier. It exploded with a bang and spurted pungent liquid all over his shed clothes. The combination of smells was too much for the foam-covered, stark naked Woodhead. He leapt through the bathroom door in a cloud of steam and vomited a spray of Dog's Tooth over the unfortunate Dora who had been drawn to the scene by the outrageous din. Horrified, Woodhead stood momentarily in stunned silence, then headed off as fast as he could in his shocked state, past the screaming Dora and into the bedroom.

'For Christ's sake, what's going on?'

Ernest immediately realised he had entered in on an excited drama that he would have done better to have missed. In the nausea brought on by the fearful smells, Dora grabbed Ernest's shoulders for support, and then threw up all over him.

*

The substance in Woodhead's hair rapidly attained the hardness of a crash helmet and the terrible fumes that emanated from it stung his eyes, making it exceedingly difficult for him to see for any more than a few seconds at a time. Fearing reprisals from the vengeful Dora Clamp, he wedged a chair under the handle of the bedroom door. No one in the bar shared the Clamp's thirst for revenge. Nor did they have any interest in the argument that raged upstairs between Ernest and his more than usually demented wife. They immediately grabbed the unexpected opportunity to help themselves to free beer. Woodhead was in utter panic. He could hear the fierce row of which he was the subject raging outside the bedroom. He turned cold when he heard Ernest plead with Dora.

'Come on, Sweetheart, put the gun down.'

Knowing Dora's predilection for armed violence, he dashed along the corridor to escape through the window.

'I'm going to kill that filthy little swine!' ranted Dora.

'Do you want me to do it for you, Dora?' Mario had no intention of instilling peace to the battle that raged. 'I'll get rid of both of them if you like.'

'Piss off, Mario,' snapped Ernest 'I've had e-fuckin-nough of you, bastard,' he said, and laid Mario out with one swipe of the pint glass he was carrying.

'Look, Dora, please put the gun down,' pleaded Ernest. 'He must've drunk the cellulose varnish I left in there this morning. I'm buggered if I know why, but he must've, can't you smell it?'

'Sodding model aeroplanes,' growled Dora. 'I'll teach you–'

Ernest didn't try to move as she brought the butt of her shotgun down on his collar bone. He collapsed uncon-scious to the floor. Dora, feeling much better for relieving her hot displeasure, went off to shower away the smelly, partly processed Dog's Tooth, leaving Ernest flat out on his back with his legs splayed, and Mario, only partly conscious, trying to raise himself from a curious praying position. Both were sadly unable to participate in the unsupervised drinking session that had moved into full swing at the bar.

★

Woodhead pulled a metal comb through his petrifying hair in a savage but vain attempt to give it some sort of shape. He managed to plough it forward but unhappily for him, by the time he'd accomplished that very painful process, the filaments were completely hardened, dry, shiny and quite impossible to comb back. The sickening crunch of wood on bone that had preceded a blood curdling scream from Ernest made him absolutely sure of his choice. He had to get out quickly. He dressed in the first things that came to hand: the oversize dinner suit that Ernest wore once a year to a Royal Air Force convention, and dress shoes into which he jumped sockless. He threw the matching bow-tie and cummerbund at the door in frustration and lunged at the window.

His chemically-created helmet afforded him surprising protection as he crashed through the glass in desperation. Moreover, in its hardened form the cellulose was less irritating to his eyes. Woodhead was terrified. He made a monkey-like descent through the prolific growth of ivy that covered the front of The Green Boar, and scrambled towards the ground. At first he gave little heed to the 'something' that he sensed fall past him in the dusk of evening and hit the gravel with a ripe pop.

Before Woodhead's violation of the ivy, it had enjoyed a comfortable symbiosis with the Clamp's ancient stone-walled dwelling. The wasp nest that plummeted past Woodhead also had had a symbiotic relationship with the ivy. But now it had just been deprived of this relationship in what was for the wasps a distressing and stirring event. Woodhead needed no explanation for the buzzing that sounded beneath him, and, with the thought that he might actually have died and gone to hell, he frantically struggled to re-climb the vine in a quest for safety.

If he'd had any doubts about his predicament they were quickly dispelled, along with any hope, as he fell backwards towards the ground, desperately grasping fistfuls of ivy. The wasps were quick to demonstrate retribution for losing their home. Unlike humans, who find it extremely difficult in the short term to arrive at a collective sense of outrage, the little striped stingers were immediately of one accord. They evacuated their broken home in a swarming and malevolent mass, and rounded on Woodhead. Despite the impact of his fall, Woodhead leapt to his feet at lightning speed and ran across the car park, energetically waving his arms and legs at the cloud of wasps that followed him. His baggy clothes had saved him from a potentially lethal stinging but he was, nevertheless, in considerable pain.

Finally, wasp-free and screaming a tirade of four letter words, he leapt into his Morgan – just as the gunshot rang out. Then another blast of the gun, and Woodhead's windscreen shattered. Covered in small cubes of glass, he sped off, showering a large group of fascinated Green Boar locals with gravel. The disappearance of Woodhead refocused attention on the free Dog's Tooth still available at the bar, and, with a resounding cheer, the rustics returned to the bar to manage the pumps for themselves.

Woodhead was seething. He had become filled with an uncontrollable desire to put as much distance as possible between himself and the suddenly violent village of Stonebeggar. He raced his Morgan along forest roads, negotiating treacherous bends at speed without flinching, and, despite that blasting wind through the empty frame of his windscreen, his rigid hair pointed faithfully in the same direction.

He was six miles out from Stonebeggar before his fury and fear had subsided and before he realised where he was. He pulled on to the verge and wept. He sat there until he regained a semblance of serenity. He put the car into gear, and tearfully drove back to The Womb to change into 'Woodhead' clothes.

'What can I do with this bloody hair?'

In the mirror Woodhead noticed for the first time the sinister, clean hole that extended from one side of his plastically fixed hair through to the other side, close to his forehead.

'Christ! Somebody's tried to kill me!' he said aloud. 'That fucking Dora.'

Woodhead then realised that Dora had a shotgun, and shotguns don't make clean holes.

'Christ, someone's tried to kill me!' he repeated.

He broke out into a cold sweat. His brain hummed with confusion. He tried to focus on his important goal. London beckoned immediately and he was on a mission.

Chapter Two

If the Lord had blessed Cynthia Flockhard-Flute with an amount of femininity and intelligence proportional to the amount of money bequeathed to her by her long-suffering and bitterly disappointed mother, she would indeed have been a very beautiful and intelligent woman. As it was, He had seen fit not to bother. Her fearsome, overpowering voice, her brittle hardness and crude approach to romance had left her without a lover, despite her incessant efforts to find a father for the heir she hoped would carry the family name into the future. Much of her driving and ruthless approach to business was born out of the frustration resulting from a lack of romantic fulfilment. She was, put simply, a very nasty piece of work.

'Frightful business, Jeremy, I've just heard. Such a talented boy too. Our best horror writer ever.'

Cynthia sighed one of her melodramatic sighs, and walked towards a window in the boardroom of Flute Publishing. Her dark-brown pinstripe suit attracted dust particles as she stood in a shaft of sunlight.

'Grindle's style had such an authenticity about it,' she said. 'What do you think he'll get?'

Jeremy Simms had been a major shareholder in Flute since the days of Cynthia's long-dead father Marcus. He was also the company's legal advisor. A retired barrister, Mr Simms enjoyed a position of considerable authority on the board. He had reservations about his relationship to the Flute empire, and these were mainly to do with the woman he now faced. Although far too professional to say so, he loathed her totally, not least because she bore a striking resemblance to the late Noel Coward, whom he had admired.

'Hopefully never out,' he replied, looking at his watch, 'not unless they can find someone else to sign the confession he rubbed his murderous little thumb prints on. And that's another thing: his mother did the writing, he just worked the chainsaw; the sod can't even read.'

'Well, we should put her under contract. She's got a great talent. I understand that the prison authorities encourage creativity in psychologically disturbed inmates.'

'Bloody good idea, but a bit late,' gasped Simms. 'She was the last thing Grindle put in the mincer before he gave himself up. Said to the police he didn't want to see another cottage pie as long as he lived.'

'Incredible isn't it, Jerry. Just when you think you know someone—'

'I'd best be going, Cynthia, the press will be expecting some sort of statement from us about this situation. We'd better be very careful how we handle them, his books will be worth a fortune to us now, and we don't have to give him a penny.'

'Don't worry about me, Jeremy,' Cynthia gurgled unpleasantly. 'My lips are sealed.'

Jeremy Simms left the building wishing he could seal the bitch's lips for ever. It was a great shame he hadn't known about Willy Grindle's cannibalism before the police. If he had, he would most certainly have encouraged a romance between Cynthia and the evil swine.

*

A crystal decanter sparkled seductively in a corner of the panelled room, and Cynthia, who was feeling the need for a bracing drink in the light of her company's most recent good fortune, was half way through her second double brandy before Jeremy Simms had reached the ground floor. By the time she'd emptied her third glass, she felt as though she were completely enveloped in soft, warm cotton wool. This comfortable mood drifted into melancholy, and as she scanned the manic gawks of her antecedents, those perched on the Flockhard-Flutes' family tree who were deemed illustrious enough to merit freezing in oil, she was suddenly shocked by her recurring and terrible realisation. If she remained childless, her infamous clan would go the way of the brontosaurus, and her portrait – she had wisely decided upon an abstract likeness – would be the last to grace the boardroom wall. She was now in panic at being childless – male childless.

It was with a sense of liberation that she eventually decided to listen to her instinctive inner voice. After slurring barely understandable instructions at Miss Rock, her long-suffering and underpaid secretary, Cynthia locked the door and fell asleep on a studded leather sofa. At peace with her meaningful baby-wise goal, she drifted into a dreamscape, searching her mind for the lucky father.

'Oh, Hollis,' she murmured, 'Hollis, you bwute.'

She had arranged to meet Woodhead later that night at The Jolly Hangman, a wine bar on King George Street in Greenwich.

*

Traffic was fairly light on the way into London – a good thing for Woodhead, whose face had been noticeably swollen by the truculent stabs of his tiny winged assailants, and not a bad thing for the motorists who were forced to avoid the wayward red Morgan and its deranged occupant. He had discovered that the throbbing lessened if he concentrated on something else, so he spent a good deal of the journey rolling and smoking cigarettes pregnant with strong tobacco. At seventy miles an hour this was a miracle of manufacture, and made possible only by applying steady pressure to the accelerator with his right foot and firmly manoeuvring the steering wheel with his knobbly knees. Although therapeutic in itself, this achievement was accompanied by ferocious teeth grinding and a virtually constant string of obscenities from other drivers.

He ran out of motorway at Sunbury-on-Thames, and sidled north east, as much as the roads would permit him until he reached Deptford. He had roughly an hour to kill before meeting the formidable Cynthia and felt the time would best be spent trying to calm his strained nerves, and cooling his swollen cheeks and forehead.

Woodhead drove around until he found a public toilet. He had lived in a fair measure of poverty and filth in his time, so he was quite oblivious to the weather-beaten and vandalised state of this Victorian pissoir. As he entered, the dank smell of stale urine hit his nostrils and reminded him momentarily of his caravan. Strange clanging noises emanated from the verdigris-covered copper piping. The dirty yellow walls were covered with obscene sexual suggestions, obviously written by badly illiterate sexual deviants. In one corner, several very large West Indian men were having a heated discussion with a uniformed police-man. Woodhead realised it was too late to back out: they'd all seen him come in.

When they caught sight of Woodhead, they suddenly lost interest in their previously intense debate. They watched in silence as Woodhead ambled to the mirror, doing his level best to appear cool. When he looked in the mirror and saw the extent of the swelling, he was so horrified that he forgot himself for a moment and let out a whimper.

'What's your problem, honkey? Hey you! You hear me, hamster?'

'Wasps! Fucking wasp stings!' screamed Woodhead, unable to contain his frustration, 'that's my problem. Satisfied? You jump into a nest of the little bastards, and see what you look like when you come out!'

Surprised into a grudging respect for Woodhead, who returned to his activities at the wash basin apparently untroubled by the threat of sudden death normally associated with sounding off at the local mafia, they whispered amongst themselves for a few moments and handed a wad of notes to the waiting PC.

'Not a penny more. Read my lips, pig, not a penny more. You tell them that, you understand?' said the muscle who had interrogated Woodhead moments before.

The young copper's ashen expression evidenced the message had been understood.

'Now get going.'

The hoods then turned their attention to Woodhead.

'Hey, what happened to your hair, mon?' said the muscle slapping Woodhead on the back. Woodhead, hands occupied, fell forward stiffly on to the point of his hardened hair, which prevented his face from hitting the wall.

'It's really wild de way it shoots up.'

'Look, I don't want to talk about it, if you don't mind,' said Woodhead, struggling silently to direct himself accurately against the porcelain.

'Hey, no problem, honkey, just stay loose and keep eway from de wasps.'

As soon as the man disappeared, Woodhead cursed everyone with a skin pigmentation other than his own to eternal agony. He stamped across to his car in a fiendish temper, and hopped behind the wheel.

★

An intercom sucked in the nasal monotone that Miss Rock hummed into its microphone, and spat it out into Cynthia's ears.

'It's five-thirty, Miss Flute. I'm leaving the office, and I'm leaving you to lock up.'

Miss Rock knew only too well that Cynthia would not be remotely capable of answering the intercom at the other end, and she used the advantage to make good her escape to her Friday yoga class.

'Bloody woman,' Cynthia cursed in a hoarse voice, 'telling me to lock up my own office. I'll show the bitch!'

But Miss Rock's victory was crowned when Cynthia fell from the sofa and landed heavily on the polished floor. Cynthia studied the ceiling for several minutes before remembering her arrangement with Hollis Woodhead and, inspired by the promise of romance, she staggered upstairs to the hospitality suite for black filter coffee and a series of hot and cold showers.

After punishing herself sufficiently for the excesses of the afternoon, she covered her nudity with an intricate arrangement of towels, sat by the coffee percolator with a box of chocolate liqueurs, and watched television. She was particularly fond of *Coronation Street*. She felt it kept her in touch with the proles. However, it was Liverpool rather than Manchester that proved to be the source of the most riveting television of the evening when *News at Ten* reported the public lynching of Simon Webster-Jones, the Conservative candidate for St Helens. Webster-Jones had apparently insisted on exercising his democratic right to walk the streets of his constituency despite the fact that most of the constituents were baying for his blood.

'Who said being overweight was bad for you?' Cynthia asked her television, before biting into the last of the liqueurs. 'If he'd been a skinny little runt he would have been dancing about on the end of that rope for hours. Most undignified.'

She switched off the television and went into the bedroom to change and it occurred to her then that life was filled with amusing coincidences. On the very night that a member of Parliament had got himself publicly topped, she had arranged to meet her beloved at The Jolly Hangman. She smiled contentedly and picked out a black velvet dress.

★

Woodhead was brooding over a bottle of wine in a shadowy corner of the wine bar when Cynthia arrived. She strode confidently to his table and kissed him on the cheek.

'Don't bother to get up, Hollis,' she said, grinning broadly.

Woodhead managed a smile, and gestured towards an empty chair. She sat down. 'It's great to see you, Cynthia. Been a little while since our last meet.'

Woodhead had become a polished liar over the years, and continued to spew flattery on automatic pilot for several minutes before being reminded that there was no need for that sort of thing when dealing with a Flockhard-Flute.

'Cut the bullshit, darling. I've got something you want, you know it and so do I, so let's not beat around the bush. Where's the ring?'

It wasn't like Cynthia to be so aggressive in Woodhead's company; he had a feeling that something nasty was brewing.

'What ring?'

'Our engagement ring, you silly boy. I've sensed the way things have been taking the two of us for some time. But you're so shy, Hollis,' she said, giggling ridiculously. 'If I left it to you you'd never get around to popping the question. I took the liberty of choosing the ring myself. Let's face facts, dumpling, neither of us is getting any younger.'

She produced a small square case from her purse, and handed it to him.

'Oh, I'm so happy, Hollis, I can almost hear the patter of tiny feet, can't you?'

She drummed the table with her long, black-glossed fingernails, and gazed at Woodhead in a way that brought to his mind a fleeting picture of insanity: a mindless smile from a dark corner of some middle age lunatic asylum.

'Patter of tiny feet?' asked Woodhead rhetorically. Rampaging bloody elephants more like it, he thought to himself.

Cynthia's tasteless sound effects became horribly amplified, and mixed madly with his own silent screams.

'I'm just going to get another bottle, Cynthia,' he said, somehow managing to conceal his revulsion.

She wanted marriage! She wanted to be a mother! Worse still, she wanted him to be the father!

Woodhead sneered and went to the bar. What could he do? If he wanted *Hoard* published, he'd have to go along with it. Yes, that's what he'd do. He'd go along with it, and pull out as soon as the book was in the shops. He could tell her that he wanted people to think *Hoard* had reached the shelves on its own merits, and not because he happened to be married to a Flockhard-Flute. How stupid he had been to imagine that his ability had got him on to Flute's list of authors.

Cynthia had put him under contract three years earlier as a writer and illustrator of children's stories. He had enjoyed the work thoroughly, thrilling the Flute editorial staff with such unusual titles as *The Dirty Raincoat Man* and *Hedgehog Eaters*. Cynthia had often commented – he had thought genuinely – on how innovative and rich his efforts in children's literature were.

'Darling Hollis,' Cynthia had said, 'as six year olds become increasingly sophisticated, we will be in a position to
publish a number of your stories. It's just that, well, at the
moment they're a little too radical, if you know what I
mean. But whatever you do, darling, don't feel in anyway
obligated to compromise your artistic integrity. I'll tell you
what we'll do. I think we'll take you out of children's
books, and put you into Adult Fiction. I'm sure you'll be a
big hit there. What we're looking for is something really
revolutionary.'

Woodhead recalled Cynthia's challenge with satisfaction.
Hoard was certainly 'revolutionary'. He gulped down a stiff
whiskey and went back to the publishing heiress with a
bottle of champagne and a renewed sense of confidence.

The remarkable power that he'd exercised over Cynthia
was nothing short of astonishing to Woodhead. They'd
been introduced some nineteen years earlier at a backstage
party given for his band, *Martian Wildlife*. Even as a teenager
she'd had a somewhat menacing and masculine appearance,
but when he'd discovered that she was immensely rich and
a passionate admirer of the Woodhead sound to boot, he'd
thought it sensible to overlook these shortcomings and
make every effort to capitalise on any opportunity her
'loving' relationship with him presented. Indeed, as it
transpired, Woodhead had consistently managed to escape
Cynthia's amorous clutches whilst screwing her for vast
sums of money. Now, finally, it seemed that time and
circumstances were catching up with him. He'd have to
play on what appeared to be Cynthia's desire for some sort
of respectability; a few well chosen words on the purity of
marriage would probably be enough. After all, she'd waited
years, what difference could a few months possibly make to
her now?

He put the bottle on the table and opened the little box
she had given him. He removed the ring, took Cynthia's

hand in his, and asked the question she'd been longing to hear.

'Will you marry me?'

'Of course I will, Hollis. You know I will.'

After a few minutes of manly hugging, Woodhead was released and allowed to open the champagne.

'By the way, Hollis, I almost forgot to say how handsome you look tonight. It's nice to see you with some colour in your cheeks for a change, and who did your hair? It's so you.'

Woodhead dodged the question with a shrug. The only thing he felt like talking about was his book – and the bitch had better love it or he'd strangle her with his bare hands.

'Now, what's this great secret that's kept you so busy?'

'Let's go back to your pad, Cynthia, I'll explain it to you there.'

'All right, Hollis, but no fooling around. I want our wedding day to be special.'

Woodhead couldn't believe his luck, and felt like saying, truthfully, that he wouldn't have dreamt of it. But after pondering on the brink for a moment or two, he decided that it might be an unwise move.

'If that's what's going to make you happy, Cynthia, then I suppose I'll have to be patient. But I respect you for it, I really do.'

They finished the champagne, and got a cab back to Cynthia's apartment in Kensington. Woodhead didn't really like the idea of leaving the Morgan, but Cynthia insisted.

'I wouldn't be seen dead in a car like that, Hollis.'

'No, you wouldn't,' he mumbled, 'you'd be locked in the boot.'

'Sorry, darling?' asked Cynthia, 'I didn't hear you.'

'Nothing, Cynthia.'

★

It was a long drive to Kensington, and made even longer for Woodhead by Cynthia's incessant chatter. They arrived at her apartment just after one in the morning. The hallway was dark, and Cynthia stiletto-spiked Woodhead's feet before she managed eventually to extend a bony finger and flick the switch.

'Let there be light,' she intoned drunkenly, and suddenly there was – a very great deal of light, far more than Woodhead's eyes could take in one go. He was very glad to escape into the softer illumination of the lounge.

'Make yourself at home, you little hunk. I'll go get us some coffee,' said Cynthia. 'How do you like it?'

'Black,' croaked Woodhead, cringing at the thought of being anybody's 'little hunk', Cynthia's little hunk especially.

'Well, what is it?' she asked when she finally came through with the coffee.

'What's what?'

'Your brainchild, silly. It must be something you believe in passionately, Hollis. I mean, to get you to come and see us yourself.'

She looked at her engagement ring and smiled.

'But whatever it is we're going to publish. From the look of the paintings, I'd say it was something pretty unusual.'

'Oh, you got them, then?'

'Yes, arrived yesterday.'

'What did you think?'

'Why, darling, they're beautiful; you're just so imaginative, my sweet. I'm afraid I only had a chance to look at them briefly when they came; we'd just discovered that one of our horror writers is a mass murderer.'

'Who?'

'Grindle.'

'Bloody hell, no wonder he was so good.'

'Quite.'

There was a slight pause while they both considered Mr Grindle.

'How did he do it?'

'Chainsaws and a meat mincer, I believe. He was a cannibal, you know.'

'No, I didn't know.'

'So was his mother. In fact, she was the one who wrote the stories. Of course, they were mainly autobiographical, but she was very good.'

'What happened to her?'

'He ate her.'

'What do you mean, he ate her? You can't eat your own mother.'

'Grindle did.'

Woodhead shuddered.

'I went out for a meal with him a couple of years ago. I could have ended up in the pot. It's bloody outrageous.'

'Let's forget about Grindle, darling, he won't be getting out again.'

'I should bloody well hope not.'

It wasn't often that Woodhead came across someone he could condemn as more despicable than himself, he was enjoying it.

'Come on, Hollis, what about this book of yours? I'm fascinated.'

'Well, to be honest, Cynthia, it was a conversation I had with you that generated the idea. You said you wanted something really different. I think your exact words were "something revolutionary". Well, I tell you, I've done it!'

Woodhead's pitch seemed to be having the desired effect on his prey. She was drunk, but definitely all ears.

'Go on, go on,' she gasped.

'The name of my book is–' He paused for dramatic effect and, as he did so, his eyes glazed in a sort of evangelical ecstasy – '*Hoard*.'

'Prostitutes?' Cynthia asked hopefully.

'No, not whores. Buried treasure! H-O-A-R-D.'

'Hasn't that sort of thing been done before?'

'Not the way I intend to go about it. Think, Cynthia, what motivates everyone these days? Money. Lots of lovely money. It's so simple, it's perfect; publish a book full of clues that lead the punter to buried treasure, a huge amount of money – a fortune. But set a time limit, and make the puzzle so bloody difficult that not even Einstein could piece it together in a thousand years. The bigger the prize the more books you sell. The point is that it has to be a huge amount of money and a very short time limit – just to be on the safe side. Let's say a year.'

'What will you bury? You're not going to bury cash, are you?'

'Of course not. I've already buried it.'

'What?'

'My grandfather nicked a casket of eight golden cones when he was in India. He was on some sort of business trip, tiger skins or something. He managed to hide the cones from his creditors when the family business folded. Well, my father was a bastard—'

'I'm sure he wasn't as bad as all that, Hollis,' Cynthia interjected.

'I mean he was illegitimate, Cynthia. The rest of the family disowned him, and he had to fend for himself. Anyway, he followed Gramps on the night he hid the cones, and, on the way back home, the old chap had a heart attack and died.'

'How awful for your father; a little boy all alone in the dark with a dead body.'

'Actually, dad was thirty at the time. As it was, he kept the cones, and when he died I inherited them. I thought they'd do for the treasure, and, at this moment, Cynthia, they're three feet under the ground in the original casket.'

'Where?'

'Well, obviously I can't tell you that. It's the whole point of the book.'

'That's just so romantic, Hollis.' Cynthia had sobered considerably and was beginning to see some real commercial sense in what Woodhead was saying. 'Have you got any photographs of the treasure?'

'No, I've only got the negatives, but I'd planned to get some prints on Monday.'

'Yes, do that, and in the meantime I'll arrange a meeting with Jeremy Simms for Monday afternoon. By the way, Hollis, how much money did you have in mind for the prize?'

'Before I tell you that, Cynthia, you must remember that this is absolutely watertight from your point of view. The only thing Flute stands to do is profit from this, and in the meantime the cash is in the bank making interest just like it would have done anyway.'

'Just tell me how much, Hollis. I love the idea, and besides, we could do with some good PR after what Willy Grindle's done for our image.'

'Two million.'

'Two million! Talk about shooting high so as not to miss the target, darling. Are you absolutely sure nobody can find it?'

'One hundred per cent.'

'Where's the *Hoard* manuscript?' she asked thoughtfully.

'I've brought it with me. It's right here,' said Woodhead.

'Okay, Hollis, we'll do it. You can stay in the hospitality suite above Flutes.' She went into the bedroom and came back with a door key and some money which she handed to him. 'I'll call you a cab. Oh, by the way, you'd better buy yourself some clothes, my boy, you're going to be in the news. You're going to meet the Schiki Micki. You know who I mean, the social set, the culture darlings in London who gather to intellectualise about art in all its forms, and drink champagne.'

Chapter Three

Woodhead didn't pay any attention to Saturday until it was almost over. When he opened his eyes, he saw from the digital clock at his bedside that it was nearly midnight. It was some ten minutes before he had pieced together the events of the previous day. During this less than incisive mental reconstruction, Woodhead staggered about in darkness looking for the bathroom. He was suffering from a headache that suggested some sort of cranial damage. He pulled the light cord and made a bleary-eyed inspection. Allowing for the natural puffiness of prolonged sleep, he could see that his face was not as swollen as it had been, but his hair was immovable – a solid, forward-pointing mass. His heart leapt when he fingered the single bullet hole that extended from one side of his sculptured headpiece to the other.

'Christ, that was bloody close!'

Perhaps Dora had other guns? And he had upset her badly. He decided to rest easy in the thought that a wrathful woman had tried to kill him.

'It's an old story,' he said to himself.

The hair presented an immediate problem. One way or another, he decided, it would have to change direction. He switched on some more lights and went about acquainting himself with his new surroundings. The drinks cabinet was about as familiar as he wanted to get once he'd found it, and he poured himself a large whiskey in honour of the beastly dog that had bitten him. The drink put a warm glow in his stomach, and settled him quickly. Satisfied that his own brand of medication was the best, he poured himself another, and went into the kitchen to find something to eat. To Woodhead's great relief there was a large cache of tinned food in the pantry.

It wasn't long before he was stirring his very own kind of hot-pot into a bubbling brew on the hi-tech hob. When he'd satisfied his hunger with the stew and a large French loaf, he lit a cigarette, got back into bed with a half-drunk bottle of Glenfiddich, and considered the various courses of action he could take against his wayward hair.

★

Whilst persons of a more hypocritical nature than himself – and he counted his wife amongst them – squirmed uncomfortably in Sunday morning pews during the strongest passages of carefully prepared religious sermons, Mr Jeremy Simms derived his spiritual fulfilment upon the verdant fairways and putting greens of Chorleywood Golf Club, where he was a senior member. He revelled in the sycophantic ineptitude of those junior members who competed amongst themselves for the dubious honour of losing to him in order to climb the rungs of the precarious social ladder he had climbed before many of them were born. They were wasting their time with Simms; he hated snivellers. On the other hand, he did not like to be beaten. He hated the few honest young men in the club who took delight in beating the shit out of him. A fatal mistake for anyone wishing to remain a popular member of the Chorleywood set.

It had been a pleasant Sunday morning's golf, a light breeze cooled Simms' face as he left the eighteenth and made for the clubhouse, having abandoned his ladder-climbing partner to search for an imaginary lost ball. A rainbow was visible in the fine mist of a sprinkler as the device rotated with a rhythmic click that lent order to the otherwise natural sounds of the birds and insects that chirped and hummed about him. Simms changed his shoes, and went inside for a drink.

'Your usual, Mr Simms?' asked Webster, the club steward.

'Yes please, Webster. Perhaps you'd be good enough to bring it out to me. I'll be on the veranda.'

'Of course, sir,' said Webster, reaching for a large cocktail shaker. 'By the way, sir, a Miss Flockhard-Flute telephoned and asked if you would be good enough to return her call. Shall I bring a telephone out to you as well?'

'Bloody woman!' cursed Simms, wearily raising his eyes to heaven. 'Is there absolutely no place on God's earth untouched by that malignant bitch? Very well, Webster, fetch the phone; but in future, if anyone calls me here, especially Miss Flute, I'm not bloody well available. Got it?'

'Got it, sir.'

Webster was a very practised servant. He'd made a healthy living at it for many years. He went inside to carry out his orders, without a shiny strand of black, Brylcreamed hair out of place. The po-faced steward glided on to the veranda a few minutes later and hovered over Simms, a telephone hanging on to the ends of the outstretched fingers of his left hand, and a filled cocktail glass balanced perfectly on a silver tray above the spread fingers of his right hand.

'Thank you, Webster,' said Simms, when he finally became aware of the ghostly figure at his side. 'That'll be all.'

'Very good, sir. Will you be having lunch in the club today?' asked Webster.

'That's a very good idea, Webster. I might need all the excuses I can get hold of not to see that bloody woman today.'

He picked up the receiver and dialled Cynthia's number.

'Cynthia? Jeremy Simms here. What can I do for you?'

'I'm terribly sorry to bother you at your club, Jerry, I know how important your Sundays are, but something really peachy's come up and I need to confirm your availability for tomorrow afternoon.'

'Is there anything you'd care to tell me about it now, Cynthia. I'd be happier if I knew what to expect.'

Simms was sick of the kind of surprises Cynthia delighted in springing on him, in particular the kind that had to do with money, as he strongly suspected this one might be.

'It really is better that you see for yourself. I'm sure you'll love it, Jeremy, it's just the most gorgeous PR idea we've had in centuries. Shall we say three o'clock tomorrow?'

'I'd rather we said four, if it's all the same to you. I've got a lot on tomorrow.'

'You're a darling, Jeremy, I'll see you at four. Ta ta till then.'

'Good afternoon, Cynthia.'

Simms replaced the receiver without experiencing the slightest twinge of curiosity. He was just relieved that whatever the mad woman had up her sleeve didn't require his immediate attention. He emptied his glass and summoned Webster to make him another cocktail.

*

Woodhead had worked hard through the night to return his hair to some state of normality. The dawn chorus had long become silent by the time he had ceased his experimentation with alcohol as a cellulose varnish solvent. Apart from a couple of small bald patches that he had torn away with a stiff wire brush, the gamble had paid off. At least his hair looked a little like hair again. He showered, threw on one of Cynthia's monogrammed dressing gowns, and grabbed a hairdryer from the bedroom. After an hour of careful coaxing with the machine, Woodhead's hair was alive with so much static it crackled audibly.

Grateful that the worst was over, he went back to bed. He woke again at eleven, and after taking a light breakfast, he showered and brushed his teeth. It occurred to him only afterwards how completely out of character this behaviour was. Perhaps, he mused, the opulent surroundings were exacting a weird psychological impact; but he quite enjoyed being clean and decided he might try it more often. He plastered his rioting hair with a gel to get it under control, put on a pair of Cynthia's Oxfords, and a pinstripe suit, and set out for Greenwich to pick up his beloved Morgan.

*

The jolly hangman painted on the sign outside the Greenwich wine bar, swung to and fro in his frame. Woodhead looked up at the sign and suddenly experienced a sinking feeling. Over the years, he had developed a spiritual oneness with some elements of the criminal class, and felt a certain revulsion from the thought that a man whose job it was to despatch others into eternal oblivion could be so happy. He suddenly appreciated the irony in Cynthia's choice of bar: the matrimonial noose was tightening around his neck. However, as he sat in his Morgan, and studied the laughing face across the street, he realised that he was laughing back at it. The early afternoon sun had warmed the leather upholstery of his beloved automobile, lending it a luxurious glow. He turned the key in the ignition and the engine started first time. One hour later, he was back at Thurloe Place, steering his car into the underground garage under Flutes.

Strangely, the main door was unlocked. Woodhead, who was by habit a very careful man in matters of security, found this rather unnerving. As he mounted the stairs, his highly polished shoes began to squeak increasingly, until the spacious stairway was filled with the noise of their conspicuous progress. Woodhead unlaced and removed his noisy, new footwear before continuing his search for human life. He reached the door to the hospitality suite, where he heard the muffled sound of a vacuum cleaner from within. He turned the door handle and entered.

The smell of air-freshener confirmed his suspicion, and dispelled his natural cowardice altogether. Cynthia had already told him – but he'd forgotten – that Mrs Bullick, the cleaning lady, tended to the apartment every Sunday afternoon. Woodhead breathed a sigh of relief as he stepped into the lounge and ambled over to the drinks cabinet. After the recent catalogue of disasters he had suffered, it made a refreshing change not to be entering into a place of violence; he had somehow found this impossible to avoid over the last few days. He was sure that brandy would make for a refreshing change too, and quickly swigged a quarter of a bottle before settling into a more methodical drinking rhythm.

As the afternoon wore on, the dull hum of Mrs Bullick's insatiable sucking machine advanced towards the lounge as surely as Woodhead was advancing into alcoholic oblivion. The empty bottle dropped from his hand and rolled away as he fell asleep in an easy chair in front of the television, snoring loudly. He was blissfully unaware that Mrs Bullick had delegated the domestic duties at Thurloe Place to her very young and attractive daughter, Olga, while she, Mrs Bullick, was in hospital recovering from a glandular operation, a recommended last resort against her obesity.

Unlike her mother, who, in her dead weight, anaesthetised state, the consultant surgeon had called Moby Dick,

Olga was a trim vision of loveliness and, naturally, the target of many male charmers. Olga's experiences with men had given her an extremely high opinion of herself, and a very low opinion of men in general, particularly drunken men, as she had quite often found in her experience men to be. This proved to be unfortunate for Woodhead. Disturbed from his afternoon nap by the closeness of Olga's foraging Hoover, Woodhead just managed to get to his feet before the violence began. This movement was a momentary gesture, and one made even more threatening to Olga by the misty, not-at-home look in his bloodshot eyes, and the friendly grin that looked to her positively wolfish.

'Rape! Rape!' she screamed, decking Woodhead with one ferocious swing of the cleaning tube and its heavy attachment.

'Fuck,' moaned Woodhead, immediately wishing he'd expressed himself with less vigour.

'Take that you filthy little pervert!'

Olga growled, and buried the front of her right foot into Woodhead's crotch. He fainted without saying another word.

'What on earth do you think you're doing?' Cynthia squawked at the demented Miss Bullick who was about to finish Woodhead off with a kick to the head. 'This man is my guest.'

'My gawd! I'm sorry, Miss Flute. Mum's in hospital at the moment and she asked me to fill in for her. She said the place would be empty. When I saw him, I thought he was a burglar or something. He was ever so threatening, and he was drunk.'

'Well, I'm sure Mr Woodhead had absolutely no intention of frightening you, Olga,' said Cynthia, reaching into her handbag for a couple of fifties.

Olga took them.

'I don't know, Miss Flute, he was very aggressive. He had a funny look to him and he was snarling at me.'

Cynthia forked out another fifty.

'Thanks, Miss Flute. I'll be off, then, unless you need anything else?'

'That'll be all thank you, Olga. Just give my regards to your mum, and tell her I hope she gets well soon.'

Olga beamed back her gratitude and, with a sour look at Woodhead, she switched off the vacuum cleaner, and disentangled the tube from around his neck.

'Mum'll be back next week. Cheerio, Miss Flute.'

Cynthia smiled weakly. She wasn't keen on lovely, lively young females; they reminded her too painfully of her own shortcomings. But there was no time for self-pity; her man needed her, and very probably needed a competent medic into the bargain. She dragged him feet first into the bedroom where he had already spent the majority of his stay, and put him on to the bed.

Undressed, Woodhead was not an attractive sight. Neither was Cynthia for that matter, but then both of them looked pretty dreadful when they were fully clad. Cynthia comforted herself in the knowledge that there was a great deal more to a relationship between a man and a woman than sex, and, although she wasn't exactly sure what that something else might be, she was certain that babies had a significant role to play in the structure of things. She tucked Woodhead firmly into bed and made him an ice pack. Satisfied that he would survive, she closed the bedroom door and went into the lounge to watch *Coronation Street*.

★

Woodhead jolted into consciousness. Cynthia's improvised ice pack had melted, presenting him with a translucent and most peculiar view of his dim surroundings. He screamed in shock utterly convinced that whatever was on his face was alive and trying to suffocate him. He frantically jerked the ice pack away. Suddenly he had an arm free, then a leg. He rushed for the door, and very nearly wrenched the thing off its hinges in his hurry to get the other side of it. Cynthia swung round at the noise and caught sight of Woodhead in his underpants, as white as a ghost, and quivering like a jelly.

'What's wrong, Hollis, what's happened?' Cynthia demanded.

'Cold,' Woodhead gasped, 'cold and wu wu wu wet–'

He staggered into the kitchen and grabbed a carving knife. It was perfectly obvious, even to Cynthia, that the man had completely lost his head. She locked herself in the bathroom whilst Woodhead, who was stark white with terror, went back into the bedroom to deal with the 'thing'. It didn't take long for him to snap out of his dreamy state of mind when he identified the source of his consternation. He stood in silent embarrassment thinking vengeful thoughts about water filled polythene bags and aggressive cleaning ladies. He got dressed, and sheepishly knocked on the bathroom door.

'Cynthia, are you all right?'

'What the bloody hell do you mean, am I all right? It wasn't me who was jumping about in the raw with a carving knife. What the fuck's got into you, that's what I'd like to know?'

'I had a bad dream.'

'Oh, well that makes all the difference in the world, doesn't it? I'll just come out now so you can stab me to death.'

'Don't be like that. Look, I'm really sorry, honestly I am I've had a bad day, that's all. That woman nearly killed me this afternoon.'

'I suppose you were having a nightmare when you freaked her out. I had to pay off the silly little bitch to keep her mouth shut. The public will be saying Flutes only employ homicidal maniacs the way things are going at the moment. Perhaps you'd like to team up with Willy Grindle; you could make pies for British Rail.'

Cynthia opened the door and took a peek at Woodhead. 'See,' he said, 'I'm all right.'

Cynthia wasn't altogether sure about that but she was prepared to give him the benefit of the doubt; after all, she was in love. She gave Woodhead a cuddle and directed him to a large comfortable-looking chair, and then went to make some coffee for them both. The hot coffee tasted good, and Woodhead sat alternating between slurps of the dark elixir and heavy drags on a clumsily-made roll-up, while Cynthia explained the plan of action for the Monday meeting with Simms.

'Trust me, Hollis, you mustn't worry about Jeremy. I'm sure he'll love *Hoard*, it's a great idea.'

'What happens if he doesn't like it, Cynthia? What if he advises you against the whole thing?'

'He won't do that, Hollis. Besides, even if he did we'd still go ahead; it's my money, not his.'

'In that case, why do we have to meet with him at all?'

'Good boardroom strategy, silly. Anyway, he's just about the best legal counsel in London. With him on our side we don't make any silly mistakes, darling.'

Cynthia swamped Woodhead with one of her deep and meaningful stares. Woodhead took a long and meaningful drag on his roll-up.

No, you're right... er, darling, we wouldn't want to make any mistakes. What time's this meeting tomorrow.

'Four o'clock, and that's just as well really. It gives us a chance to get your image sorted out. Not that I'm saying I don't like the way you look – and you've done great things with your hair. We just need to make you a little more Bohemian. We've got to sell you to the public just as much as we sell your book.'

'Sounds great to me, Cynthia. Who's going to handle the publicity?'

'Simply the best people available: Sellers and Stone. We just turn it over to them, and they'll get us everything we need: prime-time TV, radio, newspapers, the whole smash. They'll even set up our *Hoard* web-site. Sellers and Stone are very, very good. They did all the work for the PM at the last general election.'

'If they got that bastard into power then they must be very good.'

'Why, Holly, I never realised you were interested in politics.'

'You'd probably find my views on politics a little too extreme for your taste, Cynthia.'

'All right then, what's so wrong with the present government? After all, they've crushed the unions and given all the money back to the rich. People know their place in society again. I think that's really healthy. At least we don't pretend anymore.'

'They're not radical enough,' fumed Woodhead, irritated by Cynthia's rose-coloured perception of Great Britain.

His own idea of a green and pleasant land owed much to a man who'd kicked the bucket in a Berlin bunker.

'What about all the darkies then?'

'Really,' gasped Cynthia, overdoing her mock dismay at Woodhead's rampant racism. 'That isn't worthy of you, Hollis, you're meant to be an artist.'

'I am an artist, Cynthia, and what's more I've lived in a caravan for more years than I'd care to remember, while half the population of Pakistan fly over here and drive about in BMWs all day.'

'Mercedes, dear, Mercedes. Indians and Arabs drive about in BMWs. Pakistanis generally prefer a more conservative profile.'

'Very funny, Cynthia, you wait until one of the swines gets into power.'

'Well, what would you suggest?'

'Well, you might start by reading *Mein Kampf*?'

'All I can say, Hollis, darling, is whatever you do, don't say any of this in public, or they'll be buying your book just so they can burn it – and that's not all they'll want to burn.'

'Look, why don't we forget politics, Cynthia? To tell you the truth, it just makes me irritable. Let's go out for a meal or something.'

'Okay, where would you like to go? I assume curry is out of the question? What about Chinese? Got anything against them?'

Woodhead decided that it was hopeless to engage Cynthia in political debate. He was very hungry and anything would do.

'Okay, let's eat Chinese, Cynthia.'

'Hollis, dear, the Glass Dragon in Egerton Crescent has the best Peking duck and a super selection of wine.'

'I can't wait.'

Chapter Four

Monday morning was a draining experience for the author of *Hoard*. His shopping spree with Cynthia ended abruptly when one closet queen too many asked him for his inside leg measurement. The manager of the gentlemen's outfitters assured Woodhead in no uncertain terms that Julio, his boyfriend and general assistant, didn't want to eat the tape measure, and that if Woodhead didn't take it out of Julio's mouth immediately, he'd call the police. Cynthia had been quick to practise the usual form of cheque book diplomacy on the victim, who'd recovered faster than an injured Italian footballer. She didn't mind in the least; she'd had tremendous fun creating the new Woodhead image. That the object of her artistic flair had been so stubborn and unreasonable only added to the sense of achievement she felt as she watched him totter to the taxi sartorially reborn and heavily laden with boxes.

'You know Hollis, you look really–' she clenched her fists and drew in her shoulders, then released all this energy by throwing out her arms to deliver the chosen words powerfully, '– so Picobello!'

'Isn't that a stomach disease? Cynthia, do I look as bad as that sounds?'

As far as Woodhead was concerned the only pleasant mission of the morning had been collecting the prints of the *Hoard* treasure paintings. They were perfect. The golden cones glinted mysteriously from amongst the bonanza of colourful flowers and flint stones of Ernest

Clamp's rockery and, for a moment, Woodhead was back in Stonebeggar sampling Dog's Tooth at The Green Boar. But only for a moment.

*

A Victorian carriage clock filled the still air of the board-room with its resonant chimes, and filled Woodhead with a sense of self-importance. It was four o'clock and he could hear Cynthia muttering to someone just outside the door.

'Genius, Jeremy, untapped genius. Willy Grindle will be yesterday's news the second we launch this product.'

'If you don't mind, Cynthia, I'd like to reserve my judgement until I know what you're actually talking about.'

'Of course, darling, of course, just come this way.'

Simms reluctantly followed Cynthia into the board-room, doing his best to smile pleasantly at the woman he had learned to loathe above all others. The strange collection of prints that confronted him were not nearly as unusual as the man who sat beside them.

'Jeremy,' said Cynthia, 'I'd like you to meet Mr Hollis Woodhead, author of *Hoard*, the book that's going to take the nation by storm.'

Simms wiped beads of perspiration from his brow with a silk handkerchief, and sat down.

'Pleasure to meet you Mr Woodhead,' lied Simms politely. 'Perhaps you could explain a little about your work; it certainly looks very interesting. Unfortunately, Miss Flute has kept me completely in the dark until now.'

Woodhead remained seated and silent under a large Panama hat. Simms shifted uneasily in his chair. Woodhead got to his feet brandishing a copy of the *Hoard* manuscript and a short explanation that Miss Rock had typed during her lunch break.

He handed it to Simms and sat down again without saying a word. Simms looked at Cynthia and sighed; he had had a perfectly good day until he walked into the Flute boardroom.

'I hope you don't mind, Jerry,' said Cynthia. 'Mr Woodhead's in one of his non-communicative moods.'

'Really?' Simms replied. 'I really didn't notice.'

Woodhead glared at Simms from beneath his hat. He looked a little agitated.

'I need a few hours to go through this stuff,' said Simms, and he withdrew to Cynthia's library.

Four hours later the Flute director had finished his reading and was deeply engrossed in Woodhead's surreal paintings. He had to concede that the peculiar Mr Woodhead had talent, and the more he thought about the idea of a national treasure hunt the more he liked it. Two million pounds was a lot of money, but nothing in comparison to the millions Flute would make as the adventurous publishers of the book. Provided *Hoard* was marketed properly, and he would make sure it was, they could rake in millions. Every man, woman and child in the land would get gold fever, shares in Flute would go through the roof, and Simms could sell his seat on the board to the highest bidder. What utter bliss: to be rid of that Flockhard-Flute bitch once and for all! He could spend the rest of his life in California, sipping cocktails and bedding pretty young females.

'Mr Woodhead,' said Simms finally, 'you have appealed to the most loathsome facet of human nature: good old fashioned greed. And I can tell you from personal experience that there is no stronger motivation.'

'Bravo!' exclaimed the diabolical Cynthia. 'Bravo!'

'Not at all, Cynthia,' said Simms, lightly mopping his forehead for the umpteenth time that afternoon. 'Of course, our editorial staff will need to work on it a bit to raise it to a higher level of literary polish, but basically it's very good. Congratulations, Mr Woodhead. I'm quite sure you've struck the mother load with this one.'

'To the mother load,' said Woodhead, breaking his silence and raising a well-filled glass of brandy.

'Exactly, Mr Woodhead,' said Simms, pouring himself a less impetuous measure, and a much larger one for Cynthia. 'To the mother load.'

'To the mother load,' Cynthia squealed excitedly. She winked at Woodhead and wistfully thought of babies. A musical clink of brandy glasses rang out in agreement.

'I'll draw up a contract this evening Cynthia,' said Simms. 'Mr Woodhead can sign it tomorrow morning, and we'll have the first edition of *Hoard* in the warehouse by the end of the month. Shall we say one hundred thousand copies as an initial run?'

'Fine.'

'We will certainly need to open a *Hoard* home page on the World Wide Web, and establish an e-mail address too – to give people the opportunity to claim over the net,' put in Cynthia, making a big thing of declaring her knowledge of modern communication methods.

'Good idea, Cynthia, that will help spread the interest fantastically,' said Simms annoyed with himself momentarily for commending the hated Cynthia.

'That's something the editorial team below can monitor.'

The thought of providing a special, additional and costly resource to do this work was anathema to Cynthia's business sense.

'I take it we can leave Mr Woodhead to advise our printers on the layout of the book,' Simms continued. 'After all, he's the only one who understands his puzzle; and frankly, having read the manuscript and seen the paintings, I dare say he's the only one who ever will.'

'My sentiments exactly,' said Woodhead. 'By the way, Cynthia, my finances are a little strained at the moment. To be absolutely honest with you, I was rather hoping for an advance.'

'How terribly insensitive of me, darling. Of course you can have an advance. Would you be dreadfully disappointed if I were to suggest five thousand?'

'No, not dreadfully,' said Woodhead, trying a dispassionate tone.

'I'm afraid I have to consider the feelings of our other authors, Hollis; there'd be the most awful fuss if you got any more for a first book.'

'Well, as Mr Woodhead is happy with that offer I think we can consider the matter closed,' said Simms. 'I'll get everything ready for tomorrow morning as agreed.'

'Until tomorrow, then,' said Woodhead, offering a nicotine-stained hand.

'Indeed Mr Woodhead, indeed,' said Simms. 'I shall be here at ten.'

He wished Cynthia a pleasant evening, about turned, and left the room with a purposeful step. The sooner *Hoard* was available to the public, the quicker he could wash his hands of the hideous creature who owned it.

*

As the weeks passed, the enormous promotional extravaganza considered essential to the success of *Hoard* gathered momentum. Woodhead was driven from interview to interview – and he enjoyed the unusual billboard spectacle of his mysterious new image challenging the public to search for the *Hoard* treasure.

'Hollis, my darling,' Cynthia said excitedly, 'another TV appearance for you tonight. Timing's perfect for the launch tomorrow.'

52

Woodhead possessed a large measure of megalomania, and bristled at the prospect of being in front of the camera again.

'Great for me, great for the book,' he responded majestically. 'Let's go.'

The TV station was an impressive glass and marble hexagon that would have scared the life out of lesser mortals; not so the fearless Woodhead. He could not wait to get in there.

'Right, Mr Woodhead, come this way and we'll get you ready for the show,' ordered a squeaky voice in the busy studio corridor. 'I suppose you must be getting quite used to this treatment by now,' the voice continued as they marched to 'Make Up'.

'I'm always happy to oblige my public, mate,' said Woodhead arrogantly.

A few minutes later, he was led on to the stage of Studio Four to rapturous applause but was rather surprised to discover that he was in the middle of a live prime-time debate on the 'alarming decline in church attendance, and the difficulties faced by practising homosexual clergymen'. It seemed an entirely inappropriate subject for the author of a treasure hunt book, but he thought he might as well make the most of it. Unaware that his fellow guests were more than well acquainted with both problems, Woodhead suggested castration as the only sensible solution. An angry murmur filled the auditorium, and a man wearing a large pair of headphones came forward and whispered in Woodhead's ear.

'Why didn't someone tell me I was on the wrong set?' squawked Woodhead. 'Do I look like an arse bandit to you?'

'Mr Woodhead,' said the director, when he'd pacified the irate author enough to get a word in, 'this show has been sponsored by a gay organisation, and most of them are in the audience. Your sexuality is not an issue at the moment, but if you don't get off of this set, it will be.'

'What do you mean?' hissed Woodhead. 'I was voicing my opinion. It's a free country, and I can say whatever I like.'

'What I mean, airhead, is I'll be very surprised, after your little speech, if they don't try to castrate you and the whole fucking production team into the bar–'

There were muffled pleas for a commercial break as a roving camera swung out of control under the considerable strain of its new occupant, a lesbian bus driver and born-again Christian from Bradford. She used her improvised weapon to good effect on the director, two stage hands and several of her fellow marauders, as she flew away from the stage and out into the gallery before being catapulted into the ultimate journey via a plate-glass window in the upstairs bar. A security guard plunged the studio into darkness in an attempt to avert total war. The camera, considerably lighter now that it had shed its heavy female burden, furiously bucked and rotated about the studio in an unprecedented orgy of destruction. People who had been screaming abuse at Woodhead only moments before, fled for their lives, whilst the target of their initial dissatisfaction relished their plight from the safety of a portable scaffold. The carnage ended as abruptly as it had started when the wheeling demon camera keeled over, finishing off the host of the show in a spectacular display of electric fireworks as he rummaged in the darkness for his dentures.

Woodhead gave little thought to the groans of the dying and injured; it was every man for himself as far as he was concerned. He climbed down from the scaffold and sneaked out of an emergency exit, carelessly treading on screaming faces as he made his escape. Police and ambulance sirens whined in the summer night air as Woodhead climbed into his Morgan and drove back to Thurloe Place.

54

Cynthia met him outside her home. She had witnessed the televised homosexual riot in amazed silence as she calculated the amount of free publicity this new sensation would give *Hoard*.

'Hollis, my darling, you were incredible!' Cynthia hugged Woodhead's scrawny frame until his face reddened breathlessly. 'With the book signing and the national launch tomorrow, things couldn't be better. Come in and get changed; we're going out to celebrate.'

'I can certainly claim to be a little bit elevated by that experience,' he boasted.

'It's good sometimes, Hollis, to go around with your feet just a little off the ground.'

Woodhead disguised his now well-known face, and took Cynthia out with the express intention of getting very drunk.

★

Jeremy Simms sucked on a long Havana cigar with an air of deep satisfaction as he sat in his XJS watching an angry crowd of gay rights campaigners being dragged from Harrods's by the police. The First of July had arrived. Somewhere inside the great store, Woodhead was busily signing copies of *Hoard*, shaking hands with awestruck punters, and giving interviews to news programmes and the national press. Woodhead was a star; the tabloids had already seen to that in the morning.

Simms took another puff on his Havana and chuckled. He was studying a picture of Flute's great white hope on the front page of the *News Of The World*. Woodhead had been snapped clambering up a steel pole to escape the murderous clutches of the director who, still wearing the headphones that had saved him from death, was clearly unwilling to release his hold on Woodhead's shoe until he had bitten through the leather. The headline with the picture bore evidence of the outrage and chaos that Woodhead had created: 'GIVE CHOP TO PERVERTS' SAYS WOODHEAD, AS LESBIAN KILLS TEN WITH CAMERA'. *Hoard* was going to be gigantic, Simms had absolutely no doubt about that now.

Chapter Five

Professor Benjamin Kahn, Head of Eastern Philosophy and Comparative Religion at Manchester University, was not a man easily given over to rage, but the threshold of his mildness was overwhelmed when the garden sundial he was relocating for his mother slipped from his hands and fell heavily on his foot.

'I don't want it there!' she nagged insensitively from the kitchen window.

'Oh, shut up, you poisonous old bag!' he screamed, 'or I'll have you put to sleep.'

'You're not putting me in a home,' said his mother, turning up her hearing aid, 'I'll call the police.'

Kahn waved an insulting finger at her and rolled about the unkempt garden in agony.

'You're not a man, you're a big baby. Can't even move a little sundial.'

She turned down her hearing aid and shoved a spiteful fork into the vindaloo she was eating. Visions of matricide and geriatric acid-baths flashed before Kahn's bulging eyes as he crawled towards the conservatory, foaming at the mouth and praying for a good anaesthetist. His progress was hampered by the distracting level of pain, against which he gritted his teeth and closed his eyes. Too bad, for the stinging nettles he crawled into added ferociously to his anguish. Too bad also that he was wearing only shorts and plimsolls. Then came the final straw.

'You take after your uncle Rangeede,' his mother chided loudly, as she watched his antics with a malign interest, 'he was as mad as a march hare too.'

Snarling dementedly, Kahn staggered up the garden path determined to inflict grievous bodily harm on the old woman at the very least. Sensing her son's resolve, she fled into the garden, making a stand on the compost heap.

'Just try it, egghead,' she screamed, threatening him with her walking stick, 'and I'll put a crack in your shell you'll never forget!'

Kahn stopped in his tracks. As much as he loathed his mother's constant nagging and evil inclinations, she was his mother. She was also old and frail. The bitch could not last much longer anyway, and he had no intention of going to prison by speeding up the inevitable. Besides, as he watched her sway about unsteadily on a mound of potato peelings, he began to regret his lack of self control.

'I'm sorry, Mother,' he said meekly, 'please come down from there, it's very dangerous; you could fall and hurt yourself.'

'Rubbish!' she snorted defiantly. 'You're just like your father; full of crap. No wonder your fancy wife left you.'

'There's no need to be offensive.'

'As I have to live with a moron like you it's hardly surprising that I am is it?' rasped the venomous crone.

She raised her walking stick and took a savage swing at her son that caught him on the bridge of the nose. Not completely satisfied with her first attempt, she climbed down from the compost heap and hit Kahn on the back of the neck, sending his turban high into the air.

'Moron!' she reiterated, her voice thick with hate. 'You make me sick.'

She prodded him maliciously in the ear before creaking
back to her meal in the kitchen.

★

'Are you all right, love?' asked the receptionist when Kahn
checked into the hospital.

'What do you think?' he snapped, through a nose full of
congealed blood.

She put her head to one side and scrutinised him with a
thinly disguised dislike.

'Name?'

'Kahn. Professor Benjamin Kahn.'

'What happened to you?'

'I dropped a sundial on my foot, then I fell over and hit
my nose on the garden wall. Would you mind if I sat down
now, I'm feeling rather delicate.'

'I'm sorry, Mr Kahn,' said the receptionist with sadistic
delight. 'You can't receive any treatment until you've given
us your details; hospital regulations.'

'How do you deal with advanced blood loss? Wait for
the poor sods to come round so you can throw the book at
them?'

'Do you want to be treated or not?'

'I wouldn't be here if I didn't want treatment, would I?'

'Right then, let's fill in the form together, shall we?'

Kahn decided to cooperate. His big toe was on fire, and
his badly swollen eyes gave him the feeling that he was
looking through a letter-box.

'There, finished. That wasn't so bad now, was it?' said
the triumphant receptionist.

Kahn huffed irritably and flopped into a moulded plastic
chair amongst other physically desperate souls. If he'd had a
revolver on him he would have stuck it in his mouth and
pulled the trigger. The lanky Indian had wasted his life

teaching students who despised him almost as much as he despised them; his wife had left him for his ex-best friend, Julian Snode, and, to top it all, the financial burden imposed upon him by an extremely resentful divorce court judge had reduced him to cohabiting with a homicidal maniac who exhibited all the signs of advanced senile dementia. A fat, loud nurse broke his concentration.

'Can I have the emergency haemorrhoid?'

A sheepish little man rose from his chair, and gingerly walked in the direction signalled by her pointing finger.

'Mr Kahn,' she boomed, 'doctor will see you now.'

He followed her into a small cubicle.

'Doctor will be along in a mo, sweetheart. You just sit down and relax.'

She smiled inanely and, with a swish of the curtain, left him to consider his plight and the impending medical examination.

'My, that looks angry,' said the casualty doctor. He drew in air through his closed teeth as he delicately fingered Kahn's bloodied nose.

'And your foot too, Professor! Let's x-ray the lot. I'll get nurse to wheel you down to the x-ray department. Nurse!'

*

'Well, Professor Kahn,' said the doctor after studying the photographic evidence. 'I'm afraid your nose is broken, and we're going to have to do something about that quickly. If it sets in its present position you'll experience considerable discomfort when you try to breathe through it.'

'What about my foot?' asked Kahn miserably.

'Yes, I was just coming to the foot,' said the doctor, as if Kahn had stolen his thunder. 'I'm afraid your big toe is broken too, and you've also got a couple of other minor fractures in your foot. Oh, and there's some bruising to the back of your head as well. It must have been a pretty nasty fall.'

Kahn said nothing. He wasn't going to confess he'd been beaten up by an eighty-one year old woman wielding a walking stick.

'Actually we'd like to keep you in overnight,' the doctor continued. 'There's nothing to be alarmed about, it's just to make sure you're not suffering from concussion or anything like that.'

'Whatever you say,' groaned Kahn.

'Let's get you sorted out, then,' said the doctor, expertly filling a syringe. 'Don't worry,' he grinned, 'I'm just going to give you something to make you feel more relaxed. Get on to the bed, there's a good fellow.'

Kahn felt a tiny stab as the needle punctured his skin and a few moments later, he was present in body only.

★

'Wakey, wakey Professor Kahn, I've brought your breakfast,' said a pale young nurse with prominent front teeth and a receding chin. 'I thought you might like to read something as well, so you can have my *Daily Mail*.'

Kahn tried to smile but his nose hurt too much.

'Thank you,' he said, delicately feeling his swollen nostrils. They were supported internally with rubber wedges. 'How long have I been asleep?'

'Since yesterday afternoon. How are you feeling?'

'Groggy, very groggy indeed,' said Kahn.

He took a slice out of an overdone sausage and dipped it into a poached egg.

'I'll let you eat your breakfast in peace, Professor. The doctor will see you later this morning.'

Kahn had stopped listening. He chewed his food thoughtfully as he considered his dismal existence. It was quite clear that radical action was required. His biggest problem was money. People didn't get rich teaching Eastern Philosophy, not at Manchester University they didn't, anyway. He finished his breakfast and thumbed through the newspaper desperate for a hard luck story worse than his own. He didn't finish it in the same frame of mind. In fact, he didn't finish it all. Like thousands of other people who read the feature on page seventeen of the *Mail* that morning, and millions who had read similar articles appearing in newspapers and magazines throughout the country that week, Kahn became infected with a mania that would change his life for ever: *Hoard* fever. To a man in his financial and psychological condition, the report on Woodhead's buried treasure, and the staggering two million pounds prize, seemed like an almost personal invitation to participate in the treasure hunt.

Author and painter, Hollis Woodhead, whose controversial statements on homosexuality sparked off a riot at a television studio in Shepherds Bush on Sunday night, was at Harrods yesterday signing copies of his sensational treasure hunt book Hoard (Flute, £10.95). The book, which contains clues to the exact location of two million pounds worth of buried treasure has already sold out in many book shops around the country. Mr Woodhead, who first captured the public's attention in the sixties as the lead vocalist of rock band, Martian Wildlife, would reveal nothing about the whereabouts of the treasure, except to say that it was buried 'somewhere in Great Britain'. Hunters have a year in which to solve the mystery.

'Of course, we very much hope that it will be found before this period elapses,' said Mr Woodhead.

The book's fifteen surreal paintings are accompanied by the story of a twelfth century knight, Sir Lexicon, who's quixotic tendencies run riot when he discovers a mysterious map in the grave of a leprechaun queen. There are four riddles on the ancient parchment that lead the armour-clad protagonist to a mountain cave 'wherein lies the hoard of the leprechauns…'

The injured scholar had read enough. He tore out the page and grabbed his clothes from the bedside chair. What Mr Hollis-bloody-Woodhead hadn't counted on, as clever as he obviously considered himself to be, was that Professor Benjamin Kahn would be taking on the challenge. Yes, it was he, Kahn, who would find the treasure, and he alone who would receive the adulation from an awestruck press, that he so richly deserved.

There was absolutely no time to waste; the quest had already begun and the only place Kahn wanted to be at that moment was the University library with a copy of *Hoard*. The plaster cast on his foot presented a problem because it was far too thick to go down the leg of his trousers, but after a little violent persuasion, the uncompromising cloth compromised with a loud rip.

'Professor Kahn, what on earth do you think you're doing?' said the chinless nurse as he limped past her and into the corridor.

'What does it look like I'm doing?' said Kahn, as he stood by the lift waiting for the doors to open.

'I'd say you were trying to leave without—'

'Oh, fuck off,' said Kahn, with as much petulance as he could muster.

He got into the lift and pressed the ground floor button. The doors closed and Kahn descended, only his mouth and blackened eyes visible between the bandages that held his nasal plugs in place. It was raining heavily outside, and Kahn, not wishing to go back into the hospital, hid from the downpour in a public telephone box. He ordered a taxi and spent the next ten minutes conducting an imaginary telephone conversation for the benefit of an old man who stood crow-like beneath a large black umbrella, angrily pointing at his wristwatch whenever he caught a glimpse of Kahn's eyes. Eventually, the taxi arrived and the professor relinquished his shelter.

'Bastard!' snarled the old man.

'Where to mate?' asked the taxi driver.

'W. H. Smith's in the city centre,' gasped Kahn. 'As fast as you can please. I'm in a hurry.'

'What was the old geezer so uptight about?' asked the driver. 'He looked like he was going to blow a gasket.'

'He wanted to use the telephone, and I wouldn't let him because I was there first,' said Kahn aggressively.

'Bloody scandalous isn't it?'

'I thought so,' said Kahn, looking out of the window and wishing the driver would not engage him in chit-chat.

'Looks like you've been in the wars a bit lately too, you'd think people would have more consideration.'

'Yes, you would,' said Kahn ironically.

'Sorry, mate, I don't suppose you feel much like talking. I mean, being all bandaged up like that.'

Kahn nodded, and looked out of the window again.

★

'Wait here for me,' Kahn said as he stepped out of the taxi.

To see *Hoard* as the W. H. Smith's hype of the month brought an inner exhilaration to Kahn. He was surprised not to have heard about it sooner. The shop window was filled with posters and other devices that promoted the great treasure hunt.

Two million pounds, thought Kahn, I can do this.

Pushing past a huddled group of would-be on-the-spot solvers, he grabbed two copies, paid, and then took the taxi to his mother's house to pack some clothes.

'Oh, it's egghead,' said Kahn's mother spitefully when she opened the door. 'I suppose you've come back to apologise.'

Her son stood in the drizzle outside gritting his teeth. He was thinking of doing something to the old bag that would necessitate a convincing alibi, not an apology.

'I've come to pick up my things, Mother, I'm leaving.'

'Huh, there is a God after all!'

Kahn brushed past the old woman and limped upstairs. He had very little to pack. Apart from the suit he was wearing, which had shrunk in the rain, he had two jackets, a few pairs of socks and underwear, an assortment of shirts, one Shetland jumper, two pairs of shoes, two towels and an oversized dressing gown. He stuffed these, his only earthly possessions, into a large leather case and dragged it downstairs, his heart near bursting point with the injustice of it all.

'And don't come back!' growled his mother as he reached the front gate.

'Fuck you!' screamed Kahn, with the rage of an otherwise peaceful man who had reached the end of his rope.

He slammed the gate, and took a short cut through the public gardens to the university. Mrs Kahn wasn't interested in her son's thoughts on injustice. She was very strongly given to hard liquor and horror; content now that she could relax undisturbed, she lay in bed with a bottle of gin and a copy of Bram Stoker's *Dracula*.

★

After such a crushing day, Kahn's room at the university became a refuge from the world. A bag of fish and chips, a can of beer and *Hoard*. He was overcome with a sense of challenge and well-being.

Chapter Six

Visitor's day at Broadmoor Prison. Willy Grindle's fallen
arches slapped the stone floor of his cell as he paced
barefoot up and down in a state of considerable excitement.
Sister Beatrice of the Holy Order of St Joan, a Catholic
convent in the wilds of Berkshire, was coming especially to
see him. Initially, her visits to Grindle sprung from a
genuine will to encourage the illiterate murderer in his
professed desire to become a good Catholic. As time went
by, however, the Devil, in the unsavoury guise of her erring
charge, began to tempt her. She had made sterling efforts to
inculcate scriptural principles into this hardened villain, but
was increasingly falling victim to his subtle advances. As she
read scripture, she sensed his attentions, and her own
unwillingness to fight them. She tried to whip the sin from
herself, but her secret, shameful fantasies about Willy kept
on growing.

She saw in Grindle the same dawning sensitivity that
had transformed Burt Lancaster's 'Birdman of Alcatraz' into
a lover of canaries. Perhaps, she thought, there was hope for
an old buzzard like her. But as she climbed out of her Mini,
and wrestled with the patent rubber underwear she wore
beneath her habit, she realised she might never see her
Willy again. This was the pang of insecurity that
preoccupied her as she locked up and put the keys into her
carpet-bag.

Doctor Baker, the prison psychiatrist, was waiting at the visitors' entrance and, as usual, Sister Beatrice was invited to take some tea in his office.

'I must say, Sister Beatrice, you've worked a miracle with Willy Grindle.'

'We do our best,' said the good sister in a gruff Welsh accent.

'You certainly do,' said the doctor. 'He hasn't tried to bite a soul since the pig farm incident, and that was months ago. Sugar?'

'Two, please.'

'Yes, we're very pleased with his progress. I've been thinking of recommending him to the prison chaplain. Did you know he's learnt that tape of hymns you gave him, off by heart?'

'No.'

'Always singing them he is; especially "Jerusalem". Drives the other prisoners round the bend.' The doctor stirred his tea and considered his unfortunate choice of words. 'Well, I suppose you'll be wanting to see him for yourself now, Sister?'

'If it's no trouble,' she said.

Her magnified eyes shifted nervously behind the pebble lenses of her spectacles. There was going to be a bloody great heap of trouble, and she knew it. The doctor accompanied her to the cell of her beloved and unlocked the door. Willy was listening to a tape on his Walkman and kneeling by a poster of the Virgin Mary.

'See what I mean, Sister?' observed the doctor, 'It's astonishing.'

'With God, anything is possible,' she said, momentarily revolted by Grindle's mock sincerity.

'I'll be back in ten minutes, Sister,' said the doctor.

'God be praised!' shouted Willy, who had forgotten to take his ear phones off. The cell door clunked into place and they were alone.

'Did you bring everything?' Grindle whispered.

'Everything,' gulped Sister Beatrice, 'did you doubt me?'

'Not for a second, angel.'

'I wish you wouldn't call me that,' she said uncomfortably.

The conspirators were interrupted by heavy footsteps in the corridor.

'God be praised!' exclaimed Willy with all the pathos of an American television evangelist.

'Amen,' cried the nun with an equally passionate expression of faith.

The footsteps grew fainter and the danger passed.

'Now!' hissed Willy, pulling on the sister's hood. It came off at the first attempt.

'Bloody hell!' he exclaimed, taking off her glasses. 'You do look just like me.'

The resemblance was startling. Sister Beatrice had gone to some trouble with the wig, a short ginger affair secured with super-glue at the edges to achieve a merging of the natural and synthetic. But there were also astounding facial similarities between them: Grindle was a little less hairy on the chin, it was true, but their noses, their small eyes, even their general bone structures, were quite alike. It wouldn't fool anyone for long, but it would give him a good head start. They quickly exchanged clothes, knelt by the bunk breathing heavily and pretended to pray.

'Now remember, Willy, don't say anything unless you absolutely have to. Just smile and make the sign of the cross occasionally, and you'll be all right.'

'God be praised,' said Willy, forgetting himself for a moment.

'Look for the blue Mini,' said his anxious Catholic look-alike. 'The keys are in this bag. There's a change of clothes, two wigs and three false beards in the boot, and the cash you asked for is under the driver's seat. It's not much, but it's all I have. You will send for me when I get out won't you, Willy? I couldn't bear prison unless I thought you were waiting for me.'

'Trust me, Beatrice, you'll get five years at the most and it'll probably be an open prison, anyway. It won't be any different from a few more years in that convent of yours; in fact it'll probably be better, and as soon as you're paroled we'll skip the country together.'

'Oh, Willy, I do love you.'

'And I love you too.' Willy patted her buttocks lightly.

Grindle had doubted his sanity until he met Beatrice. Quite clearly, he had very little to worry about. He was an average, no nonsense, psychopathic murderer; she on the other hand was as mad as a coot. Just then, a key rattled into the lock, and the two impostors assumed a praying position with their backs to the door.

'Time's up, Sister Beatrice,' said Dr Baker. 'Willy, all right?'

The bogus prisoner counted the beads on her rosary, and the nun coughed.

'Fine,' said the nun. 'No, better than fine; he's taken a two day vow of silence, and to cleanse his body we've decided on a two-day fast. I hope you don't mind, Dr Baker; him not being able to speak and all?'

'Whatever you think's for the best, Sister.'

'When you see Willy again you won't believe your eyes; you just wait and see, doctor.'

Beatrice couldn't believe her ears: Grindle's impersonation was very convincing. Furthermore, the doctor seemed delighted with his proposal.

'Excellent, Sister, I'll escort you to the main gate.'

Beatrice nodded vigorously and continued to count beads as the door shut behind her.

'God bless you Doctor Baker,' said Grindle as they walked out of the main gate and into the sunlight, 'I'll see you next week.'

'Sister Beatrice must've been in a hurry,' said Dr Baker, sharing his amazement with Maguire, the guard at the gate, 'I've never seen a nun sprint before.'

'Very odd,' said Maguire cheerfully. 'She must have upset her star pupil too; they're asking for you in Q block. Apparently Willy's throwing a wobbler up there.'

'Get on the blower and tell them I'm on my way.'

'Yes, sir.'

'You'd better tell them to straightjacket the little bastard as well. I'm not going in that cell until he's immobilised.'

'Very wise, sir, especially after what happened at the pig farm.'

'How is Smith by the way?'

'He got a disability pension, but he still can't pee proper. Incredible what they can stitch together these days, isn't it, sir?'

'Quite.'

★

Beatrice watched Grindle race across the car park and jump into the Mini, and it suddenly dawned on her how foolish her romantic obsession had been. Willy didn't even blow her a kiss like he'd said he would. She'd been well and truly hoodwinked, and she knew it now for sure. Well, if Willy wouldn't have her, then no one would have her Willy.

'Guard!' she screamed. 'Guard! Willy Grindle's escaped!'

'I thought you'd taken a vow of silence Grindle, you grizzly bastard,' shouted the duty guard through the spy hole. 'Why don't you behave like a good little boy and *shuddup*?'

'You don't understand,' she protested. 'I'm Sister Beatrice. Grindle hypnotised me and made me give him my clothes. This is a wig, watch this!' She pulled out a chunk of hair.

'Stop it, man!' cried the guard, revolted by the prisoner's masochism.

Beatrice yanked out another chunk and then another. He'd seen enough. Two minutes later he was back with a straightjacket, reinforcements and Warden Sergeant Morse.

'Right, lads,' he said, unlocking the door, 'on the count of three. One… two… three!'

The men were astounded by the ghastly spectacle that confronted them in the cell. Beatrice sat under the window, naked, apart from her rubber knickers, and surrounded by a heap of ginger hair. The few strands of coloured nylon that remained embedded in the man-made scalp reinforced the grotesque nature of the scene.

'My God! This is bloody awful.' The bitter truth dawned on Morse. 'Grindle! He's gone. Fucking hell!'

'It's a wig,' wailed Beatrice. 'Grindle glued it on me, and I can't get the rubber off.'

'You don't have to take off the rubber, Sister Beatrice,' said Morse. 'You're naked enough. Hodkins!'

'Yes, sir?'

'Sound the alarm.'

'Yes, sir.'

Hodkins, scuttled off to activate the siren no one ever dreamed they'd hear for real. He was back just a few seconds later.

'Where is it, sir?'

'Where's what?'

'The alarm, sir.'

'I don't believe this,' screamed Morse, 'get this nun a blanket. I'll sound the alarm.'

Morse raced off along the corridor and crashed into Dr Baker, laying the psychiatrist flat on his back.

'What the hell's going on?'

'Willy Grindle's escaped, dressed as a nun! I'm gonna raise the alarm!'

'Don't do that you moron!' screamed the doctor, grabbing hold of Morse to raise himself to his feet. 'You'll have half the fucking news hounds in the country breathing down our necks if that siren goes off. Let's go and see the Governor.'

Five minutes later the Governor was on the hot-line to the Home Secretary, asking for the authority to launch 'Operation Flying Nun'. The media were informed that according to reliable intelligence sources a ruthless terrorist was believed to be hiding out in the area.

'We'll have to keep the nun here until we recapture Grindle,' said the Governor. 'We don't want this affair going public just yet.'

'Well, she's dead to the world at the moment: I've given her a sedative,' said Baker. 'I can probably hold her for a week.'

'Bloody do-gooders,' said the Governor, 'they're more trouble than they're worth.'

*

Willy's illiteracy caused him great problems as he raced along the country roads in Beatrice's Mini. He could handle a car admirably, his mother had seen to that, but she'd always been in the passenger seat to navigate for him. He found himself confronted at every junction by clusters of little boards he could not understand. Clearly, it was time to team up with somebody who could. Heavy clouds advanced the evening darkness as Willy drove into a small village. He had no idea at all where he was, but he was heartened by lights coming from the windows of the house next to the church.

Ah ha! he said to himself. I'll try the vicar! With this outfit, I should be able to get help from him. I'm okay if he's the only sod there.

The aged Father Peter Updyke lived alone. He practised a nonconformist religion that evangelised and encouraged inter-faith cooperation.

'My dear Sister,' he said when he opened the door to Grindle, 'how nice of you to call. Can I help at all?'

Willy nodded.

'Then please come in.'

'Thank you, Father.'

'Not at all, Sister, it's a pleasure to be of service.'

Father Updyke led Willy into his small living room, attached to the walls of which were many maps of various parts of the British Isles.

'Planning a trip, Father?'

'No, I'm trying to find something buried somewhere in England – or Scotland, or someplace. It's a puzzle,' answered the clergyman guardedly.

An array of books and notes lay scattered on the table in the middle of the room.

'Look, Father, it's a quarter to nine and I want to see the news on the TV at nine. Okay?'

'Fine, can I get you a drink? Tea perhaps, or milk? Nothing alcoholic, I'm afraid,' put in Updyke, anticipating a likely response from such an unlikely-looking nun.

'Be quiet for just a moment,' said Willy as stirring music introduced the TV news.

Armed police are today searching areas of the Midlands for an escaped terrorist. The man was last seen in the Eastbury area

in a yellow Mini driving south. The police warned that he is
an extremely violent and dangerous man and members of the
public should on no account approach him.

The TV displayed an old photograph of Grindle that bore
absolutely no likeness to him at all.

It seems as though the whole of Britain has gone crazy. Up
and down the country, ancient religious sites and burial
grounds have been vandalised by treasure hunters. Witnesses
interviewed said that people are digging all over the place for
the so-called Golden Cones in a two-million pound treasure
hunt that's gripped the country like an epidemic. The author
of the treasure-hunt book Hoard, Hollis Woodhead, refused
to be interviewed about the matter.

Grindle was too deep in thought over the first report to
notice Updyke shifting papers around to cover his copy of
Hoard.

'Do you have a car?' asked Willy, putting his feet on the
coffee table and scratching his nose.

'Yes, I do. Why do you ask?' inquired the priest, alarmed
by the nun's peculiar behaviour.

'Oh, just wondered,' said Willy thoughtfully. 'Can I
have a glass of water?'

Updyke decided he didn't like this peculiar and
ungracious nun, and suspected that he had made a terrible
mistake in inviting her into his home.

'Look, I'm ever so sorry, Sister, but I really have to go
out now. I'm afraid you'll have to leave.'

'Oh, please Father, just a glass of water.'

The priest looked at his watch.

'Very well, but then I've got to go. I am sorry, I really
am.'

'Thank you, father,' said Willy, following him into the kitchen.

As the old man filled a glass with water, the murderer drew a large kitchen knife from a cutlery rack on the wall. He felt its sharp edge with the tip of his index finger then tossed the knife from hand to hand. Suddenly, he grabbed the priest from behind and put the knife to his throat.

'Right, you old bastard, if you don't do what I say, I'll slit your throat.'

In desperate fear and panic, Peter Updyke elbowed Willy in the stomach, bringing the murderer to his knees, and dashed out of the back door, into the cemetery.

'Sod it!' shouted Willy, straining his eyes to see into the blackness outside.

Rain was falling and the wind whistled around the gravestones as Father Updyke searched for a place of safety. There were no woods close by in which to hide. The graveyard was his only hope. He looked back at the house and saw Grindle silhouetted in the kitchen doorway. Grindle scanned the eerie darkness with the thin beam of a torch, and made towards the graveyard.

'Oh, God, save me from this evil,' prayed Updyke in an undertone.

Creeping on all fours, Updyke scurried as quietly as he could towards the boundary wall, putting as much distance as possible between himself and the homicidal nun. He could see torchlight flashing between the headstones, and coming his way.

'Oh my God, oh my God.'

As if in answer to his plea, Updyke fell into a newly-prepared, expectant grave, grabbing as he did, the sacking that covered dirt mounds at the graveside. He quickly covered himself from head to foot with the sacking and lay still and tense in the mud of his refuge, his heart pumping furiously. Through the open mesh of the sacking, Updyke could see the occasional flicker of light followed by absolute blackness. Then there was only blackness and silence.

He's gone, thought Updyke.

Suddenly, a continuous light, softened by the sacking filled his eyes.

'Okay, Father, out you get.' Grindle's voice was slow and threatening.

Updyke lay still and silent and prayed as thoughts of death ripped through his mind.

'All right, Father, stay there if you like.'

Updyke felt the heavy thump of earth falling upon him as Grindle kicked at the dirt mound.

'All right, all right!' he screamed. 'I'm here, I'm here!'

'I know you're there,' glowered Willy.

'Okay, okay, what do you want me to do?' whimpered the muddied clergyman as he ascended from the pit.

'I'll show you,' said Willy.

Willy frog-marched Updyke through the graveyard, and back to the house.

'I think I'll just make you safe for a while,' said Willy.

He tied Updyke's hands behind his back, then secured him to the newel at the bottom of the stairs.

'Don't worry about a thing, Father, I just want to see if you have something to help me on my way.'

Willy searched drawers and cupboards for money, and returned after a short time with hands full of magazines, videos and a small metal box that contained Updyke's savings.

'Well, well, well. This is amazing! I reckon you could be put away for this stuff, Father.' Willy fanned the porno-graphic magazines on the table. 'And this one, Father, this one is a criminal offence job.'

Father Updyke hung his head on his chest. Various methods of suicide ran quickly through his mind.

'Don't worry, Father, you're in no danger, and I'm not going to shop you. My name is Grindle, and you'll be pleased to know that I am a murderer, and a cannibal, and I'm wanted by the police. Now, what d'ya think about that?'

Updyke remained silent and totally dejected. Grindle could not remove from the clergyman the extreme guilt that consumed him.

'What do you want from me, Mr Grindle?' asked Updyke meekly.

'Right, when we've cleaned you up a bit, I want you to show me your garage.'

★

The old garage door creaked open to reveal Updyke's large green Volvo. Grindle forced the terrified cleric into the driver's seat, then sat next to him and held the knife to his throat.

'Okay, reverse out until I tell you to stop. Do it right or you're dead.'

The trembling churchman stalled the Volvo three times before the car was clear of the garage. 'Now get out,' said Willy, 'you're going to drive my Mini into the garage.'

Under threat of a bloody death, the timorous Updyke obeyed Willy silently.

'All I need now, Father, is a black suit, a dog collar and something for my hair. Come on,' growled Willy.

Shortly, the murderer was dressed in an ill-fitting, freshly dry-cleaned ministerial suit, complete with dog collar, and his hair was now oily black and smelling of boot polish.

'You'll never get away with this,' said Updyke, misinterpreting Willy's intentions when he saw the murderer's new disguise. 'I'm very well known in these parts, and so is my car.'

'Don't worry, vicar,' said Willy, stuffing Beatrice's habit into the boot of the Mini, 'you're coming with me. You're going to drive me to London. I'll even pay for the petrol.'

'You'll never get away with it.'

'I'd better,' said Willy with a manic giggle, 'or you won't get away with it either.'

To reinforce the seriousness of his threat, Willy slammed the boot down hard and knelt by Updyke, sneering at him.

'I've just escaped from Broadmoor, mate, and I haven't got anything to lose; so, please, don't even think about being a hero, or you'll die. Capito?'

Updyke nodded agreement.

'Good,' said Willy, 'just let me put my beard on first, then we're off.'

'Absolutely,' said Updyke, 'whatever you say.'

Willy escorted Updyke to the waiting Volvo. They got into the car, and Willy prodded Updyke with the tip of the carving knife, drawing a squeal from the petrified minister.

'Okay, you old faggot,' he said, 'let's go.'

*

From an organisational point of view, 'Operation Flying Nun' was a tremendous success, and if the army and police helicopters that flew over Updyke's green Volvo had been looking for such a vehicle, the hunt would've been over in a matter of minutes. Unfortunately for Updyke, they were not. They were not looking for a couple of clergyman either. Moreover, nor were the police who manned the road-block he and Willy negotiated unchallenged.

'Come on, Father, let's have a sing-song,' said Willy, as they sped away from the blue uniforms and flashing lights.

'I don't really feel like singing at the moment, thank you.'

'You wouldn't want to put me in a bad mood, would you?' said Willy, pinching the old man's ear, and prodding him again with the knife.

'What do you think we should sing?' asked Updyke.

'Oh, I don't know,' said Willy, fidgeting with his beard. 'How does "Jerusalem" grab you? Yes, I think we'll sing "Jerusalem". You do know it I s'pose?'

The priest broke into song: 'And did those feet in ancient time…'

'Very good,' said Willy.

So off they went to London, Updyke singing his heart out, and Willy Grindle prodding him with the knife whenever the priest showed signs of reluctance or tiredness.

*

An early morning mist from the Thames put the finishing touches to Peter Updyke's despair as he drove, Isle Of Dogs bound, into the southern mouth of the Blackwall Tunnel. The maniacal Willy Grindle smiled at him with a sinister delight that did not bode at all well for the priest's continued good health.

'Nearly there, Father,' said Willy, 'then you can have a nice long rest.'

Updyke didn't like the sound of that at all. Willy jabbed him with his elbow to solicit a response. The one hundred and fifty eight performances of 'Jerusalem' his kidnapper had required during their nightmarish association had dried out his mouth, and made it difficult for him to reply with the enthusiasm Willy demanded. Willy jabbed him again.

'Thank you sir. Yes, a nice long rest. Thank you,' Updyke squeaked, re-animating his numb vocal cords.

'Yes, that's right,' growled the murderer. 'Sir, and don't you forget it.'

This last act of cruelty made something snap in Updyke's head. He was going to die very soon, of that he was certain and, if he was going to die, then he would do it in a brave and dignified manner. With a blood curdling scream Updyke slammed his foot down hard on the accelerator and the two men rocketed into the tunnel, fighting for control of the wheel and the carving knife that had been Willy's insurance against awkward behaviour.

'Stop! Stop!' Willy protested. 'You'll kill us both!'

Updyke gritted his teeth and defended his position at the wheel. Frantically, Willy scrambled into the back of the car and curled himself into a ball on the rear seat. The vicar's eyes, although sunken and bloodshot, showed a glint of victory; his ordeal was nearly over, the inevitable consequence of travelling at a hundred and ten miles an hour with only fifty yards of tunnel left; and, what was more, he would have the satisfaction of taking his tormentor with him. As the car leapt out of the tunnel and into the mist, Updyke prepared himself for the Kingdom.

'The Lord is my shepherd,' he shouted, 'I shall not want—'

'Oh my God!' was the only religious plea Willy could muster. But his mind was occupied with the more practical business of how to survive the horrific impact in which Updyke's reckless antics would certainly terminate. The priest had just reached the bit about 'green pastures' when they crashed through the main gate of Gardener's World. If he'd had time to read the sign that dispatched him as it dropped through the front windscreen and took off the top of his head, he would no doubt have been surprised with the speed and efficiency that trespassers would be prosecuted. The mangled Volvo slowed down but, undefeated in its argument with the gate, careered across the floodlit tarmac in search of more havoc.

From his hiding place behind the driver's seat, Willy was only vaguely aware of the commotion outside as members of a night-time delivery firm abandoned a large consignment of gnomes, and fled for their lives. The little people stood their ground regardless. The army of fixed grins, variously armed with miniature wheelbarrows and fishing rods made a defiant stand against the speeding assailant, but were unable to absorb the inertia of the battered giant as it tore through them.

'What the hell are they doing?' yelled the manager, tearing at his hair.

'It's gnome-icide,' said one of his men drolly.

'It's no bloody joke, you idiot, they're not insured!'

'What did you expect us to do about it?' shouted the foreman belligerently, 'stand in the way?'

'Don't argue with me, I'm your boss.'

'I don't give a monkey's fuck. Piss off.'

As the argument became more inflamed, Willy Grindle stirred to action amidst a heap of crumpled plaster and dust.

'Oh my God,' groaned Willy as he raised himself on his elbows.

The hazard warning lights at the rear of the car flashed on and off. Updyke had been thrown into the back of the car when it finally crashed to a halt. In the intermittent orange light, Willy could see the priest slumped next to him. Time to leave. Remarkably, the engine was still running. He got into the driver's seat, put the car into reverse and sped backwards out of the debris.

'Run for it lads!' shouted the foreman, 'the bastard's on the move again.'

With a threatening screech of rubber, Willy achieved an impressive about turn, and raced off as fast as the punctured front tyres and steaming radiator allowed. Despite the pressing nature of his predicament, he enjoyed the spectacle of workers desperately scrambling for cover; his sense of being a dangerous criminal was restored by it. He clattered over the vanquished gate, and trundled along Blackwall Way under cover of the thickening mist. The car managed a couple of hundred yards, then went into a convulsion. Willy pulled into a side street.

'Christ, I'm hungry. Uh hmm, I must eat something.'

Willy looked at the priest. Updyke's head was sliced right through like a breakfast egg.

'Oh yeah, of course, breakfast.'

*

In the dimly-lit darkness of Dogs Thames side, Grindle set off to find refuge. He just hoped that Magdelaine, his fortune-telling sometime girlfriend was home, and unattached.

*

Magdelaine's elegant fingers, heavily laden with peculiar rings, gently stroked the head of a stuffed ferret that had been screwed, like its snarling neighbour, to the arm of an antique chair. A television beamed out a late night black and white foreign movie that gave an eerie pseudo-life to the menagerie of preserved animals that hung from the ceiling and peered cautiously from glass cases around the darkened room. The faded English rose, engrossed in the unfolding drama on the tube, gripped the ferret by the neck as the tension mounted, anxiously awaiting the subtitles that would make her enjoyment complete. At that crucial moment her viewing was interrupted by a loud rapping on the front door. It was three in the morning, and she expected no one, so she ignored it at first, but its persistence pulled her, irritated, from her film.

'What do you want?' she shouted as she peered through the spyhole.

A bearded clergyman hugged himself against the cold, misty night, hopping up and down between his bursts of activity on the knocker. Magdelaine spoke to her unusual visitor through the letter box.

'What do you want, Reverend? Three o'clock in the morning's hardly the time for tea and scones.'

'It's me Magdelaine.'

'Who?'

'Me.'

'Me who?'

'Willy.'

'I thought you were in prison.'

'Well, I'm not now, am I?'

'I suppose not. What happened? Did they let you off?'

'I'm freezing my nuts off out here, woman; for crying out loud let me in.'

'Oh, I am sorry, Willy, I'll be with you in a second.'

Magdelaine liked masterful men, always had. A chain rattled, a lock clicked, and the door opened. Willy was in the hall in a flash, his teeth chattering so hard that he emitted a high frequency clicking noise.

'You've escaped, haven't you?'

'Don't worry, Magdelaine, I just need a place to hide out for a few days. I've got plenty of money.'

'That's nice,' chirped Magdelaine when Willy waved some notes at her to illustrate his point. 'We'd better get you into some dry clothes before you catch your death.'

Willy smiled and peeled off his damp beard.

'Maggie.'

'Yes, lover?'

'Have you still got that parcel I asked you to keep for me?'

'Yes, lover. I hid it in the deep freeze, next to Aunt Lily, just in case it was one of your meat specialities. I didn't like the idea that it might thaw out and rot. It would smell so awful after such a long time.'

'What d'ya mean, Aunt Lily in the deep freeze?'

'Willy, she was my favourite auntie, and I decided to give her a chance when modern medicine catches up with death, if you know what I mean. I heard about it on telly. It's called Cry of Lennox. It's a curious name, but I think it's the name of the inventor,' said Magdelaine seriously.

'Oh my God, Maggie, you're fucking stupid. Stupider than Beatrice, and she was round the twist.'

'Who's Beatrice, Willy?'

'Forget it, Maggie. Get my package from the fridge. It's just some letters.'

'That's nice,' said Magdelaine.

She took hold of the fugitive's hand and pulled him upstairs.

'Let's get you sorted out first. Let me just look at your mouth. Umm, have you cut your lip, luvver?'

★

Willy snored contentedly in Magdelaine's bed, blissfully unaware that 'Operation Flying Nun' was moving into a higher gear. A thorough search of properties within a five mile radius of Broadmoor Prison had unearthed the Mini belonging to Sister Beatrice in Peter Updyke's garage, and, following the discovery of the vicar's smashed-up car and mutilated body a mile from Magdelaine's Dewberry Street home, the massive manhunt had switched from Berkshire to London's dockland.

'For God's sake, sir, look at the vicar's legs. Somebody's taken bites out of both of them. That's bloody awful.' The policeman stood quickly back from the car, repulsed by his first encounter with cannibalism.

'Yes, Constable, that's our Willy. He's a bloody monster,' said the detective. 'He's a real nasty, and we'd better get him. He prefers his food warm, you know, when it's been recently killed, just like the vicar here.' The detective examined the vicar's head. 'I didn't realise he went in for brains, though.'

Chapter Seven

Ernest Clamp went through the pre-flight checks of his Piper Archer thoroughly. He was airforce trained, and a damned good pilot. He loved to fly, and it had hurt him badly when he was grounded. In the twenty-one years since his less than esteemed retirement, he had put in a great many flying hours, *unlogged* flying hours. After buying the Green Boar, Ernest had never had enough money to join a flying club, let alone buy his own plane. That was out of the question. But unbelievable good luck ensured a continued, albeit black, flying career. It had started a long time ago, and his introduction to his unbelievable good luck was at first something altogether nasty.

A cold night, then, and the last of the drinkers had gone home. It had snowed heavily. Ernest was making the usual check at the back door of the Green Boar, and that the light of the outside toilet was switched off. The light from his open door fell upon a strange and frightful group of four strangers standing before him. Ernest was shocked to see a naked, bound and gagged unfortunate in the middle of two heavies; his face and body were badly beaten.

'Are you Ernest Clamp?' said an accented but educated voice from behind the group.

'What?' Ernest was too shocked to make any sense of questions.

'Yes, you're Clamp. My first name is Marek. You would not be able to pronounce my second name, but don't worry. You and I are going to do business together for our big company, but first we want to show you something. Okay, Dicky, your time has come,' said the voice to the wriggling naked form.

One of the heavies forced a pistol into Dicky's mouth and pulled the trigger. The blast spattered blood over the white snow, and stirred the wild life in the surrounding forest. It also brought Dora from her bed.

'What the hell's going on?' flustered Dora.

'Stay indoors, lady,' said Marek, 'and nothing will happen to you.'

Ernest remained silent.

'Ernest, this was for your benefit,' said the stranger leading the heavies into the warmth of the pub kitchen. 'We know quite a lot about you. You're a pilot, and we are going to employ you. I want to point out, though, that Dicky outside was also a pilot, and he tried just once to leave our firm.'

'What must I do?' The blood had drained from Ernest already and the cold had got to him; he shook uncontrollably.

'You have only to make a decision: work for us or both of you die here and now.'

Dora grabbed the lapel of her dressing gown, and bit hard on it.

'We've checked up on you. You had an excellent record in the RAF before you were caught drinking in the cockpit. What a shame for you. But I am offering you a new and exciting flying career with lots of job satisfaction. It's not jets, but it is a job for life, with excellent pay.'

'Well, I like to fly,' said Ernest.

'There, it wasn't hard to make a decision, was it? And I do so like my work to be easy. Well done. Are you wondering why we picked you, Ernest?'

'Not really.'

'I understand,' said the sympathetic, educated voice. 'Your particular flying experience – lots of low-level night flying – and your set-up here in the pub, which is strategically placed on a delivery route. It will all work out fine. We won't even take the pub from you.'

That's all that was needed to introduce Ernest into the association of the ruthless and brutal London-based Mafia. Ernest discovered over the years that they controlled a large ring of drug couriers and pushers, and operated in all the other usual illegal business opportunities one might imagine, through connections in Europe, Asia and America.

'I'll make sure you get your plane, but you will be expected to be loyal, Ernest. You will make several trips a month from this point, fly a predetermined charted route, deliver some goods, and return with a briefcase to the airstrip from where you first took off. No questions asked, no answers given. I want to make one thing clear to you, Ernest: now that I have told you these things, you would be silly to refuse. Do you understand what I'm saying?'

It was not the heavy threat that convinced him he should take the job, but the delightful thought that he would fly and have it paid for; and, what's more, spend pleasurable hours away from his uncaring and detestable Dora.

'Look, no problems. I'll take the job,' said Ernest.

'Okay, fine, Ernest. By the way, don't forget to get rid of the body outside.'

*

Since then, Ernest had operated a simple routine that brought him immense pleasure, and more money than he had ever expected to earn for such a simple task. Money for old rope. The work was well organised, and he admired the clock-work precision of the operation that involved him. He would drive his car, on a few irregular nights each

88

month phoned to him in code, to a remote airstrip about ten miles away. The flight chart and destination were always the same, and he assumed that flight controllers along the way had either been paid off or threatened, or both. The airfield at each end of his course seemed to be set up especially for his Piper aircraft, obvious to him after seeing the spare parts arranged on shelves at one side of the hangar. His plane was always in excellent working condition and replaced every three years. The ground crew never acknowledged him but serviced his plane efficiently and well. He received only polite words of greeting from the small cluster of guys with the smart suits and big cars who were always there to make the exchange of goods, whatever they were. The exchange was mostly the same though: a couple of large, heavy suitcases or bags from Ernest's end for a briefcase at the other end. Ernest never asked about what was exchanged; he absolved himself from guilt by remaining in ignorance of the true nature of his job. He never got to know names directly, but he had plenty of information from investigative reports in the national press about individuals suspected of being involved in a big, big Mafia operation, individuals he had often met face to face. Ernest had obeyed the rules and had kept his mouth tightly seated on the matter. And he was surviving still.

*

He went through his take-off check-list, then set the plane in motion. Rotation velocity, stick back, and the exhilaration of lifting up into the sky and flying again. Flying low in the dark the instruments were the most important things. But he had made the trip many times now and he was relaxed. These flights had become important to him. He indulged himself in the privacy of his darkened world with the green, red, and white lights and the fancy displays with a variety of adult accessories.

'And what will it be today?' he joked to himself. 'Ah yes, the penis expander. Or is it extender? Or enlarger? Shit, who cares. Just check everything. Yep, autopilot's in, and we're okay.'

He lowered his trousers, fitted the enlarger, and operated its hand pump.

'My my, that's what I call a swell job!'

With no control tower directions to listen to, he put on headphones and rested back to listen to his usual late evening music and chat show.

'Ever dreamt of digging up a vast fortune in buried treasure?'

This curious question raised Ernest to alert consciousness.

'Fortune?' He sat forward in his seat as the rasping voice of radio presenter, Gordon Bates, continued with his promise of wealth.

'Here's your chance to find a fortune. Our guest on today's show is none other than Hollis Woodhead, author of *Hoard*; and just in case you've been out there living under a rock and haven't heard of his book, then pin back your ears. We'll be talking to him after this little number by James Last and his orchestra.'

Ernest Clamp's startled disbelief obliterated the melodious 'Smoke Gets in Your Eyes' from his hearing as he stared open-mouthed at the radio before him.

'Hollis Woodhead? Buried treasure? Christ, I must have been dreaming. Bloody hell, I'd better do something to keep myself awake.'

He turned up the radio and settled back into his bucket seat again, opened a quarter light to let in some air and then lit up a cigar. As the tune faded, the prattling voice of Gordon Bates broke the end of the music.

'That was James Last with a great, great sound from the past. Now to our guest spot on today's show and, as I said, it's someone who's very much in the news at the moment, and a really talented guy: Hollis Woodhead, author of *Hoard*, the treasure hunt with a two million pounds prize! Staggering! What gave you the idea, Hollis?'

Ernest Clamp's befuddled brain was buzzing in an attempt to make some sense of this revelation. He did not hear Woodhead's well-practised explanation of his treasure hunt. All he could see clearly in his mind was the huge prize. Two million pounds! Two million! How could a loser like Hollis ever get hold of two million pounds? The bastard hadn't breathed a word! By the time Ernest had come to terms with Woodhead's good fortune, he had drifted wildly from his course and lost a great deal of altitude.

'Oh, fuck me! Where am I?'

In confused panic, Ernest peered out into the blackness and then at his instruments. He had trained for emergencies but that was a long time ago. His confusion was total, exacerbated by the black anger he felt towards Woodhead. He made no sense of what his altimeter was telling him: that he was flying too low. It all happened so fast. No time to make corrections. The reality hit him only when his fixed undercarriage started striking the tops of the trees. The nose dipped. Then suddenly the cacophony of dreadful noises as the propeller tried vainly to cut its way through the trees and the wings were ripped from the fuselage. Then quiet.

Ernest sat there for many minutes, upright but in stunned shock, and puffing frantically on his cigar. He was covered totally in white powder from the large bag that had burst open in the crash. His brain became fuzzy, and all he could hear was the now sickly voice of Hollis Woodhead prattling in his headphones. He wrenched the phones from

his head and sat there to recover his senses. He was angry,
very angry: at himself for losing control; at Woodhead – his
'friend' – who had not confided in him; at his predicament.
What's more, the mob would wipe him out for crashing.
He licked at the white powder around his mouth.

Not bad, not bad – but not the real thing, he thought –
and then licked the powder from his hands and wrists.

He became quickly relaxed, and his anger at Woodhead
and his fear of the mob gradually subsided. He pumped up
the device still attached to his groin, rested back and closed
his eyes.

*'If you survive an accident, remove the "goods" and burn the
plane. Call the coordinator on the mobile telephone.'*

He suddenly remembered his accident procedure.

'Fuck the coordinator,' he shouted loudly and laughed
uncontrollably. 'Where the hell am I?'

He ran his hand over his chest but detected no injuries.

'Christ, that was bloody good luck,' he said loudly to
himself. He peered out of the side window, but could see at
first only the blackness and then he saw the white face
peering in at him from outside. He gaped in fright and the
cigar dropped into his bare lap. His whole body whipped in
reflex. He crashed his head on the cabin hood and fell
backwards out of the plane to the ground – fifteen feet
below him.

*

It was morning and light when Ernest returned to consciousness. His mind was dazed and his body ached all
over.

'Oooooooo! Oh, fuck! Woodhead… I'll kill the bastard!
Two million fucking pounds! The bastard.'

Ernest looked at his watch.

'Six-thirty and a bit. Oh god!'

He laid himself on his back and looked up into the trees at what remained of the aeroplane. He saw just the ragged outline of the pilot's cabin above him, jammed firmly in the stout branches of an old oak.

'My Christ, I haven't delivered the case!'

He was suddenly struck with anguish and the image of Dicky in the snow biting on the end of a pistol. It might have been a long time but the events of that late evening were ever vivid in his mind. He tried to stand and felt an intense burning pain between his legs.

'Oh, my God, oh, my God!' he screamed out.

The penis enlarger was still firmly attached. He relieved the pump's suction but that didn't free it from him.

'It won't come off!'

He pulled gingerly at the glass tube.

'Ough, oooo, oooo!'

Tears welled in his eyes as he gradually pulled the thing free. He looked down in stark horror at his very dark blue penis. He laid out on his back in dreadful pain and sobbed. After an hour or so of exposure to the cool morning air, the painful throbbing subsided, but his schniddelwutz was still very blue.

'I must get out of here,' he said, remembering his danger.

There was one of the cases. It had split open on impact with the ground.

'The other must still be up there in the cockpit. Jeesh!' he murmured.

The open case contained sticks of dynamite (the small hairs on the back of his neck prickled at the thought of carrying explosives all those years), at least ten hand grenades and three handguns. Airforce survival training in a hostile country: he had all the knowledge but could he make use of it now? They would have been looking for him for hours, and they would be very angry that he had not delivered or phoned.

'Too late now,' he said to himself.

He had to make a move. Grunting under the pain of his injured crotch, he shoved the case into position under what remained of the plane. He loaded a pistol with bullets, and stuck it in his belt. He was no hero or killer, but he didn't know what to expect from the mob for ditching the plane. Would they understand that sometimes aeroplanes crashed?

'Shit, this will probably kill me.'

He pulled a pin, jammed the hand grenade into the case and ran as best he could to the safety of a huge tree – and counted.

'… six, seven, eight, nine…'

The explosion was enough. The pilot's cabin blasted into the air, along with the tree it was resting in, and white powder filled the woods about him. Ernest remained crouched behind a tree, still panting heavily from his dash to safety and out of sheer fright, and still feeling the heat from his enlarged blue end.

'Oh, my God! They'll hear that for miles around. I'd better get out of here fast.'

★

'Hey, what are you doing?'

Ernest tried to wrestle the pistol out of his belt, but succeeded only in shooting several rounds wildly into the earth, gyrating frantically and falling flat on his face right on his Blue Peter. He screamed in agony. The two strangely dressed figures looked on amused, and then smiled at each other.

'Christ! Who the hell are you?' he shouted. 'One moment. Wait. Can you help me?' he said, remembering that he was lost and injured.

'Are we safe?'

'Yeah, yeah, no problem. I thought you were someone else,' he reassured them. 'It's okay, I'm no killer. But if we don't get out of here soon, I reckon we'll be murdered.'

Without questioning why, the two strangers turned and ran towards the sunshine and Ernest, waddling painfully, followed as best he could. It was hard to say whether the strangers were men or women, or one of each. They both had long, well-groomed hair, faces colourfully made up like he'd never seen before and woven white druid-like robes. They were not druids but clearly some sort of sect.

They led Ernest to an open field in the centre of which stood a white, polished building that resembled a small temple. No windows, though. Five people in robes stood quietly and waited for Ernest and his companions to arrive.

'We heard the explosion. We've been waiting for you,' said an old man who seemed to be the leader.

'What are you talking about? Would you please just hide me somewhere, I'm in great danger. Where am I anyway?'

'My man, you are at the centre of knowledge. We are its guardians and you are here to witness fantastic things before we leave Earth together.'

'Ya, ya good, but can I please just hide, there are people out to kill me.'

Ernest was beginning to panic – and his groin ached again.

'You should take a shower and get cleaned up. If you don't, you cannot put on one of our sanctified robes – and that's the best hiding place. What do you think?'

'Yep, good idea.'

★

'Ah, you look much better. Are you still in pain?' Without waiting for an answer, the old man pointed to the temple.

'Come with me,' he said, 'we are going to start an interaction.'

Ernest had no grasp of what the old man was saying, but obeyed to ensure his personal security. Mafia killers were very good at finding their man. He was amazed to find the 'temple' contained a complex array of computers and instruments, of which only the radio altimeter was familiar to him. Clearly a space craft. A highly polished silver sphere about six feet in diameter, emitting sparkling pins of light all around, stood centrally under a dome. Suspended above it, was what appeared to be a holographic book.

'Your bible?' Ernest asked.

'No. But you will come to know the truth of it.'

Bloody weirdo, thought Ernest who had no time for mystical talk.

'You're not going to sacrifice me?'

'No, no, no. Nothing like that. Just pull your hood over your head and take a seat amongst the other members.'

Ernest sat in the only vacant seat of eight, disposed equally about the sphere. A beam of light directed Ernest's eyes towards the book.

'Dear friends, I have selected a test of our powers. Given your immense technical abilities, this is a trivial test, but a necessary one to determine that your microcircuits have not deteriorated on this trip to Earth. We cannot travel comfortably unless we operate totally. Our two objectives for returning to Earth this time are close to fulfilment. I have identified the location of the eight Golden Cones, and I have also identified a good candidate to replace our dear friend Igor. His place has been empty long enough, and it's not easy operating with less than eight members. I cannot remove the Cones from their place in the ground yet because they are currently part of a contract between the author of this book,' – he pointed to the hologram – 'and all the people who have bought it. That contract ends on the

1st of July next year. Not long to wait. Then we should be able to return them to their rightful home in Omitek. That's our next destination. I know where they are now. I will give you my vision of where they are and you must return that vision. Naturally, when I register receipt of your mental transmission I know you are fully functional. Only you realise what these Cones mean for us who have extraterrestrial experiences. Right, close your eyes and interact with me.'

Ernest looked at the spot-lit book and could see clearly Woodhead's name under the title, *Hoard*, printed on its cover. He had no good reasons for believing in visions or mental transmissions, so he was tempted to do a bunk. Then he remembered his crotch.

The session lasted less than half an hour and the members filed out. Ernest just sat there. Just the old man was there with him.

'Your treasure and happiness, Mr Clamp. I repeat, *your* treasure and happiness are in the ground near your home.'

A loud burst of sustained gunfire brought Ernest quickly to his feet. The Mafia! And nowhere in the temple to hide.

'It's okay, the battle's over,' shouted one of the seven from the door. 'Just two hoodlums with guns. They're dead.'

'You have guns?' queried Ernest.

'Certainly not.'

Ernest looked at the multicoloured face before him for some time before being able to form the obvious question.

'How did you do that?'

'It's really just science advanced beyond what is known generally. The knowledge I have is confidential to the seven of us who, because we have shown a commitment for space travel, have been permitted to have this knowledge and the power that goes with it. These two were neutralised by a serial particle beam from our leader, a beam just one particle wide, but accelerated beyond the speed of light. Not even CERN has been able to do this with their huge accelerator, although they have been trying for years. I guess you could think of it as a laser beam, but much more intensely powerful. The concentration of power is super fantastic in comparison with what is available in ordinary so-called modern science.'

'My God! Is this really true?'

'Believe me, Mr Clamp. I am a flesh and blood human but changed to be very different. The power I possess comes from ordinary bodily electrical functions, but amplified millions of times by concentrators and power containers. I have several implanted within me – as do all seven of us you have met today. Our power comes from advancement driven by a need to survive the eventual devastation. It's not God-given magic but sophistication. You will know the truth of these things soon. We travel space and visit planets, but have need to return to gather the raw materials of our power. We don't travel through time. And we sense no distortion of time – as many thought there would be from travelling at fantastically high speed – but then we don't reach the speed of light, so that might still be a reasonable theory.'

Ernest stood there understanding well what the traveller was explaining. He was now convinced that he could find the *Hoard* treasure: he just needed to get his hands on the book.

'You can take the book with you,' said the departing traveller, as though he were reading Ernest's mind. The hologram disappeared but the traveller handed a physical copy to Ernest. Ernest stood dumbfounded for a second, then grabbed *Hoard* and left the temple. He saw only the two dead gangsters with their Kalashnikovs lying near them. No one else in sight.

'I'm dreaming. Either that or I'm still on a high from the drug. This is all bloody madness,' he said loudly to himself. 'No one around to ask, and no landmarks either.'

He tried to recall his position in the air just before the crash.

'I was flying west, and the sun is there, so home is generally in that direction,' he deduced. 'Ah ha, problem: the Mafia will be waiting for me. Shit!'

Still dressed like a druid, he set off to find a road.

★

'This will do,' he said to the driver, 'thanks for the lift.'

To spot any Mafia activity, he climbed Moll Hill and studied from this vantage point the Green Boar and the village centre. Six police cars and two ambulances stood in the pub's car park.

'My God, that looks like serious business,' he muttered to himself. 'I guess she's dead. And bloody good riddance too, the bitch.'

No! There she was walking out of the pub with her shotgun under her arm. Ernest could see three grey, plastic coffins being packed into the ambulances. The police cars started to leave. A policeman shook Dora's hand and put his arm around her shoulder as if in praise.

'This is a very weird day,' he said to the sky.

He looked at the village pump just across from the pub, and thought about how he could dig up the Woodhead treasure without Dora seeing him.

'A night-time job. All my real work is at night,' he complained.

★

The sky above Stonebeggar was now overcast and rumbling with thunder. Suddenly, heavy rain beat against the window of the garden shed. Ernest studied *Hoard* and was impressed by the complexity of the story, and the quality of its presentation. He had felt compelled to start digging, even in the pouring rain.

'You bastard! Where have you been?'

Dora Clamp suddenly presented herself, large and angry, in the doorway of the shed, before her surprised husband.

'What's wrong, Dora?'

Unfortunately, the luckless Ernest was not to discover. He was swiftly laid unconscious by the bottle of Dog's Tooth that Dora crashed down on his head.

★

The next morning, Ernest's impulse to set things right with Hollis Woodhead overcame the pain of his throbbing head, and he rose early for the first time in several years. If Woodhead was going to treat him like dirt after all the free beer and cocaine he had taken from him during their long association, then Ernest would show him that nobody put the squeeze on a Clamp and got away with it lightly.

'I'll teach that bugger,' threatened Ernest. 'First, the treasure. Tonight, I'll dig it up. I just can't wait.'

★

Since Woodhead's bathroom incident, Dora had barely uttered a word to Ernest but, when she saw him tucking into a fried breakfast at seven-thirty in the morning, she was stunned into confused silence by the sudden change in his habits. Dora gathered her composure, and sensed irritation welling in her at the thought of this sloth corrupting her ordered, busy morning.

'What are you up so early for, you big oaf?'

'No reason in particular,' said Ernest evasively.

He finished his breakfast without saying another word to Dora, and left the room. He drove the fifteen miles into town. He had to find out first what the excitement was at the Green Boar the day before – he had no intention of trying to discuss the matter with Dora since there was the distinct possibility that she had behaved heroically – and he needed to know more about the *Hoard* treasure hunt. The poster outside the newsagents shop said it all: '*Hoard* – success for local man!' Ernest was astounded.

★

Woodhead's publishers, Flutes, were also astounded. *Hoard*'s success was well beyond their expectations: £4,500,000 in the first four post-publication months, and the release of two reprints. But that was of no interest to Ernest. He was simply irritated that Woodhead hadn't bothered to tell him about the treasure hunt.

'The silly sod could've let me know. I was his best friend, for God's sake! But he'll be bloody annoyed when he discovers that I've found it.'

Ernest hardly noticed the journey back to Stonebeggar. He sloped into the Green Boar, and did his utmost not to distract Dora who was busy on the phone, ordering stock. Unseen by his wife, he stole furtively past her and went to his bedroom.

'A pint, a pickled egg and a cigar to get me in the digging mood.'

Ernest was eager to make a quick start with the treasure hunt, but he had no mind for such physical activity before beer had passed his lips. He concluded his meal with an amazing belch that relieved his feeling of heavy indigestion.

'Whew, that's better.'

He turned to *Hoard*, and re-examined the pictures.

'This is a really nice book.'

He felt some pride that he knew Woodhead, and was also very pleased to see that the pictures clearly included features of Stonebeggar.

There's the water pump! The pump had been encircled by its previous owner.

This is it. It's got to be.

Sir Lexicon was pointing at a water pump that looked exactly like the one on the village green! As if this wasn't convincing enough in itself, the text on the very next page confirmed beyond all doubt the incredible disclosure at the temple:

At the bridge that crossed the emerald stream a strange beast with green skin was casting a net into the evening sky.

'May I ask what you're trying to catch with your net?' inquired Sir Lexicon.

'The end of a rainbow,' the beast replied, pointing towards a shimmering arc of light that danced in the rays of the setting sun.

Ernest closed the book, and lit a cigar triumphantly. The end of the rainbow always marked a pot of gold, and the green beast in Woodhead's story was clearly a reference to the Green Boar. He didn't need to look at the pub sign to know that the snout of the boar pointed directly at the old water pump in the centre of the village green, and from there it was but a short step for Ernest to deduce that the treasure was buried at the foot of the pump. He wouldn't be able to dig for it until early in the morning. He lay on his bed fully dressed and ready to go as soon as he was sure Dora was asleep.

'I'll just close my eyes for a couple of minutes,' he said to himself.

★

Ernest awoke with a jolt. He could just make out the grey half-light at the bedroom window.

'Oh, Christ! What time is it?'

He was momentarily in panic. He switched on his small bedside lamp. It was four-twenty in the morning and he had slept much longer than he had intended. He felt acutely irritated that he had fallen asleep and left himself so short a time to find the treasure before Dora was up and about.

I'll have to work bloody quick to get that stuff indoors before the old dragon wakes up, he thought.

Dora's heavy snoring allayed Ernest's fears a little; she was obviously in a deep sleep.

'Pity the witch isn't in a coma,' he mumbled.

He crept out of the pub and into the back garden. He had prepared for this moment: pick, spade and flashlamp. As if to give the furtive treasure hunter away, an owl hooted loudly in a tree just above Ernest's head. It hooted again and again. Dora's bedroom light suddenly came on and her window opened. Ernest had no time to move; he simply looked up at the window and stiffened when the barrel of Dora's twelve bore poked through the curtains. He wanted to shout to her that it was only him, but in less than a second the gun flashed and the trailing noise rang loudly in Ernest's ears. Dora's shot evaporated the owl and half the tree. Then her window shut and the light went out. The widely distributed white feathers from the unfortunate creature fell gently, like snowflakes, around Ernest who stood shaking, still staring at the window.

He eventually gathered his wits, collected the tools and set off for the water pump. It stood shrouded in a mist made uncanny by the moonless night and, as he staggered towards it, clasping his shovel, he was in seventh heaven; his greatest moment had arrived. His moment of release – from Dora and the Mob.

'Here goes,' he said, and sunk the blade of the spade into the soft turf to begin his dig. The first ten inches or so were easy enough, but the deeper he dug the harder it became. He had to widen the original hole several times to get to a reasonable depth. At three feet things were beginning to get impossible as one large chunk of flint after another impeded his progress. Gritting his teeth, Ernest dug fiendishly at the unyielding ground with the pick until, at last, he heard a promising metallic clank. He'd found the casket of gold cones!

He sat on the edge of the hole exhausted but happy. He pulled a Corona out of his pocket, bit its end off and lit up, considering as he did how best to undertake the exhumation of the treasure. The casket seemed robust enough, but Ernest didn't want to take any chances by being heavy handed. He finished smoking, got into the hole and picked away at the earth and stones surrounding the casket with his fingers. It was big. It was enormous! He shone his flashlamp over its smooth surface. There was strange writing on it that he couldn't make out in the dull light of morning. The words certainly were not English, and if he hadn't known better he would have taken it for an unexploded bomb. He took a closer look in the light of the flashlamp and could see clearly in large characters the only word of German he knew: ACHTUNG! A whirring sound came from within the metal casing, then a soft click as the mechanism within performed its intended function. In the ominous silence that followed, the horrible truth dawned on Ernest.

'Oh, bugger!' he gasped, as he frantically clawed his way out of the hole.

The old man from the temple stood before him like a ghost.

'Ernest, I said that you would find your real treasure. Now we can go.'

A second later, Ernest and most of the village green vanished as one thousand pounds of German cordite detonated with a force that rocked the foundations of every building in the village and bathed the surrounding countryside in a flash of blue-white light.

Chapter Eight

Woodhead took the news about Ernest Clamp very badly. It was his fault that his good and kind friend had blown himself to pieces. It was the tail-end item of the national news on TV, and Woodhead had seen the devastation. The Green Boar was also dead. Woodhead phoned his old neighbour, Stan Taylor, for the details.

'Hi, Stan, it's Hollis. I suppose you've heard about Ernest? What happened?'

'Hello, Hollis. Ernest was digging for something at the old pump on the green, and struck an unexploded Gerry bomb. He was just totally blown to bits. Identified him from his wallet or something, a book perhaps, I can't remember. Poor old Ernest. Bad luck, eh? We nearly all got killed. The pub's a ruin.'

'And Dora, what's happened to Dora?'

'Hollis, where have you been? Stonebeggar has been big news recently. Dora killed three Mafia assassins at the pub. But she got it too, the following day – along with her little Italian mate – when the pub went.'

Woodhead was stunned into silence. No question about it, the Mafia men had been searching for him. *Hoard* had focused attention on Woodhead. There were lots of very greedy people who would do anything – indeed, had already tried – to get him to disclose the burial place of the Cones. He suddenly became alert to the idea that he was in mortal danger. He had made a great deal of news lately. Bad press that did wonders for Flute's sales figures. But because of *Hoard*, many people had died and the heritage sites of Great Britain had suffered immense damage at the hands of frantic treasure hunters. There was bound to be revenge of some sort.

'Time to go to ground,' he declared.

Woodhead's face and hands were sweating at the thought that there were people out there preparing various ways to put him in his grave. He gripped the telephone nervously, and called Cynthia at her Flute's office.

'Cynthia, listen. I've got to get away for a while. I think people are out to get me, and I need to find a hiding place.'

This need to confide in Cynthia was necessary while she was still providing funds and a place to live.

'Hollis, darling, aren't you being just a bit too paranoid? Who on earth would want to kill you just for writing an exciting book?'

'Just think about it, Cynthia, two million pounds might not be all that much to you, especially after what *Hoard* has already raked in, but to everyone else it's a fucking lot of money.'

'Well, yes, darling, if it's really worrying you. But I was hoping for more of your company as our wedding day approaches. We have to make plans, don't we?'

'Of course, lover, and we will. I just need to disappear for a couple of weeks.'

'Oh dear, Hollis, I will miss you dreadfully, even if it's only for two weeks. Where will you go?' she said in a tone that rose to an irritating whine.

'I want to keep it a secret so that you aren't burdened with dangerous knowledge, my love. When I've found a safe house I'll give you a call. Goodbye, Cynthia.'

Desperate to end the conversation, he put down the phone before she could say any more.

★

He could hide in London easily. And there were plenty of small hotels in West London.

No problem even at this time in the evening. Money was no problem either.

'Just look at you, Moggy,' Woodhead said to his neglected Morgan sports car.

He looked at the shattered windscreen and remembered the shooting as he was running frantically from The Green Boar.

'Who the fuck was it?' he wondered.

The double door swung silently upwards as he approached it from within the spacious Thurloe Place garage. He set off down the private drive towards the road. The gates opened to let him through, and then closed behind him. As he pulled out into the road, a BMW raced past him and then suddenly braked and stopped right in front of the red Morgan. Another car screeched to a halt behind him. Trapped! He waited for the blast of a gun.

'Good evening, Mr Woodhead,' said the toothy, smiling Indian-looking face politely.

A group of eight men, all wearing turbans, appeared.

'If you're lost and want to know the way to Delhi,' shouted Woodhead, 'you can have my world atlas. I always carry one. Always pleased to give you foreigners directions back home.'

'Mr Woodhead, your good English manners are legendary. However, we know where we are. And we know who you are. We will not respond by doing you harm just yet. We'd like you to come with us. We need to talk to you.'

★

The blindfold let in no light at all, but Woodhead recognised the noises of London through the open window of the car. The din of a multitude of people, the buses, the distinct sound of the taxis.

Piccadilly Circus, he guessed.

Within ten minutes he was escorted up some steps and into a building.

'Okay, Rashid, remove the blindfold, but leave the hands tied.'

It was an Indian Temple in the heart of London. The stained-glassed windows had been replaced by Indian forms; however the 'trinity' windows told him that it was once an Anglican or Catholic church. An added frieze around the walls of the large nave depicted a great variety of sexual activities, which reminded Woodhead of the post-cards he had once received from a friend visiting the temples at Karnak. Although he'd never entered a temple of any sort in his whole life, he perceived this one was somehow not the place for normal Indian worship, but something more sinister. The whole place exuded evil. Through the subdued lighting and smoky atmosphere Woodhead could see a large three-headed figure standing before some sort of altar in a curious, crouching, bow-legged pose and wielding a curved sword. In each head eight highly decorated and fearsome staring eyes. Its warrior dress was covered with the dreaded Nazi *Hakenkreuz*.

'I didn't know there was a Delhi National Front.' Woodhead constantly feared a violent death but had an amazing propensity to draw it near to him.

'Ah, the swastikas. You are a great fool, Mr Woodhead. This cross is a symbol from antiquity and represents a powerful god. Our god Yamati,' said the Indian through closed teeth in an irritated tone. 'He is a killer of infidels, and we live and act in the image of our god.'

'Yamati? Hmm, sounds bloody Japanese to me.'

'Mr Woodhead, you are in great danger of losing your head. And you may yet, when we have finished with you. Aren't you interested in why you're here?'

'I already know. You've abducted me against my will, and now you're going to convert me – against my will. I don't want to be evil and vicious, thank you.'

'If you had read your Indian history well, Mr Woodhead, you might have remembered that the Yamati were a thug tribe that did immense work in convincing the British Raj that they should go home. We strangled, stabbed and poisoned a large number of your brave young men – around the first part of this century especially.'

'Are you sure you're not Delhi National Front?' asked Woodhead, treading close to the edge of danger.

A heavy door near the altar creaked open and a tiger-headed being wrapped in an orange sari and carrying a long staff entered, and walked slowly to the altar, followed by a guard of eight solemn-faced men with oiled bodies, painted faces, wearing only baggy linen pantaloons. It suddenly dawned on Woodhead that everything about this group so far had been in eights: his captors, the eyes in the altar god, the ritual guard. Even the swastikas had eight elements. Except the image: it had three heads. Woodhead remembered that many pagan deities were trinities. Perhaps this was such a representation.

'Look Mr Woodhead,' shouted the voice from the tiger's head, 'look here.'

The priest pointed with the staff to a carving at the rear of the altar.

'What do you see, Mr Woodhead?'

In this temple it was difficult for Woodhead to see anything that was not extraordinary.

'What am I supposed to be looking at?'

'Come closer, you fool, and you will see!' boomed the tiger.

'My Christ! The Cones!'

The nonplussed Woodhead narrowed his eyes to peer closely in the dim light at the religious emblem built into the front of the altar. Eight Golden Cones, the same number, shape and pattern as those he had planted in the ground, depicted in plaster in a ring in the altar stone.

'But that's been made recently,' said Woodhead.

The tiger turned to Woodhead.

'That's true. This emblem is in all of our temples, and some of them are new. But what about this?'

The tiger directed Woodhead's gaze to a framed photograph attached to the altar, an old photograph of a very large rock that dwarfed the sacred people bent over in prayers before it. No question, the same emblem engraved in the rock.

'The thing is, Mr Woodhead, you have the golden originals – and we want them back,' said the tiger in a slow determined whisper, 'do you understand? We want no part of your low-minded treasure hunt. We are dignified, dedicated and strong Yamati warriors, and we want to restore full Yamati ceremonies. We can only do that when we have the Cones.'

A great mistake. Woodhead recognised now the folly of publishing pictures of the original Cones. Anything would have done. Someone was bound to make a connection to the religious significance of the Cones and the robbery in India so many years ago.

'We feel very privileged that we – *we* tracked you down. Although it really wasn't difficult. The secretary at your publishers was very helpful.'

'I'm in the shit,' admitted Woodhead.

'You certainly—'

The tiger was interrupted by the incongruous alerting tones of his mobile telephone, which he took from a pocket in his breeches.

'Oh, hello, Rodney darling, it's you,' said the tiger, putting his left hand to his ear and turning his head away from Woodhead. 'Look, umm, I can't talk to you just now, dear. Yes, yes, okay. But remember to bring the catalogue.'

'Tiger, tiger burning bright,' Woodhead chortled, 'you're a poofter, aren't you? A candy-striped tiger.'

Members of the guard broke into belly wobbling laughter, and the tiger threw down his staff angrily.

'Strip him and throw him into the lock-up, right now!'

The tiger was in absolute fury.

Woodhead was thrown unceremoniously into a small, cold and empty concrete bunker with no light, wearing only his underpants.

★

'Would you please come out, Mr Woodhead,' said a cheerful Bombay accent.

'Why are you people always so bloody polite? Why don't you ask me if I'd like a cup of your best Darjeeling tea – and a biscuit too?'

Woodhead hated politeness generally, but considered it especially repugnant when associated with violence. A couple of silent heavies led him down a set of old stone steps to a room filled with implements of torture. Déjà vu!

'Look, don't waste your time. I'll tell you where they are. I don't need the bloody things anyway,' said Woodhead, suddenly realising that the Golden Cones were not absolutely necessary for the success of his plan. 'Nobody would find where they were buried anyway. Get me to Miss Candy Stripes and I'll explain everything.'

★

'Knowing you as we do, Mr Woodhead, it will not surprise you to learn that we don't trust you,' said the tiger. 'You won't be leaving here tonight.'

'When's the interrogation?'

'Interrogation is overdoing it a bit, Mr Woodhead. I have only one question of you, and it needs a very simple answer. You know the question already. What's the answer? Think about it. You don't have to strain yourself with an answer right away. We have all the time in the world. You simply don't eat or drink until you've told me where our blessed Golden Cones are.'

'Can I have a cigarette?'

'We Yamati do not smoke common cigarettes, Mr Woodhead,' said the tiger with effeminate indignation.

'Pardon me for living,' Woodhead retorted sarcastically as he was being manacled to a wall, 'but there are some in my trousers.'

'Tonight is Hasamachi, and we are going to celebrate the birth of our god, Yamati. I have to lead the ceremony, so you are going to be alone for the rest of the night, so there.'

'Why does everything about this religion of yours sound Japanese?'

The tiger and his guards left without answering.

Woodhead was soon unbearably cold.

'Hey, somebody!' he shouted as loud as he could. 'Get me out of here. I'm fucking freezing.'

The door of the torture chamber opened almost immediately.

'We were just coming to get you, Mr Woodhead. We want you to join our celebration.'

Two guards this time, in ritual dress. They led Woodhead into the large nave of the temple, which was now filled with at least a hundred people, all adults, and all dressed ceremonially. They turned and watched as Woodhead was secured by a rope to a ring on the wall at the side of the altar. The tiger stood facing the altar, and the members of the ritual guard stood equally spaced in a square in front of the steps leading up to him. A helper to the side of the altar beat a small gong just once, and everyone except the priest and the ritual guard knelt down on the carpets and bent over until their heads touched the floor. Then a procession of eight figures, all covered from head to foot in brightly coloured, muslin robes, entered the square formed by the guard.

'Jahashi yan tasha, jahashi yan tasha!' chanted the tiger, and the auditorium responded with incomprehensible murmuring.

Woodhead stared at the proceedings and wondered what it all meant for him. Throughout, the tiger chanted what Woodhead assumed to be religious entreaties to Yamati, and the attendant followers raised themselves, knelt and bowed obediently.

'Yamati, Yamati. Yesh Yamati! shouted the tiger.

Immediately, the guards pulled the robes from the covered figures. They were lovely young women, all in their late teens, completely naked, but highly decorated. Laces of pearls hung around their waists; they wore golden bracelets and anklets; and bright rich colours were daubed on their faces. And their black shiny hair was long.

'My God, they're beautiful,' said Woodhead, sensing his prejudice slipping away.

'They're maidens. Not my scene really,' confessed the tiger.

'No, I suppose it isn't,' said Woodhead with uncharacteristic honesty.

'Silence!'

Woodhead sunk to the floor as far as his fettered arms would allow. Coloured lights flashed through the haze and pricked his eyes.

'Okay Hollis,' said a familiar voice, 'don't worry, I've got you.'

'Hollis! Who called me Hollis?'

'It's me, Ernest Clamp. Just let me carry you.'

Woodhead was shocked into semi-consciousness. He strained hard to look at the face; he couldn't make out the features but the voice was unmistakable.

'Ernest, Ernest...'

'Just let me carry you, Hollis.'

'Am I in touch with you, or are you there?' said Woodhead deliriously.

'I cannot stay with you, Hollis, because they're waiting for me. I asked only that I be allowed to rescue you. Perhaps you will remember this: I am not dead. I was taken by the travellers.'

'Ernest, why have you painted your face so brightly? That's not like you.'

Woodhead laughed loudly, and fell into a deep sleep.

Chapter Nine

The gothic spire of St Ansalph's Church towered into the blue sky above Greenwich, and Hollis Woodhead stood beneath it wishing he were somewhere else. He pondered on the gargoyles that looked down upon him with petrified cries of anguish that reinforced his own deep sense of depression. A man stood at his side wearing the uniform of an undertaker and a sombre expression.

'It's time to begin,' said the man. 'We were beginning to think you'd changed your mind.'

The undertaker snapped his fingers, and Woodhead and the man were standing in the church either side of a coffin. A faceless figure turned to the undertaker and pointed at the box.

'Remove the lid,' it said.

There was a gasp of expectation from the pews as the oak cover hit the floor.

'Do you have the ring?' it continued.

'I do,' said the undertaker in a monotone.

'Then let the marriage take place.'

Strains of 'The Wedding March' rattled into the rafters from a wheezing Wurlitzer organ, and Cynthia Flockhard-Flute leapt from the coffin into Woodhead's trembling arms.

'Quick! Give me the ring!' she barked. 'We can't let him get away now!'

A menacing chant came from the shadows:

'The ring... the ring... the ring... the ring...'

'Never!' screamed Woodhead, 'never, never, never.'

He reached for the bedside lamp and switched it on. Ever since Cynthia had publicly announced her intention to marry him his dreams had swiftly graduated from the vaguely disturbing visions he was prone to suffer from time to time – a legacy of his unusual life – to nightmares that made him afraid to go to bed. She had not even bothered to consult him before blabbing it to the newspapers. He'd stormed over to Cynthia's apartment immediately after reading the offending gossip columnist, determined to put her in the picture once and for all but she had been waiting for him with a sweetener she knew a man like Hollis Woodhead could not possibly resist. Sure, he was already rich from the monumental returns on *Hoard* (a fortune that continued to grow daily), but the contract that Cynthia handed him, a contract assuring him the two million pounds prize if the treasure remained hidden after the closing date, had been more than enough to cool his rage.

'After all, darling,' she'd said, 'you've got to be rich in your own right or everyone will say you married me for my money. Besides, you deserve it after what your book's done for Flutes. All our other titles are selling like hot cakes too. I suppose the punters are hoping they'll find extra clues to the treasure in them.'

Woodhead sat up in bed and rolled a cigarette. He had at least managed to negotiate a few days of separation from the wretched woman.

'I could do with a little space,' he had told her.

There was nothing for it: he would have to arrange something for Cynthia – something unpleasant and terminal. He spent the day mulling this considerable problem over in his mind as he sat in his office checking on the usual pile of mail from treasure hunters. He never answered any of the letters, but felt it was in his best interest to look them over. Many were from admiring young women who tempted him sorely with promises of physical fulfilment. Woodhead's diligence in scanning all the letters had one objective, though, and that was to make sure that no one had unravelled the clues. If anyone ever did, serious action would have to be taken, the sort of action he already had in mind for Cynthia. It was early evening by the time he'd finished reading the last letter.

★

For a number of weeks he had enjoyed the company of shapely Olga, the daughter of Cynthia's cleaning lady, Mrs Bullick; and, although a vacuum cleaner had figured heavily in their first encounter, Olga's attitude had changed beyond recognition after she'd seen Woodhead on the television. He'd accepted her apology without hesitation, and her body in much the same grateful way. As he drove to her flat in Knightsbridge, he remembered fondly what she had said to him the following morning:

'I think you're really nice, Mr Woodhead.'

'Call me Hollis,' he'd said generously.

'Sorry... Hollis.'

He realised he was getting soft, but it didn't worry him. Once Cynthia's funeral was over, and all the fuss had died down he might even ask Olga to marry him. After all, he wasn't getting any younger. He pulled up at her flat, and noticed a large Harley Davidson motorbike parked on the kerb outside the front door. She obviously had a visitor. Woodhead didn't like bikers. He rang the doorbell and took a step backwards to see if she was at the window. Olga's voice came over the speaker.

'Yes?'

'It's Hollis.'

'Oh... hello... you'd better come up.'

Olga sounded strange over the intercom as if she'd rather he hadn't come. A buzzer sounded and the lock clicked. Woodhead opened the door and scaled the stairs. Her expression was cold and, instead of the customary warm hug, she simply beckoned him into the apartment. He kissed her on the cheek, but she didn't respond; her hands remained in her pockets.

'What's wrong, Olga? Are you feeling all right?'

'Fine.'

Woodhead felt the ice in her voice. The balloon was about to go up, and he didn't have the faintest clue what he'd done to deserve it. What had happened to his beautiful Olga? She was usually so affectionate and bubbly; now, suddenly, it seemed she had no feelings for him at all. He followed her into the living room. A man Woodhead had never seen before was sitting on the sofa tinkering with an oily lump of metal.

'Engine trouble,' he explained. 'Must've seen my Harley as you came in. I love bikes. Like to get my leg over.'

He gave Olga a knowing wink.

'Oh, Herby,' said Olga, 'you are naughty.'

'Pleased to meet you Hollis, Olga's told me a lot about you.'

He extended a filthy hand that Woodhead, who had absolutely no desire to be sociable, found himself shaking out of reflex.

'Who?'

Woodhead was lost for words.

'The name's Herbert old chap – well Jeremiah Herbert Longfellow, actually. Magdalen, Oxford,' he added as though it were his customary line. 'You see, my mother was very keen on the Bible.'

He erupted into a raucous fit of laughter that made Woodhead feel sick.

'Anyway,' he continued, when he'd recovered his breath, 'you can call me Herb.'

Woodhead stared at the man open-mouthed. He was no picture himself, he knew that, but Herbert was the most disgusting human being he had ever set eyes upon. The man was a loathsome large lump of fat with an ugly, pock-marked face, and tattoos wherever there wasn't a covering of black leather; and, to top it all, he must have been sixty at the very least.

'Herbert's my new boyfriend,' Olga announced callously. 'He's a viscount, and we're going to go around the world on his motorbike.'

Woodhead sat down, and struggled internally with this revelation for several minutes. Herbert finally broke the silence with a rattling of chains.

'Can I get you a drink, old chap? You look a bit under the weather.'

'No, I don't want a fucking drink!' snapped Woodhead.

'Temper, temper,' said Herb, 'cause me and Olga any trouble and I'll send some of the boys around to experiment on you.'

Woodhead couldn't believe what was happening to him. He was being threatened by a Hell's Angel pensioner who had just poached his girlfriend from under his nose. He felt as though he was about to blow up, self-destruct. He turned his attention to Olga, who was standing by the door with her arms folded. Olga's obvious enjoyment from this confrontation cut Woodhead deeply.

'Why?' he asked pathetically.

'I love him, that's why.'

'How can you love that? Look at him. The man's a fucking moron!'

'I love him!'

'He's got tattoos!'

'I love him!'

'I think you'd better leave,' said Herbert.

'Don't worry, fatso,' said Woodhead. 'I'm on my way.'

'And don't ever come back!' screamed Olga as he staggered down the stairs in a state of shock.

At the bottom he turned and looked back at them as they studied him from above.

'I wouldn't come back to you if you begged me on your hands and knees! I wouldn't come back to you if you were the last woman on the planet! I wouldn't even come back to you if my life depended on it, you silly little bitch! Satisfied?'

'Yes!'

'Good!'

He got into his car and reversed into Herbert's motorbike, an act of vandalism he enjoyed more than anything he could ever remember doing in his life. He then drove off in search of succour. He spent the rest of the evening drinking heavily.

'I could have made her happy,' he said aloud.

As the evening went on, he became argumentatively drunk, and was forcibly ejected from the bar with the familiar words of a little earlier: 'And don't ever come back!' He staggered into a nearby park, and tried to sleep it off on a bench.

After a few hours, he awoke feeling very cold and still very drunk. He rolled himself a cigarette and stood up, pulling his jacket collar up against the night. The dreadful events of the day dawned on him as he swayed to and fro in a light rain, drawing on his roll-up.

'When it rains it fucking pours,' he moaned drunkenly.

There was a flash of lightning as he spoke, and suddenly it was pouring. Woodhead raised his eyes to the sky for inspiration and, as he did so, his cigarette was extinguished and he fell over.

'Olga! Why?' He tried to get up but fell over again. He howled. He couldn't stop himself.

Chapter Ten

Irwin Axelburger III was a man who knew exactly what he wanted, and more often than not, whether by fair means or foul, that was exactly what he got. The second Irwin Axelburger had clawed his way out of the poverty trap by manufacturing display fireworks for America's rich and famous. It was only natural therefore, that the third Irwin should follow in the footsteps of his enterprising father. This he had done with distinction. By the time he was thirty-five he was selling arms to the United States government and every developing country they felt like starting a war in. In short, he was, at sixty, an immensely wealthy and powerful man. He was also as bald as an egg and, as he was forever telling his three common law wives (Lola, Mary Anne and Iris) and ten children (Irwin IV, V, VI, VII, VIII and IX, Marsha, Mona, Catherine and Lucy), 'real pissed off with everything.'

He had cultivated an appallingly ruthless outlook on the world before leaving his teens. It was a philosophy that did not require the smallest atom of goodness, and one that any arms dealer worth his salt since the beginning of hostilities between human beings, would have been proud to harbour. It kind of went with the terrain, and it had to be said that Irwin was worth more salt than most. He loved to mix it with the military big wigs, especially American generals – they knew about making war.

The Axelburgers inhabited Charlbury Hall, an Elizabethan manor house set in several hundred hectares of

Oxfordshire. Although outwardly elegant and inwardly lavish, the house held little appeal for Mr Axelburger. He was more preoccupied with his nuclear shelter and state-of-the-art weaponry, including two tanks with the latest computer control systems and communications gear, and an assortment of heat-seeking missiles, all of which lay beneath its sixteenth-century foundations. Not even Irwin's butler, Bracebridge, knew the full extent of the dormant arsenal.

Axelburger pressed a buzzer on the marble desk in his study, and waited impatiently.

'You rang, sir?' asked the butler solemnly as he opened the study door.

'Why do you always say that, Bracebridge?' demanded Axelburger hotly. 'You know damn well I did... five fucking minutes ago.'

'I'm sorry for the delay, sir. I'm afraid I had my hands full.'

'Play with the maids in your own time. When you're working for me I want you here on the double.'

'As sir wishes.'

'And don't give me any of that superior English bullshit. I can see it in your eyes. You're an asshole, Bracebridge – an English asshole. You know it, and so do I.'

'If it pleases sir to think so,' said the butler, raising an eyebrow, 'then far be it for me to contradict an opinion so firmly held.'

'It pleases the hell out of sir to think so. Now, fuck off and get me some breakfast, and Bracebridge–'

'Sir?'

'How long have you been an employee here?'

'Eight years, sir.'

'Well, if you want to keep on being one, don't call me sir anymore. It gets on my tits.'

'What would you like me to call you instead, sir?'

'My lord will do.'

'My lord, sir?'

'Don't push your luck, Bracebridge.'

'No, my lord.'

'Now, go and get my breakfast. After that you can take me over to the lab in the helicopter. I want to see if those idiots have solved that frigging book yet.'

'As my lord wishes.'

Axelburger enjoyed insulting Bracebridge.

*

An hour later the two men were on the roof of Charlbury Hall walking towards the helicopter pad.

'Bracebridge.'

'My lord?'

'When we get back from the laboratory, I want you to go down to the bunker and baby-sit.'

'But they don't like me, my lord – and there are so many of them.'

'Of course they don't like you. That's because they know an asshole when they see one.'

'Then why do I have to look after them?'

'Because I said so, damn it. Now start up the whirly-bird and stop whining.'

Irwin III suspected – and with good cause – that at least three of his ten children were the offspring of the poker faced butler. Unfortunately, he had no way of proving it. However, he could think of few punishments more fitting for the adulterous swine than taking charge of the Axel-burger brood for an afternoon. They were extremely disagreeable company, largely because they spent most of their time underground – but then, the way things were going on the planet, Axelburger couldn't see any reason why they shouldn't get used to it.

Bracebridge climbed into the helicopter and pressed the ignition as his resentful American master sat in the passenger seat. The rotor-blades picked up speed, and the flying butler busily mumbled obscenities at the control panel.

'What was that Bracebridge?' shouted Axelburger above the noise.

'Nothing, my lord.'

'Let's move out, then.'

'As my lord wishes.'

Moments later they were airborne and rising.

*

The Axelburger research laboratory was only two miles to the north-west, but Irwin III rarely travelled there by car. A helicopter had a much bigger psychological impact on a workforce than a car. You couldn't be thought of as a god descending from heaven to terrorise the inferior beings that worked for you if you arrived in a limousine, not even if it had eight wheels like the one under wraps in his garage. And Irwin III liked the god idea a lot. Even before they'd touched down, an embassy of men in pinstripe suits were walking briskly towards them making obsequious gestures. They looked suitably terrified, and quite ridiculous, as they cowered in the mini-tempest blowing at them from the helicopter rotors.

'See that, Bracebridge?' bellowed Axelburger, nodding at the miserable creatures who stood to attention with wildly bulging eyes and manic grins. 'Assholes, every one of them, just like you.'

'Yes, my lord.'

'Do you know what I call them, Bracebridge?'

'Turkeys, my lord.'

'Do you know why?' The butler's quizzical expression made it clear that he didn't. 'I call them turkeys, Bracebridge, because they're always standing around waiting for fucking Christmas or something.'

'Yes, my lord.'

'I think I'll sack a few today. It'll keep the others on their toes.'

Bracebridge shut down the engine and hopped gracefully on to the helipad. Much to the annoyance of his overweight boss, the butler was remarkably agile for a man in his early fifties. It was an agility for which his boss's wives were forever finding intimate and exciting new challenges, and Bracebridge was always very keen to accommodate them if he could.

The pinstripes kept at a respectful distance as he walked to the other side of the aircraft and opened the door for Axelburger. The American climbed down and scowled at his assembled slaves.

'Why aren't you people in the lab working on that treasure book? Do you think I pay you to show me around my own goddamn property?'

'Excuse me, my lord I—'

'Shut the fuck up, Bracebridge, I'm busy.'

'But, my lord—'

'One more word, dickhead, and you'll be crop-spraying whatever part of this god-forsaken island you were crop-spraying before I brought you here.'

Bracebridge took a brisk walk back to the helicopter, and Axelburger spun round to continue his inquisition of the pinstripe suits, but they were running for the lab.

'Where in the Sam Hill do you people think you're going? I was talking to you!'

Like Bracebridge, and unlike Axelburger, they'd seen the escaped guard-dogs, four very hungry Dobermans that were now gaining ground on the bewildered American. He was not bewildered for long.

'Bracebridge!' he screamed, pulling a gold-plated nine-millimetre Browning automatic from his shoulder holster as one of the dogs sunk its teeth into his buttocks, 'I'm gonna fucking get you for this!'

Bracebridge read his lips from the safety of the helicopter, and Axelburger promptly shot himself in the foot. He spent the rest of the magazine trying to hit the vicious pooches as they fled from the first bang; but in his agony, and to his great annoyance, he didn't bag one of them.

'The bastards! The bastards!'

Axelburger wheeled on his one good leg and shot another salvo. He missed the dogs again, but hit a chemical storage tank next to the lab, which exploded. The explosion levelled one wing of the lab, and a huge fire ball rose into the air.

'That's the way to enforce compulsory redundancies, Bracebridge!' he screamed. Bracebridge calmly called for emergency services on the radio telephone and went over to inspect his wounded employer.

'Are you all right, my lord?'

'You asshole, Bracebridge,' gasped the American huskily, 'you fucking asshole!'

He pointed the empty gun at his butler with a trembling hand, and fainted.

*

Olbury Hospital was a beautifully converted large '30s country house. Bracebridge stood at reception, and studied the attractive nurse walking along the carpeted corridor towards him.

'Mr Axelburger is comfortable,' she said as she neared him. 'He has a hole in his right foot that should heal quite well, but his foot will be in plaster for at least a couple of weeks.'

'Comfortable, you say?' said Bracebridge politely.

The butler had been hoping for something a little more severe, and didn't feel in the least bit 'comfortable' himself. Axelburger had just summoned him to a bedside consultation.

'Are you sure he's well enough to see me, nurse?' he asked hopefully. 'He's very excitable at the best of times; I would have thought it better for him to rest.'

'Well, it's up to you whether you want to see him or not, but he seemed very keen on seeing you.'

'Oh, what the hell. It's been a good eight years, and I suppose there are worse things in life than crop-spraying.'

'Mr Bracebridge?'

'Never mind, I was thinking aloud. Where did you say his room is?'

'Along this corridor, turn left and third on your right. Number thirteen.'

'How fitting. Good afternoon, nurse.'

When Bracebridge entered the room, it was clear to him that neither his current employment nor his licentious romantic liaisons at the Axelburger home were in jeopardy. Axelburger had the company of five attentive nurses, and he was being his usual flamboyant, woman-pleasing self with them. He had been indirectly responsible for the death and wounding of many, many war heroes, now he felt like one of them. And he loved it.

'Oh, Mr Axelburger, please keep your hands off my bottom,' giggled one of the nurses as she adjusted his pillows.

'Ah, Bracebridge old fellow, how the hell are you?'

'Well, my lord... and you?'

'Fine, have you found out who's to blame for the dogs yet?'

'Yes, my lord, it was the handler. Quite drunk, apparently. Kept on about animal rights when he was questioned. I took the liberty of firing him, and I understand he's helping the police with their inquiries at the moment.'

'Too fucking right, Bracebridge. Was anyone injured?'

'Three dead and five seriously wounded.'

'Golly, that's too bad. Okay, Bracebridge, I want you to move the boffins working on that book over to the manor. I'll see them when I get out.'

Bracebridge left the room to a chorus of giggling nurses.

'What an asshole,' he muttered.

Chapter Eleven

A month of living with Magdelaine in her dreary three-roomed apartment had taken its toll on Willy Grindle. She was a very demanding woman, and he was running out of energy. He was also running out of money. Willy hated his relationship with Magdelaine, but he was stuck with it. He needed time. The media had not helped matters for him either. From the moment 'Operation Flying Nun' was launched, his face had been indelibly imprinted into the consciousness of everyone in the country. He had to leave the country, and had clear ideas about how to obtain the money to do so – by blackmailing Cynthia Flockhard-Flute. But, until interest in his whereabouts died down generally, he could not leave the house, let alone get away from Magdelaine. He had no confidence that his disguises would guarantee him security. Someone would certainly recognise him in this part of town.

He paced up and down the bedroom wringing his hands with paranoid agitation, desperately wishing that his nymphomaniac landlady owned a telephone. Blackmailing Cynthia Flockhard-Flute presented no difficulty, it was how to manage it without getting nicked again, that was the problem. It was no good, he would have to get Magdelaine involved in his plan.

'Maggie! Wake up Maggie! Maggie!'

Magdelaine emerged from beneath the covers, one eye open, the lids of the other firmly stuck together with stale make-up.

'You are a wicked Willy.'

'Pack it in, Maggie! Don't you ever think about anything else?'

'Like what?' she asked, as though there was nothing else.

'Just listen to me, will you,' said Willy, on the edge of losing his temper. 'I've got a plan, and I need your help to make it work.'

'What are you talking about, Willy. Just give me time to wake up.'

Magdelaine raised herself on her elbows, and strained at focusing her eyes on the picture that hung from the grubby wall of her bedroom.

'What is it, then?' she asked.

'Just listen for a moment, and I'll tell you.'

'I'm all ears.'

'Blackmail.'

Willy reached over her, and took from her bedside table the parcel previously deep-frozen with her Aunt Lily.

'Open it. I want you to read what's inside.'

Magdelaine had been anxious to open the parcel ever since Willy had told her it contained letters. She tore at the wrapping and pulled out a pink envelope.

'Nice colour,' she said inanely.

'Read it aloud,' said Willy.

'*Dearest William,*' she began, glancing at Grindle, '*how I've longed for you these past few days,*' Magdelaine paused for a moment to scoff at the dreary Cartlandesque romanticism. 'Hell, Willy, it's enough to make you heave. Who is this?'

'Just read it will you.'

'All right, all right.' She focused on the letter again. '*When I think of our last time together, the cuddly bear suit you wore, the exquisite texture of the fur, and the way it glistened with oil! You put me in touch with myself and reawaken feelings I thought had died for ever. Come to me, darling, soon. I am yours for eternity, Cynthia.*'

'Good, isn't it?' said Willy.

'Cuddly bear suit!' said Magdelaine scornfully.

'I had to wear all kinds of things.' And barely audibly he said, 'and do all sorts of things.'

Magdelaine looked at the other letters. All had much the same tone, except that the weird manner of Willy's dress obviously differed for each occasion.

'Who is she?' asked Magdelaine.

'Her name's Cynthia Flockhard-Flute,' said Willy. 'She's the one who published all mum's... er... my books. She's worth a fortune, Maggie, and so are these letters.'

'What are you going to do with them?'

'What do you think I'm going to do with them? I'm going to use them to blackmail her.'

'Will she go for it?'

'Of course she will. She doesn't want to be associated with me. I'm the "Beast of Broadmoor", remember? All I've got to do is tell her I'll give the letters to the press if she doesn't cooperate, and she'll give me what I want.'

'What do you want?'

'Just a million pounds.'

'My, that is a lot of money!' Magdelaine's pupils dilated.

'Don't worry, she can afford it. Besides, the bitch is raking in all the profit from my books. Now listen, I want you to buy a mobile telephone. Do you think you can do that?'

'Why?'

'So I can telephone her, stupid. I can hardly use a blinking phone box at the moment, can I? You're going to have to do all the leg work, Maggie, but I'll pay you well, don't worry about that!'

Magdelaine crossed her arms and shrugged her shoulders.

'I hope it's not too complicated for me,' she said.

★

'Cynthia Flockhard-Flute speaking.'

'Hello, Cynthia, guess who this is.'

'Willy Grindle!' A chill ran through her as she recognised the voice.

'I wouldn't put the phone down if I were you, Cynthia. Not unless you want a scandal. You're getting married next month, aren't you?'

'What do you want?'

'I've got all the letters you ever sent me, and I want to give you an opportunity to buy them back.'

There was a nervous silence on the other end of the line.

'Very simple, Cynthia, give me a million pounds, or I'll send the letters to the press. Imagine the headlines: "*Publishing heiress sends sordid letters to Broadmoor monster*".' Willy could hear her breathing heavily over the phone.

'You're insane!'

'So they tell me,' he said, giggling for a moment. 'I hope you're going to be sensible, because if you don't give me the money I'll ruin the rest of your life.'

'How do I know you still have the letters?'

'I've got them all right. All you have to do to get them back is leave the money in a locker at Victoria Station tomorrow. I'll phone you tomorrow evening and tell you where to put the key.'

'How do I get the letters?' It suddenly occurred to her that she should play for time. 'All right, I'll do it.'

'There's my girl.'

The phone went dead. Cynthia tried to collect her thoughts. Hollis would know what to do. She phoned for him immediately.

'Hollis Woodhead.'

'Oh Hollis, it's Cynthia. I'm in terrible trouble, you

must come over straight away.'

'Can't it wait until this evening?' Woodhead coughed and sniffed from the cold he had caught sobering up in the park. 'I'm up to my ears in mail – and I don't like some of it.'

'This is serious, darling and I simply don't know what to do,' sobbed Cynthia.

'Fuck it,' swore Woodhead under his breath. 'All right, Cynthia, I'm on my way.'

A little later he was with Cynthia in her apartment, trying hard to figure out what she was saying. It was so difficult to make much sense out of her while she was sobbing bitterly. Her emotions were stirred only indirectly from Grindle's threat, but most certainly directly from the many brandies she had downed between phoning Woodhead and his arrival. Between deep braying noises and the frequent pauses she took to blow her nose, he was able to deduce it had something to do with Willy Grindle. What though, he couldn't yet tell.

'For crying out loud, Cynthia, pull yourself together!' he said, snatching the brandy bottle from her angrily. 'I can't understand a word you're saying! What about Willy Grindle?'

'He's trying to blackmail me,' she sobbed.

'How?'

'It was a long time ago, darling. I didn't know what he was like. He seemed so nice, you see.'

She started to whine again.

'What was a long time ago?'

'I had an affair with him.'

'Oh, I see,' said Woodhead pretending to be hurt.

'I wrote him some letters, love letters, and they were... well, a little bit personal.'

'Correct me if I'm wrong,' said Woodhead haughtily, 'but I think you're trying to tell me that they're not the sort of thing you'd like anyone else to read.'

She nodded and dried her puffy eyes.

'He said that if I didn't give him a million pounds he'd hand them over to the press.'

This situation held distinct possibilities. Woodhead was delighted. He stalled for time while he thought it through.

'Well, we've no choice in the matter, we'll have to phone the police. The little bastard's a convicted cannibal, Cynthia. No one would publish the letters. We'd see to that.'

'Oh yes they would,' she said, howling again.

'All right then, what do you suggest?'

'He said I should leave the money in a locker at Victoria Station. He's going to phone me back tomorrow evening and tell me where to leave the key.'

'And you agreed?'

'Oh Hollis, what am I going to do?'

'Did you agree?'

'Yes.'

'I suppose you want me to take the money to Victoria Station?' asked Woodhead, giving no hint of the elation that filled him. He had already formulated a plan of his own.

'Would you?' gushed Cynthia, suddenly relieved.

'I'd like to say right here and now that I'm against this, but if you think it's the only way, then I'll do it. I wouldn't do it for anyone else, though, I can tell you that.'

'Oh Hollis, I do love you.' Woodhead got to his feet before she could grab him and went to the door. 'I'll be back this evening to pick up the money,' he said, 'so you'd better sober up and go and get it. I'll have to go. Can you really get your hands on a million at such short notice?' That it really didn't have to be accomplished so quickly – with the promise of a million, Grindle would surely wait a few days – occurred to Woodhead, but he was anxious to get all issues associated with Cynthia resolved as soon as possible.

'I'm sure I can with no trouble at all. If you want a gun, Hollis dear, I have a very nice, shiny pistol that father gave to me. He said I'd need it sooner or later.'

'Okay, give it to me.'

Not really knowing what he would do with the pistol, but nevertheless feeling more adequately armed to meet this particular foe, he left.

*

Later in the day, he picked up a smart new briefcase containing lots of fifty pound notes from a more sober and reassured Cynthia.

Why is she worried about people knowing she was having it off with Grindle? Woodhead wondered. People do such things all the time. Besides, it would make super publicity.

He drove directly to his own bank and deposited the briefcase in a safety deposit box. He then drove back to Thurloe Place and waited for things to develop. Willy Grindle would be getting his money all right, but he would have to work extremely hard to get it.

In the large pile of mail that Woodhead had received that day was a letter submitted by a certain Dr Beinegger from the Department of Astrophysics, Bournemouth University, containing a solution to the whereabouts of the Golden Cones. Although he did not specify the actual spot that marked their burial place, Beinegger gave the correct general location. It required only one small step more to locate the Golden Cones precisely. Perhaps Beinegger already knew!

Woodhead needed Grindle urgently, and Grindle had put himself into Woodhead's game-plan fortuitously – perfectly.

*

The following evening, the 'Beast of Broadmoor' telephoned instructions to Cynthia and, shortly afterwards, Cynthia telephoned Woodhead.

'Woodhead speaking.'

'It's Cynthia, Hollis. Grindle said I have to put the locker key in an envelope, go to the Mayflower Hotel in Hackney, and slide the envelope under the door of room nineteen.'

'When?'

'Nine o'clock this evening.' Woodhead checked his watch. It was seven-thirty. 'Have you told the police?'

'Lord no, Hollis. I don't trust what the police would do in this case. It's my good name I'm protecting – the good name of the Flockhard-Flute family.'

'Okay, Cynthia, I'm on my way.'

'Please be careful, my darling.'

'Don't worry about me, Cynthia,' said Woodhead, loading Cynthia's .45 automatic with a full magazine. 'I'll be fine.'

*

The Mayflower Hotel was a large and seedy-looking building that faced Hackney Marsh and the gas works beyond. Woodhead parked his Morgan nearby, and waited for nine o'clock. Magdelaine was waiting for nine o'clock too, and it seemed to her to be a long time coming. Room nineteen of The Mayflower Hotel was dirty, and harboured cockroaches. Magdelaine had never been able to cope with anything that had more than four legs, so, after seeing their dark shapes scurrying across the carpet she stood on a chair in the darkness, staring at the line of light beneath the locked door. In this discomfort her wait seemed interminable.

At precisely nine o'clock, Woodhead slid the envelope under the door. He was careful to leave a little of it showing so that he would know the moment it was picked up. He then walked to the end of the corridor and waited for the fish to take the bait. Very shortly, the envelope disappeared into the room.

'Bingo,' said Woodhead under his breath.

Magdelaine put the envelope into her handbag and hastily returned to the chair to wait out the further ten minutes after the drop that Willy required of her, before leaving the room. But in the darkness, she imagined hundreds of cockroaches climbing on to her chair, and her fear of them drove her quickly from the room.

'Not another moment in this terrible place,' she said to herself, 'I'm leaving.'

Woodhead nonchalantly followed Magdelaine to reception, watched her check out, and then followed her the short distance to where she had parked her little car. As she opened the car door, Woodhead walked up to her and pointed the .45 automatic at her head.

'Just stay where you are, lady,' he said.

'What do you want?' said Magdelaine, in a trembling voice. Her bulging eyes disclosed the terror within her.

'I want to see Willy,' said Woodhead, pushing the gun at her face.

'Willy Grindle? I don't know anyone called Willy Grindle.'

'You really are dumb. You must be Magdelaine. Don't give me any trouble, Maggie,' said Woodhead menacingly. 'Where is he? I've got a deal for him.'

Magdelaine had no spirit to play killer games – she frightened too easily.

'What kind of deal?'

'One that he can't refuse.' Woodhead pulled the hammer back on the gun. 'Now, where is he?'

'He's staying at my house.'

'Well, you'd better take me to him, then. Get in the car, you can drive.'

Magdelaine obeyed without a murmur, and the two of them set off for her little terraced house in Dewberry Street.

★

The street was washed clean after the rain but it did little to enhance its appearance in such derelict surroundings.

'You go first,' said Woodhead when they got to the bright red front door. 'Don't try anything stupid either, or you'll regret it, and so will your boyfriend.'

Woodhead was overdoing the power bit with Maggie. He would have to try the friendly approach with Willy.

'Hello, Woodhead,' said Grindle, raising his hands in surrender when he saw the gun. 'Quite the little star at the moment aren't we.'

'No problems, Willy, I've got a deal for you.'

'I'm all ears,' said the murderer, throwing Magdelaine a disgusted look. 'You want money and you want to get out of the country. Am I right?'

'Right.'

'Well, you're going to have to earn it.'

'How?'

'Willy, I want to talk to you alone.'

'Magdelaine, piss off for a while. Hollis and I have to be alone.'

'Okay, ducks, but don't let him talk you into anything that's crooked. I'll go and do some shopping.'

From the window, Woodhead and Grindle watched Magdelaine walk along the street until she was out of sight.

'Willy, I have an urgent problem, and a not-so-urgent problem; and you can earn yourself all the money that you're blackmailing Cynthia for by solving them for me.'

'You're a cheeky bastard, Woodhead. And where's the money now?'

'Don't worry about that yet, Willy. Cynthia gave you a million but asked me to handle it for you. These are the conditions, Willy, and they both need to be fulfilled. A certain Dr Beinegger is threatening to ruin me, and I want him put away. No problem for you, I think. The second thing is that I want Cynthia put away because she's threatening to ruin the rest of my life. It's sort of personal and hard to explain. I want you to kill Cynthia for me, and I don't care how you do it. Just make sure you do. Then, when she's dead you'll get your reward.'

'Look, Hollis, that's all your business. I'm hiding from the police. How the hell can I do two jobs in my predicament?'

'You must be getting old, Willy, you never had such problems before.'

'Okay, okay. How can I trust you?' Willy knew Woodhead well enough to understand that he was capable of cheating.

'You'll have to. Otherwise you'll be back in Broadmoor by morning. Anyway, my need is as great as yours, Willy, you can see that. In the meantime, you'd better give me those letters. I want Cynthia to think you're history.'

'All right, Woodhead,' sighed Willy, 'you're on: but you'll have to give me some money now. I need to buy some stuff – and me and Maggie have to eat.'

'I'll come back tomorrow and give you all the details about your contract; and, when that's completed, you'll get your money and a helping hand to get out of the country. Now, give me the letters.'

Woodhead took the letters, and left the house. It had been a good day's work: he had acquired a million pounds in cash to pay for his future peace and good fortune. Willy was a reliable assassin.

★

Willy's recent normal morning routine was to grumble at Magdelaine about the time it took her to use the lavatory and bathroom. Today, his mind was filled only with thoughts of planning and executing two foul murders in order to get his money. It was Willy's style to make murder foul. Lots of blood and gore. In other words, he was not a clever murderer and, if it were not for his cannibalism, he would have no need to kill anyone. So, the commission from Woodhead was putting Willy into a new category of killer. But he had no scruples about that; as long as he got his money it didn't matter.

'Willy, pick up the telephone. Willy!' shouted Magdelaine.

'What?'

'Answer the telephone, I'm running my bath.'

'What? I can't hear what you're saying because of the noise of the bath.'

'The telephone's ringing!'

'Oh.'

Willy feared the telephone. He placed it against his ear and listened... and listened.

'Hello! Hello! Hello... hello! Is any body there?' shouted the caller at the long, curious silence.

'Is that you, Hollis,' asked Grindle quietly.

'For Christ's sake, Willy, why don't you say something when you pick up the phone? I could be here for ages just saying bloody hello.'

'Sorry, Hollis, but I gotta be careful. Might have been the police.'

'Willy, I want you to do the first job today. It's very urgent. I had a call from this guy today, and he's close to bringing me to ruin. We must do the job today. Do you understand? Today!'

'Where is he, Hollis?'

'Down near Bournemouth. He's got a private laboratory there. But don't you worry about that, I'll drive you. Just bring whatever you need to do the job. By the way, what *do* you need?'

'Now, just what do you think a cannibal needs? A carving knife, a simple carving knife with a good sharp end, of course.'

'I needn't have asked. Tell me, Willy, how do you go about killing someone? What's your method?'

'Well, Hollis, I'm not a classy killer, you know what I mean? It's just opportunity and craving. It ain't hate or anything of my victim. No, just the occasional craving for flesh – human flesh. I think I'm psychological, Hollis.'

In the excitement generated by the threat of losing his two million, Woodhead had given little consideration to the crime he was committing. Something like 'conspiring with others to…' to do something or other. He'd read the words often enough in crime reports but his present fluster impaired his memory. After this call to Willy Grindle, he became fully aware that he was entering into atrocious acts.

★

The journey to Longway took Woodhead to familiar country. Longway was halfway between Bournemouth and

Ringwood. The lush green trees and clean air reminded him of The Womb, his caravan home not all that far from Longway. The Womb! Perhaps it was no longer there?

'Ah, Mr Woodhead,' said Dr Beinegger recognising Woodhead from his picture in *Hoard*. 'My name is Beinegger – that's Bein-egger. I say that because some people call me Beinegger.' Beinegger turned slowly, deliberately, like a royal personage, to Willy Grindle. 'And you must be Mr Pearson.'

Grindle had totally forgotten his code name for the day, and looked behind him expecting a fourth person to be there. 'Oh yeah, ah yeah. Good day.'

'Please do come in.' Beinegger had a trace of German accent. He was quite tall and slightly porcine and he held himself stiffly erect, chin tucked firmly into the rolls of flesh that hung beneath it. His face was large and concentrated. 'I'm an astronomer,' he went on.

'I am also a space scientist. My professions are, of course, complementary, and I take them very seriously.'

That Beinegger should introduce himself this way was strange for Woodhead. Beinegger was clearly egotistical and self-assured, and this strong self-presentation made Woodhead feel uncertain, inferior. Willy Grindle was never interested in a person's personality and busied his mind only on what might be the best method of dispatching his prey.

'It's nice of you to come, Mr Woodhead. I would not normally have expected a visit from the author. Your phone call was a surprise. You obviously take my solution seriously.'

Beinegger led the two miscreants through his house and garden to a large rectangular red-brick building with lots of metal and glass forming its upper half. It was a monstrous erection, and quite out of place in the green setting of the forest.

144

'This is my lab. I solved your puzzle here. Not at all that hard really.'

The laboratory was filled with scientific instruments, shiny cylinders and interconnecting pipes, mirrors reflecting pencil-thin beams of light and computers.

'Are you going to explain your solution?' asked Woodhead.

'Do I need to? Both you and I know I'm right. I have given you the exact location of the Cones, so we both know the explanation. Don't you agree, Mr Woodhead?'

When he saw the large telescope at one end of the laboratory, it dawned on Willy Grindle what Beinegger really was.

'Look, Hollis,' he whispered in Woodhead's ear, 'look at his face, you can tell he's spent all his life looking one-eyed through a telescope.'

'Shut up, Willy.'

'Come here, gentlemen, I want to show you something amazing.' Beinegger pointed to a very large photograph pinned to the wall that showed the sky at night. 'I took this photo with a computer-controlled telescope which feeds digital information into other computers for measurements, and also produces photos like this. The telescope runs continuously throughout clear nights. Can you see this trace?' He ran his index finger up a white line on the photograph. 'Some object has travelled up from the Earth at a fantastic speed, according to my instruments, at something approaching two thirds the speed of light. No one else has reported this. The point about this is that the evening when this was taken an explosion happened at a village close to here called Stonebeggar. It was caused by some poor chap digging for your treasure, Mr Woodhead. My telescope camera was covering the sky area above Stonebeggar, and the object in this picture, whatever it was, ascended from the Earth at Stonebeggar, of that I am sure.'

'Now wait a bloomin' minute,' said Woodhead, angered by the reminder that he had caused the death of his friend. 'How d'ya know he was digging for the Golden Cones?'

'I don't absolutely know that for certain, but the only thing found after the explosion was your book, Mr Woodhead – *Hoard*! A certain Mr Ernest Clamp had written his name on the inside front cover. And why else would he be digging outside the confines of his own garden? His body was never found, no bones, nothing – completely evaporated; so the only evidence to explain anything at all is circumstantial.'

Woodhead stepped up closely to the large photograph, and peered at the streak clearly visible at its base, and then fading into the starry night. He was awestruck. Willy also gazed at the astronomical photograph, but failed to understand the significance of what Beinegger was showing them. Instead, he took the brief opportunity given to tug at Woodhead's sleeve, a 'let's get-the-job-done' tug. Woodhead shook his head.

'Do nothing yet, Willy,' was all he had chance to whisper.

'Now,' continued Beinegger, 'the reason I was so keen to accept your offer of a visit was the fact that your book, *Hoard*, was left at the scene of the explosion absolutely unscathed. That's amazing, don't you think? I wanted to see what was so special about you, Mr Woodhead. But you're not special at all, as far as I can see. Perhaps the content of your book is? But I rather think that our Mr Clamp was special.'

'How did you get involved in all this?'

Woodhead only wanted to know about Ernest, and what had happened. The truth was erupting in his brain. He had not dreamed that Ernest had released him from the Yamati ritual. How else could he have found his way to a hotel?

Ernest lived! What had he said? *'The travellers are waiting for me'*. Or some such words.

Beinegger was on a roll. He was lecturing.

'I feel it's possible that we'll see Ernest Clamp again – perhaps. My project centres on what is called magnetic saturation and propulsion. Magnetic saturation is when every single molecule of a body is magnetised and able to be levitated. It's been done with small creatures, but my project work so far indicates that very, very much larger bodies can be not only levitated, but propelled, by combining the forces of magnetism with that of "power routes" that already exist all around spatial bodies – like the Earth. These power routes follow the general principles of magnetic acceleration described by Laithwaite – but they are invisible. Do you know of Laithwaite?'

The two shook their heads in unison. They had followed nothing of what Beinegger was saying, but Woodhead was listening intensely in order to learn more about what had happened to Ernest Clamp.

Beinegger continued his lecture.

'Somehow, it is necessary to tune to these routes in order to use them. I have good reason to believe this trail on the photograph was made by some sort of craft that can travel rather quickly,' he said, with understatement. 'A craft that can use these routes effectively. I can only speculate about where the space travellers come from. Perhaps the Earth?'

'Ernest is alive!' Woodhead was beginning to make sense of his dream-like discussion with Ernest at the Indian Temple.

'What did you say, Mr Woodhead?' Beinegger glared at Woodhead with half-closed eyes as though he were an inattentive student. Grindle was right, he did look as though he'd spent all his life looking one-eyed through a telescope. Beinegger opened the top drawer of his metal desk and took out a gun. 'These are all very interesting things, gentlemen, but I'm afraid, of only academic interest to you. For the moment, I am especially interested in why, Mr Woodhead, you should want to visit me,' he said pointing the gun at the two men. Woodhead and Grindle looked at each other startled.

'What are you doing, Dr Beinegger?' said Woodhead sheepishly.

'I am not stupid. You would only come here for one reason, and that's not to congratulate me on solving the *Hoard* puzzle.'

'We've just come here to check out your solution, Dr Beinegger, nothing more.'

Beinegger shifted to his other foot and scratched his ear with his gun-bearing hand.

'Let's say that I don't believe you. You've obviously conspired with your publishers to cheat the public. For most people your puzzle is incredibly difficult, and you expected no correct solutions. But I'm a genius. It's not that I have anything against cheating, but I'm not letting you wipe me out before I get a chance to wipe out the whole of living Earth.'

'You're a nut case.'

'I need that prize money to continue my research, which I assure you I will complete very soon.' Beinegger stiffened himself regally. His eyes blazed. 'Then, I will travel space for as long as I can survive. But I will leave mankind a dreadful legacy – a real nuclear bang that will blast the sun and all its planets to the far reaches of the Universe. I hate humankind – and when I see such creatures as you I understand why. Humankind must pay for my hate. Everyone will have to pay.' Beinegger's eyes glazed over and he stared into the distance.

Both captives recognised simultaneously that Beinegger had entered a megalomaniac trance, and set off at once to different parts of the laboratory for cover. Woodhead raced towards an exit, and ran behind a tall cabinet as Beinegger's gun rang out. Willy Grindle inexplicably ran towards the telescope to place himself between Beinegger and the only wall with no exit and no windows to break open. Woodhead felt for Cynthia's .45 automatic. It was still there in his jacket pocket, but he could not bring himself to shoot at the crazed astronomer.

'Humanity, I hate humanity!' screamed Beinegger. He gave out a loud, spine-chilling guffaw. He had gone psychotic.

Woodhead's eyes alighted on three large cardboard boxes with 'Zenith Probe Rockets' printed on the side of each.

'I'll give the bastard what for. Blow up the world will he?'

Woodhead tore open one of the boxes and lined up two astronomical probe rockets in the general direction of the scientist, who was still screaming madly about mankind, and shooting alternately and wildly at his would-be killers. The rockets were fairly large and complicated and had battery fuses. On each, Woodhead selected 'Fuse: 6 Sec', and pressed a red button. He then ran for the exit at the far end of the building. He strained for immediate blasts but six seconds in an emergency is like eternity. Beinegger could easily move away from the target area in that time. But there he was standing high up amongst the complex of laser equipment, arms outstretched and screaming wild things at the sky visible through the glass roof. Woodhead could see him clearly, WHOOSH, WHOOSH, in quick succession. The rockets were fuelled to reach ten miles into the sky, and when they burst open on impact with the tangle of solid surfaces of the laboratory equipment the place became a blazing inferno of terrific fireballs and loud explosions. The telescope was no longer standing. Equipment exploded, windows were blasted out – fire and glass were everywhere. The mad scientist had certainly been incinerated in the explosions. Grindle? Where was Willy Grindle? Woodhead ran for the safety of the woods. He could see hot red flames amid the thick clouds of dark grey smoke pouring out of the twisted frame of the devastated laboratory.

'Hollis! Are you there, Hollis? Hollis, where are you?'

'What have you been up to, Willy? Your face is black as the ace of spades. Come on, let's drive home.'

Chapter Twelve

The view from Professor Kahn's office could hardly be called inspirational. Indeed, he was beginning to wonder if those who wielded the power at Manchester University were trying to tell him something when they had arranged for the new gymnasium to be built twenty feet from his window. Now that the huge red brick building was completed, Kahn was lucky to get an hour's sunlight in a whole day; scant compensation for the Roman garden they had demolished to build it. He snarled at the monstrous structure as he looked up from his copy of *Hoard*.

There was a knock on the door.

'Who is it?' he barked.

A weak voice answered from the other side.

'It's Mumford, sir. Sorry to bother you, sir.'

Kahn had a low opinion of all his students, a dislike brought on by his poor position in life compared to theirs. Mumford, however, was a special case. Kahn had a particular loathing for this creature: Mumford was a confused, obsequious moron.

'What d'ya want, Mumford?'

Kahn shouted through the door that he had no intention of opening.

'It's my marks, sir.'

'What's wrong with them?'

'Nothing, it's just that no one's ever given me five As in a row before. I just wanted to thank you,' came the pathetic voice.

If Mumford was not so universally despised, somebody would have told him that all Kahn's students were receiving top marks, no matter what the quality of their work was. This was the only way the professor could ensure uninterrupted time to concentrate on Woodhead's puzzle.

'Okay, Mumford, you've thanked me, now piss off.'

'Yes, sir.'

As the sound of Mumford's footsteps faded, Kahn returned his attention to the puzzle. *Hoard* had a soothing effect on him. The thought of winning all that money, of being free from the pressure of work and the despair of extreme poverty kept him from going out of his mind. It also kept him from thinking about his ex-wife. His darkest moments were those spent away from Woodhead's mysterious world; in the real world his mind would ramble in an endless nightmare of might-have-beens. If only he'd never met Julian Snode. If only he had never trusted the bastard, and never allowed him to play squash with Veronica on Wednesday evenings. If only he'd given her more attention instead of being at the beck and call of the university all the time.

He had believed he was doing all the right things: building a good life for her, trusting her, never questioning her long absences. In reality, he had been a fool; one of the world's last innocents. He had committed the cardinal sin of believing in the goodness of human nature, a mistake he had no intention of making again. God bless Hollis Woodhead, he thought – and God bless *Hoard*, and God bless the god of money. After all, money was the only truth, and that was quite a liberating thought for a professor of comparative religion and eastern philosophy.

It was dark when he finally dragged his eyes away from Woodhead's tale of buried treasure. With a weary sigh he locked his office, and headed for the staff shower. At least nobody questioned his strange living arrangements. After freshening up, he ventured outside, his mind buzzing with one all-enveloping activity: analysis of the *Hoard* puzzle. Kahn was oblivious to the world at large, and automatically walked towards the only place in town in which he could afford to eat.

*

The Albatross Café was a grubby little place whose characteristics were reflected perfectly in Joe, the greasy little man who owned it. The tables were veneered in a dismal plastic that had yellowed and chipped through years of use. The ashtrays upon them had not been emptied for some time. A tall, pristine new glass-fronted drinks cabinet stood incongruously in one corner.

'Evening, Professor.'

Joe's greeting returned Kahn to earth. Joe was always pleased to see Kahn; the scruffy scholar had become his most regular customer.

'Do you want your usual, Prof?'

Kahn nodded. Joe dipped a large piece of cod in a tray of white batter, then dropped it into the hot fat. Kahn grimaced uncomfortably as he watched the frenzy of boiling fat consume the fish. He considered for a moment the horrific pain he would suffer were he to be dunked in boiling oil.

'It would be over in a moment, but what a dreadful way to go,' he mumbled.

The scholar looked around the cafe and sighted the only other customer, a bag-lady who sat by the window clutching a mug of tea. Kahn had always sympathised with social outcasts, and felt sorry for the woman – until he realised suddenly that he was on the brink of his own separation from mainstream society. He shivered uncomfortably at the thought and sat down.

'There you go, Prof, get your teeth into that,' said Joe cheerily as he shoved a generous helping of cod and chips under Kahn's nose with a satisfied grin.

Kahn's unhappy mind dulled his appetite, but he ate the whole meal, believing it to be necessary for the operation of his brain later that evening when he would attack the *Hoard* puzzle once again. He left the cafe to seek comfort and fortitude in the alcohol served at the Ball and Chain. Like the Albatross Café, the pub reminded Kahn of his reversed circumstances in life. Horse hair protruded from the ruptured leather upholstery of his seat, and the coiled metal springs beneath it threatened to pierce the leather, and him too. But the seedy public house offered him sanctuary from the university crowd. Not one of his colleagues or students, not even Mumford, would come to such a place.

He sat back in his seat, thoughtfully sipped his beer and mulled over the work he had done on *Hoard* that day. His painstaking study of the book had led him to the conclusion that the text held no clue whatever to the whereabouts of the treasure. Logically, this meant that the pictures held the puzzle and its answer. There was just no doubt about it, he thought happily, as he went to the bar to order another pint. At last, he could discount the story. Having arrived at such a brave decision, he saw that it made perfect sense. The story, although weird, described the illustrations too accurately; it had obviously been written after their completion, more as a complementary smoke screen than anything else.

After his second pint of beer, Kahn began to feel happier. Woodhead was a far better painter than ever he was a writer; Kahn saw this as more confirmation that he was at last on the right track. If a man was going to hoodwink a nation out of two million pounds, he'd use his strengths rather than his weaknesses to conceal the puzzle. This, the last lucid thought the professor had before the beer took over, improved his mood no end.

He emptied his glass and went to the bar for another. He found that he was actually smiling to himself as he watched the landlord strain at the pump and hand him the refill. With only six months to go before the *Hoard* competition closed, things were suddenly looking much better. Kahn swayed drunkenly into the street, remarkably spirited by the beer and the enlightenment that it had brought about. He realised suddenly that he was not alone.

'Hello, love,' said a sweet, low voice. 'I was watching you in the pub. You looked ever so lonely.'

Kahn rocked slightly from side to side as he tried to study the blur standing next to him.

'Who er... Who er... Who er,'

'No, I'm not a whore, my love. Let's say I'm a hostess.'

He was suddenly aware that he was no longer coherent and struggled desperately to identify this attractive woman.

'I mean, who er... who er you? Wa sher name?'

'My name is Mandy. Don't you worry about a thing, I can look after you for the rest of the evening. What's your name, love?'

'Kahn. Benjamin Kahn. Call me... call me Benji. Na good, youooo look after me. I need to be looked after.'

Mandy had studied Kahn for the last half hour in the pub and had concluded that he was intellectual, and, therefore, probably well off enough to part with a reasonable sum of money in exchange for a pleasant evening. Mandy had made the understandable mistake of not trusting her eyes. It is modish these days to dress cool, somewhat scruffy and for men to have a four-day growth of beard. This was especially so in the big cities where fashion rules the minds of the masses. And Mandy was as fashion-conscious as anybody. No question, Kahn was sort of good looking too, so it would be easy for a working girl like

Mandy, whose every day was full of risks, to make a mistake about Kahn's statement of account.

'Come on, Benji, let's go to my place. It's not far.'

Kahn enjoyed the soft, enticing tone in Mandy's voice.

'Yes, let's go to your place.'

'It's just across the old iron bridge. It's not far.'

The two set off arm-in-arm, with completely different expectations about what the rest of the evening would bring. Kahn looked forward to being 'looked after' whatever that meant. Mandy anticipated receiving enough money to pay her rent for the month.

'I'm dying for a pee,' said Kahn loudly.

'Just wait a while, and we'll be at my place,' assured Mandy.

'I can't wait, I'm bursting! I meant to go at the pub, but forgot. Ah, the bridge.'

Kahn ran fifty yards or so until he was at the middle of the iron bridge that spanned the Manchester Ship Canal. He clambered up on to the iron railing and teetered on its edge until he grabbed a bar above his head.

'Ahhh!'

He let out a sigh of relief as he urinated a zigzag stream on to the water below – and on to the foredeck of the pleasure cruiser passing under the bridge, the table arranged with freshly-charged champagne flutes, and on to the newly-married couple being photographed at one end of the table.

'You dirty bugger,' came a loud and incensed voice from the boat. 'You dirty sod!'

'Whoopeeee – and up yours!' shouted Kahn raising a middle finger at the boat.

Suddenly the deck of the boat became very animated, and cameras flashed at Kahn blinding him momentarily.

'Can we help you down, sir?'

Kahn turned to face the voice.

'Would you mind tucking your tool back inside your trousers, sir?'

Mandy pressed her clenched knuckles against her mouth anxiously. Jumping to the ground very unathletically, Kahn half fell into the arms of one of the two policemen who, with Mandy, had watched his superbly entertaining performance.

'What d'you think you're doing? It's people like you who give people like me long hours of unnecessary work.'

'Ah, good evening, Constable.'

'What's your name?'

'My name. Umm. My name is Professor Benjamin Kahn.'

'Yea, and I'm Sir Richard fucking Attenborough.'

'Ah ha, then I'm pleased to meet you, Sir Richard.'

The genuinely serious intent of Kahn's reply impressed the constable not one bit.

'Don't you be bloody clever with me or you'll wish you'd kept your mouth shut.'

'Take it easy, George,' said the other officer, 'he's okay if he's with Mandy.'

'It's okay, Tommy, I'll take care of him,' said Mandy.

'Let me explain, Mandy,' said the second constable, 'we're here to make sure nothing untoward happens to the wedding party that just passed under the bridge, and we don't want any bother.'

'Ah, I see. Who got married?' asked Mandy.

'Daughter of the local Tory MP. It was a posh do. But that's it for us tonight; the excitement is over.'

'And what's fucking more,' blasted George at Kahn, 'we operate a "zero tolerance" system in this town, and that means that we run in *every* offender, no matter what they've done. You're fucking lucky Mandy's with you.'

'Oh, come on, George,' said Tommy, 'it's a waste of time: we've taken practically every tramp and vagrant off the street tonight. We'll lose our credibility if we take in a guy just because he's piddled over the bridge. Let's go and find some real problem people. Besides, Mandy will lose a customer.'

It was hard for Mandy to understand that the two policemen had not seen just exactly where Benji had urinated. Nor had they noticed the uproar it caused on the boat.

'Okay, okay. Piss off, Professor – not over the bridge again – and I don't want to see your pisser or any other part of your anatomy any more.'

'Come on, Benji, let's get going.'

Mandy wrapped an arm around Kahn's shoulder and led him away to the safety of her home.

★

'I'm hungry, Mandy, d'you have something to eat?'

'Oh yes, love, I'll make some sandwiches. But I have to talk to you, Benji. To stay with me the whole night it'll cost you quite a bit. But I'm sure you've got a bit of spare cash, Benji,' she said sidling up to him.

'Money? I thought you said you would look after me? Isn't that what you said?'

Kahn had sobered considerably from the walk through the cool evening air, and had the sudden realisation that he was with a prostitute – apparently as green as he was.

'Don't give me that, Benji,' she said stepping sharply back from him. 'You knew very well what you were doing. What have you got? Enough for a couple of hours?'

'Mandy, I've got no cash whatsoever!'

Mandy walked coolly to a bedside table and pressed a button.

'Just you sit there for a little while, Benji. Somebody's coming to see you.'

Kahn recognised the hidden threat of special personal treatment and ran for the door.

'Going somewhere, buddy? Yeah, you're coming with us.'

A thick-set thug stood at the open door.

'What's this about taking up with one of our girls and saying you can't pay? We all have to make a living, and if you cheat us we find it hard to live.'

He dragged Kahn to the street below and thumped him in the face, sending him headlong into the road. Kahn grazed his forehead, hands and knees on the gritty road before he slid to a stop.

'And a little bit of bootsy for you,' said the thug as he kicked Kahn several times in the lower part of his back. 'Now piss off.'

In considerable pain, dazed and winded, Kahn's uppermost thought was why so many people wanted him to piss off. He lay there for several minutes before dragging himself to his feet.

'Where's the university? I've got to get back to the university. The bridge is that way – I think.'

Kahn was in a dingy, unfamiliar part of the city, and really had no idea what direction would lead him back to Manchester University. He walked to where the lights were brightest.

'Hotel Paramour. The porter will know.'

'Excuse me, sir,' said a harsh loud voice as Kahn entered the hotel foyer, 'tramps are not allowed in this hotel.'

Kahn heaved a depressed sigh and stared at the floor. The thought that he had come to such low circumstances brought actual pain to his stomach. He turned to leave the way he had come, but noticed a party under way in a room to the side of the reception desk. He peered in and was startled to see the Dean of Manchester University, Dickey Liverton-Smith, his boss, standing at the head of a formal dinner, papers in hand, apparently delivering a speech. Kahn pressed his nose to the bevelled glass window of the door to get a clearer look at little Dickey Liverton-Smith MP. Kahn despised him.

'Little stuck-up bastard.'

The window steamed up as he murmured hate through it.

The door swung open and a tuxedo-jacketed man with a frame like a rugby forward grabbed the stooping Kahn by his shirt collar, which tore his shirt open at the top button and pulled his tie up around his eyes.

'I know you. You're the dirty bugger who pissed on my boat.'

'Get your fucking hands off me, you ape!' screamed the normally sheepish Kahn.

Kahn had had a nasty beating earlier, and had survived it, so what could the ape do? Without another word, the ape hit Kahn in the stomach. In response to this Kahn let out a terrifying howl and fell unconscious into the party room. Every pair of eyes strained to see the commotion at the door.

'Do you mind telling me what's going on here?'

The unmistakable dulcet tones of Little Big Man MP himself.

'This nasty little tramp urinated on the champagne we had arranged on the boat,' said the ape.

'Are you sure?' asked the MP. 'Don't I know you, sir? It's Professor Kahn. My word, what a nice surprise.'

Liverton-Smith turned to the ape.

'Don, you're in charge of this situation; I'll leave it to you.'

'You ass-licker, Smith,' was all Kahn could throw back as he was punched in the face and ejected bodily from the hotel.

'Ho fucking, fucking hell!' he screamed.

Numbness replaced pain as Kahn set off in the opposite direction to that which he had previously taken.

'Thank God, the bridge, the iron bridge,' he exclaimed eventually.

Seeing the bridge reminded him of his earlier performance, and the fact that his bladder was again in need of discharge. He pressed himself against the iron railings and relaxed until a long arc of internally-processed beer connected him to the water below.

'Well, I'll go to bloody hell! He's at it again.'

'You know, Tommy, this professor guy is a bloody pervert.'

'You're right, George, let's take him in.'

Chapter Thirteen

The holiday season was at its peak, and Terminal Four of Heathrow Airport was filled with people. Hollis Woodhead weaved and bobbed his way through to the Concorde area of the airport. He checked in his suitcases and, clutching a small travel bag and his tickets, he made his way to the cool and comfort of the Concorde Lounge. He was suddenly blinded by the flash of a press camera.

'Mr Woodhead, I'm Bonner – *Gazette*. Would you care to tell me where you're going?'

'The Concorde Lounge,' replied Woodhead without hesitation.

'Ah, you're going to the US,' asserted Bonner.

'That's right, I'm going to Los Angeles for two weeks' holiday.'

'A holiday – or are you just trying to dodge answering all the accusations against you, Mr Woodhead?'

'What accusations?'

'I can't believe you don't know that the Government is up in arms about your treasure hunt. Look at today's paper.'

Front page article in the *Mail*: 'PM promises to end *Hoard* hunt.'

Yet more publicity, thought Woodhead.

'It's in every national, Mr Woodhead. They're trying to get your treasure hunt stopped. You know very well that it's causing devastation all over the country. What are you going to do about it?'

162

'Nothing, I'm going on holiday. And it seems like a good time to be getting away, doesn't it?'

Woodhead was pleased with this intrusion: it was fortuitous that the nation would know he was absent from the country when Cynthia Flockhard-Flute 'committed suicide'.

★

Concorde was a totally new experience for Woodhead. He was stimulated by the prospect of travelling as fast as a bullet, whilst simultaneously guzzling champagne. He strapped himself in, eyed the stewardesses hungrily, then relaxed for the journey ahead. Unfortunately, he found the hard engine noise at take-off and the steep, fast climb into the air disagreeable in the extreme. He panicked and grabbed the arm of the woman sitting next to him, digging his nails into her flesh.

'Let me go, you idiot,' she shouted, beating him about the head with her copy of *Vogue*.

'I'm sorry,' he said, 'the take-off scared me.'

'I'll scare you in a minute,' said the woman indignantly, 'keep your filthy little hands to yourself.'

'Newspaper, Mr Woodhead?' The stewardess bent over close to Woodhead and beamed him an I-know-you smile. 'I see you've made the headlines today.'

'Yes? Yes?' He had lost touch with newspapers over the last two years, and had to strain his mind to recollect what papers he preferred – then he remembered he hated them all.

'Oh, umm, the *Telegraph*, *Mirror* and *Guardian* please.'

At least these would convey the general mood of the nation. Woodhead realised he was starting to get ideas about his importance as a news-worthy personality. But, there it was in the press. The balance of the *Hoard* account so far, as given in the newspapers, graphically illustrated the amazing efforts people were making to find the treasure. The reading gave Woodhead a glowing sense of satisfaction:

Marble Arch undermined; police arrest four treasure hunters during the night.

American woman, 63, dies after fall from TV mast in Oxford; convinced she had located 'Hoard' treasure, say relatives.

'Hoarders' ruin Stonehenge.

Ancient sites on Yorkshire Moors laid waste by 'Hoard' hunters.

Man shoots wife who would not share 'Hoard' secrets.

Geoffrey Whitley MP proposes bill to ban all treasure hunting.

Indian tribe claim ownership of Cones – hunting Woodhead.

These were some of the headlines of articles that covered the two-page centre spread of the *Telegraph*. Woodhead ordered a quick succession of whiskeys and very soon he was drunk and asleep.

*

He was still very drunk three hours later when he staggered up to the US Immigration desk in Los Angeles airport. He could not make himself understood. No matter how hard he tried, he could not synchronise his mouth with his brain.

'Better wait over there, sir,' said an immigration officer politely. 'We'll deal with you when you're sober.'

Woodhead was put in a chair, and left to sleep. Two hours later, he awoke with a thundering headache, and a mouth as dry as a desert. His travelling baggage had been tied to his legs, and his disabled focus and shaking hands made it impossible for him to free them.

'Can you please help me,' he called angrily to the officials manning the immigration desk.

'Ah, Mr Hollis Woodhead, good day, sir. We were just talking about you. We took the liberty of taking your passport and your billfold from your pocket – for safe keeping.'

Woodhead's hands flew to his chest in reflex to feel the emptiness of his jacket pockets.

'Are all limeys like you, Mr Woodhead?'

The customs official cut the ties from around Woodhead's legs.

'What d'ya mean?'

'Waal, sir, yer a bit of a mad character. We've read about you in the newspapers.'

'Can I just have my things back, so that I can get out of here?'

'Why, Mr Woodhead, don't be so hasty, we haven't finished with you yet. You're a stranger to our country, and we have to make sure that we can let you in. Now, are you goin' to be a friendly guest, or are you goin' to give us trouble?'

'I don't want trouble, I just want to get to my hotel.'

'I understand.' One of the immigration officers looked at Woodhead with a questioning, wrinkled brow. 'Are you bringing food into the country?' he asked.

'What sort of a stupid question is that?'

If Woodhead had been fully sober, he would have noticed that there were four immigration officers, that all were much larger than he, that they all carried guns, that they all had authority to give him a whole lot of trouble. Before he knew what was happening, Woodhead was grabbed, and frog-marched, with his baggage, to an interrogation room.

'Okay, wise-guy, go behind the screen and take your clothes off.'

'But I don't want to take off my clothes.' Woodhead was petrified.

'Listen here, bub, either you take off your clothes, or we give you an unpleasant time taking them off for you. Now, what we want to do,' explained one of the officers slowly, determinedly, 'is find the Golden Cones we've been reading about. We believe you are nothing more than a limey cheat, and the people in your country are just too dumb to realise it. We think you've swallowed the Cones – don't we boys – and we are gonna make every effort to take them out of you.'

At this point, Woodhead realised that these officers had time to waste during arrivals and they were going to fill it at his expense. They kicked Woodhead's shed clothes unceremoniously into a corner of the room, and folded the screens that had immediately before afforded him cover. There he stood, in all his skinny, white – apart from his neck and forearms – pimply nakedness, hands crossed over his crotch, his knees pressed together in a peculiarly English futile act of modesty. The officers looked on, at first in amazed silence at the sight of what was before them and then they erupted into uncontrollable laughter.

'Have ya ever seen anything like this before in all your life?' roared one of them, slapping his thighs. Tears of laughter were running down his cheek. 'Get the airport doctor, I think we need to give this guy the works.'

'Look, please – I'm sorry, really, I'm sorry. Can I please have my clothes back?' pleaded Woodhead.

'Well, we can't really do that now, sir, it's too darn late. We've started a formal process that has to be thoroughly completed. We've called the airport doc and he'll be here soon. We've just got to find those precious Golden Cones,' said a sergeant before he fell into another fit of raucous laughter.

A very short, thin and bespectacled man who was dressed like and looked very much like a doctor, entered the room and joined the huddled conspiracy that engaged the topic of how best to remove the Golden Cones.

The doctor broke into a chuckle, and then loudly addressed the group.

'First, it's an x-ray job. What do these Cones look like Mr Woodhead? How big are they? Are they metal?'

Woodhead could only gawk silently.

'Well, don't worry, Mr Woodhead, we'll find the little jokers, whatever size and shape they might be. I guess we can use a suction extractor, or a pressure ejector. Or we might have to put the rod up his arse. Perhaps the whole lot if they're hard to move. There are always complications with metal objects. Could take a long time – and it will be painful.' The doctor made sure every single word was heard by the victim. 'But I have to tell you, from the look on his face they're certainly inside him.'

'I've got nothing inside me but food,' screamed Woodhead loudly. His face was covered in beads of sweat, and he was shaking violently. 'This is against the Geneva Convention,' he shouted as though these were his last words before being shot. 'You're making a dreadful mistake!'

'We think you're the one who's made the dreadful mistake, Mr Woodhead, sir,' said the sergeant emphasising the last word. 'You really should not have swallowed those Golden Cones. But don't worry, we're confident we can extract them from you. We're doing this for the people of England, the people you have cheated.'

The x-ray machine against which Woodhead was forcibly held was very cold. Following that humiliation, he was made to stand naked for an hour in an empty room, guarded by two burly customs officers.

'Okay, we have the x-ray results. The Golden Cones are at his rear end,' declared the doctor in over-exaggerated mock excitement. 'I think I can do this job by hand. Or perhaps I should use the anal extractors – you just don't know what this guy's been up to. Anyway, we'll have to clean him out first.'

The rear-end clear-out and search that followed was the greatest humiliation Woodhead had ever suffered. Two hours later, and completely sober, his innocence was established to the satisfaction and great amusement of the US authorities.

'Here are your documents, Mr Woodhead. You're free to go now, sir. Have a nice day.'

The 'piss off' that Woodhead ventured in reply cost him dearly: a repeat physical examination and extraction operation – just to make sure – and overnight detention.

★

It was a plush office in Park Lane: a very fine address. The office furniture was selected from the best of Regency antiques and included a desk that exuded greatness – perhaps from the home of the great and crazy George himself? It had a delicate arrangement of fan-tracery at each corner – not over done, though. Quality Regency wallpaper adorned the walls, alternate tones in vertical stripes of equal width. All this made Jeremy Simms' every work day a proud and pleasurable' event. His visitors, mostly board directors and high-level politicians, were always greatly impressed with Jeremy's office. Americans loved it. In this citadel he felt very much in control of his life and his several large companies. He liked to be in control. With

Cynthia Flockhard-Flute, however, he was not in control – and it ground his guts to the core.

He sat on the front rim of his treasured desk, and studied the rich pattern of the carpet that spread out before him. He played with fitting the toe of his shoe into its lines, angles and arcs. But his mind was on Cynthia. What would he do? A scenario drifted through his mind.

'Good morning, Miss Rock.' He would speak to Cynthia's secretary strongly, proudly.

'Good morning, Mr Simms.' This was always her curt reply.

'I hope you are well.'

'As well as can be expected working here,' she would say.

'I know how you feel.'

'You do?'

'Yes my dear, I do. Happily, it's something I no longer have to endure. Is Cynthia in?'

'The old cow's in the boardroom.' Miss Rock hated Cynthia only a little less than Simms, and only out of tolerance built on the need for continued employment. There was no loyalty in Miss Rock. She fawned, cowed and cringed only with a pension in view.

Simms would walk in the door without knocking.

'Cynthia,' he would say, 'I've sold my shares in Flute and I am chucking in my Flute's directorship.'

'But Jeremy… why? You've always been so happy here.'

Then he would launch into the vitriol he had prepared for the occasion. His words would be measured and heartfelt. He would present them like the barrister he had once been, summing up for the prosecution in a sordid murder trial, and would enjoy every syllable.

'Miss Flute,' he would say grandly, 'I can't begin to tell you how desperately I've longed for the opportunity to say to you what I'm about to say. I have suffered your monumental stupidity in silence for so many years that it sickens me to think about it: your ridiculous whims and fancies, your dreadful jokes, and thoroughly offensive taste in literature and music. You are without question the most repulsive individual it has ever been my misfortune to work with. Not only are you stupid, you are unbelievably ugly, and supremely unlikeable into the bargain. I didn't think I'd ever sympathise with Hollis Woodhead, but that was before I learnt he was going to marry you. Personally, I would rather cut off my head with a blunt saw. As long as I live, you loathsome creature, I never want to see your face or hear your awful prattle ever again. Now what do you say to that, Miss – I repeat Miss Flockhard-Flute?'

'Bastard!' Yes, she would certainly say that.

But then Simms decided that the large dividend he received from Flutes – a large amount of money, especially since *Hoard* hit the shops – was better than losing out because of some silly principle. 'I think I have a much better way of dealing with this situation.' He sat down in his sumptuous leather chair, rested his left elbow in his right hand, creased his chin with the fingers of his left hand, and swivelled round to look out on to the life being acted out in Hyde Park.

*

Willy Grindle found Magdelaine's stupidity and incompetence hard to deal with. He was exasperated that it took so much to make her understand such a simple concept. For Willy, murder was easy, but he took no account of the emotional strain it imposed on Magdelaine.

'I'm so nervous, Willy. What if something goes wrong?'

'Look, Maggie, there's nothing for you to worry about. All you've got to do is ring the bloody doorbell, and say:

170

"Interflora, Madam, flowers from Mr Hollis Woodhead."
Simple, isn't it?'

'Yes, Willy.'

'Good.'

'Willy?'

'What is it now?'

'What if she's superstitious? I mean, it's a bit late for
Interflora to call, isn't it? We won't get there till gone
midnight.'

'What has superstition got to do with it? Maggie, you're
driving me crazy.'

'Well, it's late and she'll wonder…'

'You mean suspicion, you… silly bitch! Look, if she asks
you why you're delivering so late, just say you run a
twenty-four hour service.'

'Yes, Willy.'

'Let's go then.'

'Willy?'

'Bloody well shut up, Magdelaine or I'll murder you
instead.'

'Sorry, Willy.'

Grindle put on his mackintosh and a black homburg hat,
and stepped into Dewberry Street. It was the first time he'd
been outside for weeks. The sensation of breathing fresh air
after being so long in Magdelaine's oppressive little terraced
house made his brain swim but it was heavenly. Until this
point, he was beginning to feel as dead as her collection of
stuffed animals.

'There's no need to be nervous, Maggie.'

Willy's voice, far from comforting her, increased the
tension she felt about being inveigled into serious crime. All
Willy's crimes were serious.

She parked her car around the corner from Cynthia's
Kensington apartment, then she and her ruthless boyfriend
walked the rest of the way.

'Just do it like I said, Maggie,' said Willy, 'and everything will be okay.'

Magdelaine trembled behind the large bunch of flowers.

'Yes, Willy.'

When they reached the door, Magdelaine rang the bell and they waited in silence.

'Who the bloody hell is it?' rasped Cynthia's tinny voice from the loudspeaker at the door.

'Interflora, Madam.'

'What d'you want at this time of night, for Christ's sake? I hope you realise you've woken me out of a deep sleep. I will suffer in the morning because of you.'

'Flowers from Mr Hollis Woodhead,' Magdelaine squeaked.

Cynthia brightened immediately.

'Oh, okay, I'm on my way down.'

Willy kissed Magdelaine on the cheek, then moved to one side, out of sight.

'I didn't realise you delivered so late,' said Cynthia as she eagerly opened the door and grabbed the flowers.

'We run a twenty-four hour service,' said Magdelaine.

'We certainly do,' added Willy in a sinister tone.

'Willy!' screeched Cynthia. It was all she could manage before the 'Beast of Broadmoor' cupped his hand over her mouth and forced her upstairs. Magdelaine closed the door, and walked back to the car. She felt vaguely guilty – but her mind soon filled with things of an astrological nature, and the feeling quickly passed.

★

The dash up the stairs had drained Willy of energy. He sat on Cynthia's bed, and fought to recover his breath. His heart was pumping so hard he thought he would pass out.

'Wait… a minute. Hoow… wait a minute,' he panted.

'What are you going to do to me, Willy.'

Cynthia's voice carried an edge of appeal.

'Wait a minute, you silly sod, can't you see, hoo... I'm out of breath?'

Cynthia lay on the floor where he had thrown her, too terrified to move.

'Do you know what this is, Cynthia?'

'Of course I do, Willy, it's a gun. Wait a minute, that's *my* gun! You got that from Hollis Woodhead. Have you killed him?'

'No, Cynthia, but he wants me to kill you – and this is just one way to do it.'

'You cannot be serious, Willy. Hollis loves me, and is going to marry me. Besides, we still have such plans for you and... well, how can we reward you for such wonderful novels if you kill off the CEO of your publishing company?'

Willy struggled with Cynthia's quick-fire question, and couldn't make good sense of it. He was now very confused. He stared at Cynthia for a whole two minutes before responding.

'What's a CEO?' was all he could think of to ask.

'The chief executive officer, silly billy. There's so much I can do for you. Let's talk about it, for goodness sake.'

'I don't know,' said Willy looking dumb-brained at the floor. 'Hollis has promised me a lot of money, and I got to have that money to get out of the country and live.'

'Money? Listen, Willy, I have absolutely pots and pots of money, and you can have as much as you want. I can also help you get away. I have lots of friends and influence.' The noise of creaking parquet from the lounge drew Cynthia's attention. 'Did you hear that, Willy?'

'Yes, I did. Be quiet.'

Willy tip-toed quickly to the switch by the door, and turned out the bedroom lights. He walked stealthily to the bedroom door, opened it a crack and peered into the darkness of the lounge. The net curtains were breezed gently inwards as the large window door was pushed slowly open. The heavy, black form of a man was entering from the balcony. Cynthia was in a frenzied dilemma: she could scream for help to try and save herself from a bloody death and possible cannibalism, but the intruder might also be after her blood. Besides, she just felt that Willy had taken her bait – her promise of as yet unspecified good things. There was nowhere for her to run: Willy was at the only exit from the bedroom.

Suddenly there was a flash and thunderclap sound of a gun, and the heavy black shape fell noisily to the floor.

'Don't shoot me, fer Christ's sake,' screamed the man.

Willy Grindle flicked on the light.

'My goodness me, my goodness me,' he drawled out. 'Arbuthnot Paltrey, what the hell are you doing here?'

Cynthia appeared at the door clearly flabbergasted and scared. 'What's going on Willy?'

'This is my old cell-mate, Arby Paltrey; and I don't know what the fuck he's doin' here. C'mon Arby, tell us what your doing 'ere.'

'Willy!'

'I just can't believe you're so dumb as to rob the place by coming in the window. Real burglars are much cleverer than that, Arby.'

Arby dragged his awkward rounded shape off the floor, and grunted as he straightened up.

'I climbed down from the roof. It was very difficult.'

'Lookin' at you, Arby, I would have thought it was bloody impossible.'

'I'd better have a quiet word with you, Willy.' He drew Willy away from Cynthia's hearing. 'I'm supposed to top the dear lady here, what's 'er name, Flockhard-Flute,' he whispered.

'You what? And who's paying you to do that?'

'I got this contract from a gent in the Hardy and Gresham, a gentlemen's club in the West End. I often do work for him. He asked me to do it for his friend. It's all anonymous. Why are you 'ere, Willy?'

'Same idea, Arby – but I'm doing it for a friend… money too, of course.'

The long-winded brain power at work between Willy and his ex-cell-mate trying to work out what to do next gave Cynthia time to think about escape.

The bedroom window and the balcony… but then what? she thought. No, it was hopeless – just impossible. She just had to trust that she could cajole Willy into accepting the promise of a gift so grand that it would set him up in luxury for the rest of his life.

'Tell me, Arby, how were you going to do it?'

'Do what, Willy?'

'Arby! Arby, you're as daft as Magdelaine. How were you going to top the lady?'

Arby drew what looked like a gift box for a fountain pen out of his pocket and opened it slowly, carefully.

'Look, Willy. A syringe, already charged with a milky white liquid. "Cyanide".'

'Willy, I have a proposition to make.' Cynthia interrupted loudly, anxious to break the whispered planning discussion which she correctly assumed to be about her immediate future. 'What do you say to three million pounds, Willy? Two for you, and a million for your sweet friend.'

'I don't know about you, Willy, but I'm here to do a job, and I'm a professional.'

Willy looked round at Cynthia then, with a shrug of the shoulders, threw an enquiring look at Arby Paltrey.

'What d'ya say, Arby? That's lots of dough!'

'Sorry, Willy, I'm a professional and I just got to keep my reputation. I'd never get another job if I couldn't be trusted to go through with it.'

Willy turned to Cynthia and pulled the gun from his jacket. Cynthia closed her eyes and cupped both hands over her face. The blast shot Arby Paltrey through the open balcony door he had come in through. Willy picked up Arby's syringe lying intact at his feet.

'Okay, Cynthia, you've got a deal.'

'Oh Willy, darling Willy.' She ran at Willy and wrapped her arms around him. 'You're a wonder…'

She looked at Willy in anguished horror as he stuck the syringe into her bosom.

'Aren't I a bastard, Cynthia? Sweet dreams,' he whispered, 'it's been a pleasure. Just a pity I could never trust you.'

In the kitchen, Willy helped himself to a sip of Brandy, and then turned the gas cooker dials fully on.

'Right, Mrs Bullick,' he said after checking that all windows were shut, 'the rest is up to you.'

He left by the front door.

Cynthia's cleaning lady, Mrs Bullick, prided herself on the high standard of her work – but she smoked almost continuously.

Chapter Fourteen

Illicit drugs were not only available in Los Angeles, they were also, in Woodhead's opinion, of the highest quality, and he spent the majority of his Californian adventure trying to discover which ones he liked the most. LA was a home from home for this hippie at heart. The cocktail bars, the cocktails, the beach and the lazy, 'high' days were totally compatible with Woodhead's philosophy. But as he lay on the sand towards the end of his visit, soaking up the sun and enjoying some of the finest Mexican grass he'd ever laid his hands on, he decided that he could bear the suspense no longer. Either Willy Grindle had done away with Cynthia, or he hadn't. He returned to his hotel and dialled Magdelaine's number.

'Hello,' squeaked Magdelaine.

'Is Mr Sandman there?' Woodhead asked. 'It's Mr Hope.'

'Mr who?'

'Mr Hope, you silly cow!'

'Well, I don't care who you are, you're not speaking to me like that, and there's no Mr Sandyman living here.' Magdelaine slammed down the receiver.

'Who was that?' asked Willy.

'Oh, Willy, he was so rude,' replied Magdelaine. 'I put the phone down on him in the end. He wanted to speak to a Mr Sandyman or Hope, or something like that anyway.'

'You moron!' screamed Willy. 'How many times have I told you? Hope and Sandman, Hope and Sandman. Oh, get out of my way!'

Magdelaine burst into tears. She had become increasingly stressed since Willy had come to stay. He shouted at her constantly, and she was beginning to fear for her life. Willy rushed to the phone and waited for Woodhead to re-dial. He didn't have to wait for long; Woodhead was re-dialling frantically. His nerves were so frayed after the first call that he dialled the number incorrectly three times before getting through. Magdelaine had sounded very peculiar on the telephone, perhaps they were being recorded, perhaps Grindle had been caught by the police.

'Sandman here,' said Willy.

'Hope here; what's the news?'

'The baby went up with a bang on Sunday. Suicide, that's what they're saying.'

'When?'

'Sunday, just like you said.'

'Great, I'll be in touch.'

'How long? I can't take much more of Magdelaine.'

'Couple of weeks at the most.'

'Okey dokey, Mr Hope, I'll be seeing you.'

After his transatlantic exchange with Grindle, Woodhead stretched out on the floor wondering if he was about to suffer a heart attack. The thought of dying at the very moment when everything he most desired lay within his grasp, was something too terrible to contemplate.

'Don't be bloody stupid, Woodhead,' he told himself as his breathing became more even, 'you're as fit as a fiddle.'

*

Cynthia Flockhard-Flute, at least as much of her as the fire brigade managed to salvage from the charred rubble of her apartment, was carried in a heavily bedecked coffin to the family burial place in the graveyard of St Ansalph's Church. Jeremy Simms, who had cancelled a round of golf at Chorley Wood to gloat at the spectacle, studied Hollis Woodhead, standing a few paces to his right, with intense interest. The man looked grief stricken enough. He was wearing a black suit and was stone-faced behind impenetrable sunglasses, but Simms had more than a sneaking suspicion that the author of *Hoard* harboured a view of Cynthia's 'suicide' very similar to that of his own; namely, that on the whole, it had been extremely decent of her to be so considerate. There was a comic element about the proceedings that brought Simms to the brink of laughter. It made marvellous theatre, he thought. There he was, surrounded by people all of whom had loathed the dearly departed almost as much as he had, but here they all were, trying desperately not to show their true feelings. As the highly polished casket was lowered on white, silk bands into its allotted final place in the earth, the vicar began his perfunctory chant.

'Ashes to ashes,' he intoned with a weary professionalism, 'and dust to dust.'

The vicar's dry dispassion and the irony in the words, opened the flood gates on Simms' control. He broke into a raucous belly laugh that bent him double and welled up tears in his eyes.

'Oh, my God, how funny, how bloody funny!' he roared.

Those around him were stunned by his humorous outburst. The retired barrister made no attempt to justify his strange behaviour, but walked back to his car, stopping occasionally to catch his breath between bursts of loud merriment. He turned round one last time and looked at the hundred funereal faces all looking at him. His laughter was uncontrollable.

'Oh, my God!' he roared, as he got into his car.

★

The day after the funeral, Woodhead was back at Dewberry Street settling accounts with Willy Grindle and Magdelaine.

'I did it just like you said, Hollis,' said Willy. 'Now, where's my money, and how are you going to get me out of the country?'

Woodhead smiled, and put a heavy briefcase on to the kitchen table.

'It's all there,' he said, snapping the catches and swinging the lid open, 'you can count it if you like.'

'What about my share, Willy?' broke in Magdelaine. 'You promised.'

Grindle looked at the woman with such open aggression that Woodhead interceded on her behalf.

'Come on, Willy, there's no time for bad feeling, we've got to go. How much did you promise her?'

'Three hundred,' said the murderer through gritted teeth.

'Three hundred what?'

'Grand.'

'Well, you'd better pay her then, hadn't you?' said Woodhead, reaching for the briefcase.

'Where're we going, anyway?' asked Willy suspiciously.

'My caravan in the New Forest. You know where it is. Remember the mad scientist? I'm going to take you down there tonight. From there I've organised a nice little boat trip for you.'

'What do you mean by boat trip? I'm not bloody well rowing anywhere.'

'No, no, Willy, I'm talking about a yacht. A big one too. Cost me twenty thousand to get you on it.

'What! Out of my money?'

'I paid for it myself. Consider it a farewell gift. The captain thinks you're a bank robber.'

'Where's this boat trip to?'

'Spain, old chap. From there it's up to you.'

'Thanks, I'll do the same for you one day.'

'I sincerely hope not,' said Woodhead, ignoring Willy's sarcasm. 'Now, shall I pay her, or will you?'

Magdelaine waited nervously.

'You'd better do it,' said Willy.

Willy wasn't very good at figures. He wasn't very good at keeping promises either. He glowered at the fortune-teller with murder in his eyes.

'There's no need to be unkind, Willy,' she said. 'I didn't make that many mistakes. Besides, you promised.'

'Oh, shut up!'

'Now, come on, Willy,' said Woodhead. 'She's done her bit.'

Woodhead paid Magdelaine, and then walked Willy to his hire car for the journey to the New Forest.

'I'd like to bloody strangle her, Hollis,' said Willy emotionally, from the back seat. 'I would've done too if you hadn't been there. She's been driving me round the bend with her stuffed animals and fucking star charts.'

'Just keep your head down,' said Woodhead, 'or we'll both be stuffed. Well and truly.'

Magdelaine saw her opportunity now to do what she had always wanted. A bungalow in Brighton with a garden full of flowers and sea shells. A life with no more crime and no more Willy Grindle. She had had enough of the rough bully; she would be looking for a little refinement in future. She switched off the lights, carried her suitcase to the waiting taxi and left Dewberry Street for ever.

Chapter Fifteen

'Well, this is where I used to live, Willy.'

Woodhead pulled the car to a stop at the edge of the woods, as close to his old caravan home as the shrubbery would allow. The Womb resembled a giant hibernating beetle unaware of the moss and fungus growing on its dull green shell. It was difficult to judge whether it had deteriorated in the eight months or so since Woodhead was last in it; it had always looked as though the lightest wind would simply blow it away in a dust cloud.

'How long have I got to stay here?' moaned Willy, when he caught sight of Woodhead's old home.

'Until Wednesday night. Don't forget the important thing: here you'll see no one and no one will see you. It's a good hideout.'

'Well, I've stayed in worse,' sighed the 'Beast of Broadmoor' philosophically, remembering his prison cell.

The two men tramped across a fifty-yard sea of tall ferns to The Womb. Woodhead pulled hard to open the caravan door, which yielded with a terrifying screech and released powdered dust into the air.

'You won't be troubled here,' Woodhead reassured Willy. 'I was here for more than two years and never had a visitor. It's all yours.'

'My God, Hollis, this is the pits!'

Willy threw his travelling bag into The Womb, and it crashed through the plywood floor and into the dust below it.

'Fer Christ sake, Willy, look what you've done to the floor. What the hell have you got in that case?'

'Oh, I just brought along a little bit of protection.'

'What sort of protection, Willy? Show me.'

Woodhead gaped when Willy Grindle laid the travelling bag open before him: a 0.38mm hand gun and an array of hand grenades.

'Listen, Willy, where you're going you won't need those bloody things – unless you want to start a war, of course. You're going on a bleeding yacht. Why don't you just bury them in the woods?'

'Just leave it to me, Hollis, I have lots of experience. Trouble just seems to follow me around, know what I mean? I want to be able to protect myself.'

'Willy, you're bloody paranoid. Please yerself.'

They confirmed the plans for Willy's trip to Spain, then Woodhead drove back to London.

★

From the moment Gwendoline Butterworth invested in a copy of Woodhead's *Hoard*, her interest in Great Britain, and its ancient monuments in particular, became obsessive. While most of the population of Leeds slept peacefully in their beds, she was enduring yet another restless night on a floor carpeted with Ordnance Survey maps. In the eight months since the madness had struck, Miss Butterworth, and her neurotic cat, Pudding, had either slept upon, walked upon or looked upon the entire land in print.

'Look at that, Pudding; another standing stone. I wonder if the treasure's there.'

The ginger tom gave her a soulful look, and padded off across Wales, kitchen bound. Gwendoline had to agree with Pudding's assessment: it was a waste of time looking at maps. Woodhead could have buried the *Hoard* treasure anywhere; and when one worked for the Tax Office, as Gwendoline did, one could not afford to drive off with a shovel at the tiniest provocation. She had done that too many times already. There just had to be another way. She rolled her formidable bulk, all eighteen stone of it, on to the south east of England, and fell asleep with a frustrated sigh.

Whilst Gwendoline's principal interest was treasure hunting, Pudding was much more down to earth. Indeed, his only interest was food, something Gwendoline's *Hoard* obsession had, for her, relegated to second place. Pudding nosed around the kitchen, but there appeared to be nothing about. The hungry cat finally clawed at a large brown bag by the fridge. Pudding loved Kitty Crunches. He scratched at the bottom of the bag until it tore open, and then gorged himself on the large blue chips that spilled on to the floor. Pudding had no knowledge of the latest highly absorbent cat litter that Gwendoline had just brought for the first time, he just loved the taste. Pudding suddenly felt very full and extremely thirsty. He waddled over to his water dish and drained it dry. The cat litter within him swelled and swelled until Pudding was twice his normal size. Without so much as a whimper, the cat took three short steps and then stopped solid, stone dead and still growing.

*

Gwendoline screamed in stark horror as she walked into the kitchen the next morning. At first she did not recognise the large ball of ginger fur that confronted her.

'Oh, Pudding! What's happened?' she howled.

The Pudding she knew and loved was barely recognisable in his altered state. He stood, bolt upright on his now stubby legs, with his eyes bulging to the point of popping out. He was the size of a small beer barrel.

'Poor Pudding,' she cried, cradling him in her arms. 'What am I going to do with you?'

Pudding responded with a loud post-mortem passing of wind. Gwendoline had no garden in which to bury the unfortunate animal, so she stuffed him into a plastic rubbish bag and placed him, ready for collection, with the rest of her garbage, then drove off to work. As sad as Pudding's final circumstances were, he was only a cat – and there were plenty of potential replacements in Leeds.

As she drove through the city centre, Gwendoline was far more occupied with the irreplaceable nature of the *Hoard* treasure. She desperately needed an extra clue or two to put her on the right path. There was only one thing for it, she needed to get Hollis Woodhead on his own and have a heart to heart with him. He was bound to let something slip; especially when he saw how keen she was. Working for the Tax Office had its advantages if you wanted to trace an otherwise untraceable individual; and Gwendoline, who had never been inhibited about using tax office facilities for her own purposes, wondered as she logged on to the central computer and entered Woodhead's details, why on earth she hadn't done it before. Gwendoline's chubby little fingers danced up and down the terminal's keyboard with a practised ease, and within minutes the author's address flashed on to the screen:

Mr Hollis Woodhead,
The Womb,
Oaktree Lane,
Nr Stonebeggar,
Dorset.

'Bingo!' she exclaimed, slapping her hands together excitedly. She was in business.

She left a note for her boss, Mrs Treen, explaining that, for personal reasons, she would be absent from work for the next two days. Then she left for Stonebeggar in a mood of grim determination. The treasure belonged to her and she was going to get it.

★

Willy Grindle's first night in The Womb had been an unpleasant one. His efforts to sleep were futile. The bed was smelly and damp, the blankets were inadequate and the small gas heater radiated very little heat. Finally, he sat upright and wrapped the blankets around himself and the heater.

'Christ, it's cold in this damn box,' he cursed.

He dozed – but only until the flames from the burning blankets shocked him into action to save his life. Shouting and stamping, he extinguished the flames, then threw himself out of the door to escape the smoke that filled The Womb.

★

The first light from the sun sparkled through the trees as Willy Grindle re-entered The Womb. He slumped on to the bed, oblivious of the lingering smell of smoke, burnt carpet and decaying plywood, and slept soundly through to early evening. He was woken by a loud banging on the door.

'Anyone there?' shouted a gruff voice.

In his half sleep, Grindle believed Woodhead had returned to take him to the yacht. He pushed the door open and began a tirade about his dreadful night.

'This fucking matchbox…' he started.

The sight that confronted him was entirely unexpected and menacing. A large woman – a very large and powerful woman – bustled past him and into The Womb.

'You're Hollis Woodhead. Are you Hollis Woodhead? You are, aren't you?'

She sounded very threatening. Willy didn't know what to say.

'It's no good pretending you're not,' she continued, her eyes glazed with violent intent, 'I've seen your picture in the papers.'

'What do you want?' asked Willy, visibly trembling in his stocking feet.

'Some fucking answers.'

'Answers to what? I've never seen you before in my life.'

Gwendoline took a menacing two paces towards him, completely eclipsing the grubby window.

'*Hoard*. I want some clues.'

'*Hoard*? I don't know anything about *Hoard*, you daft bitch. Clear off, and leave me alone.'

'Don't give me that, you little weasel! Pudding's dead because of you! I loved Pudding, and I'm going to find the treasure for him!'

'It's not going to do him much good,' reasoned Willy, trying to edge his way around her to the door. 'I mean... if he's dead n' all. Who's Pudding, anyway?'

'My cat, and it's because of you and this damned treasure that the poor little bugger's dead!'

'Don't be such a silly sod,' shouted Willy. He made a sudden dash for the door.

'Oh no you don't!' Gwendoline grabbed him and threw him against a rickety wardrobe standing at one side of the caravan. 'You're not going anywhere!'

'What are you trying to do?' squawked Willy. 'You could've killed me!'

'If you don't cooperate, I will.'

Willy pushed at Gwendoline's breasts in an effort to put space between her and him, then made another desperate rush for the door. But such physical contact was rare in her life, and she did not intend to let the possibility of bodily fulfilment pass.

'Why didn't you say you wanted sex? I'll do anything you want, just give me some answers.'

'I don't want sex with you!' shouted Willy, losing his temper. 'Now get out!'

The rejection cut Gwendoline to the core. That Woodhead was not being the least bit helpful was bad enough in itself but he had now scorned her, and she hated it. She wasted no time evidencing her anger. She grabbed a greasy, blackened frying pan from the stove and hit Willy just once on the top of his head. She left him out cold on the floor, hands and legs tied together and his head down in the hole he had created earlier. She walked through the long grass and bushes to her Mini for a few bottles from her plentiful supply of good Yorkshire bitter, which always accompanied her on long trips. She quietly needed to consider what might happen if Woodhead didn't cooperate.

*

In her drunken state, the bitter resentment she felt for the man she'd left in the caravan escalated into seething hatred. Willy heard her swearing drunkenly outside. He'd bitten through the last length of knotted cord that constrained him. Gwendoline crawled out of her car and into the undergrowth. She stumbled through the vegetation with surprising speed, stopping occasionally to sniff at the soft peat. She sensed an earthy oneness with nature that she had never before experienced. She was the hunter sounding out her quarry; she was a powerful and dangerous beast; she was many things and, unfortunately for Willy Grindle, she was very, very drunk.

A fox screamed from the woods and Gwendoline answered its call with a loud roar. Suddenly, she ran blindly headlong at The Womb like an insane rhinoceros, snapping the twigs that got in her way. Willy leapt from the caravan just as Gwendoline delivered an incredible resounding head butt. The plywood splintered as her head crashed through it. She was after Willy's blood, but he was not there. The terrified murderer ran stark naked into the late evening darkness of the woods, feeling no pain as the thorns tore at his legs. With another roar, Gwendoline extracted her head from The Womb, and sped after him. Willy sensed the monstrous woman was gaining ground. He stopped to hide behind a clump of bushes and were he not making so much noise trying to regain his breath he would have been safe. But he could not keep going; he was just too unfit.

'Got you! Yeeaghh!' Gwendoline let out a piercing, terrifying battle cry as she lunged for Grindle. 'Yee haaa!'

Willy could only stare into the blackness that seemed to be crashing around him, and wonder from where the raging attack would come. Then everything went silent. Willy cringed, motionless, for several minutes, expecting an outburst. But then he saw her – she was upright but obviously dead. In her rugby-like lunge at Willy, the luckless Gwendoline had impaled herself on a strong, pointed branch protruding from the trunk of an old oak. She was very dead.

The late evening woods were pitch black. Willy could see nothing. He was completely lost. He was also naked. He could not stay in the woods, though. Even though the days were warm a night in the woods with no clothes would be extremely cold. He walked in the direction that offered the least resistance from trees, shrubs and long grass, and eventually came to a road.

*

'What you doin' 'ere, then?'

The severe, formal voice disturbed Willy Grindle's attempt to sleep off the events of the previous evening. Through bleary eyes he could make out the pointed shape of a policeman's helmet silhouetted in the large hole in the caravan's side, made by the late but unlamented Gwendoline's super head-butt.

'We don't want any tramps around 'ere. Come on, clear off. Don't I know you from somewhere, mister?'

'It's okay, Officer, I'm a friend of Mr Hollis Woodhead. He owns this caravan.'

'I know Mr Woodhead – curious bugger he is too – but I think I know you too. Have we met before? What's your name, sir?'

'My name's Trevor Baker.'

'Do you mean Trevor-the-weather Baker, who's on TV?'

For someone not of those parts, the policeman's words held no particular meaning. Willy remained silent, wondering how he could extract his hand gun from the case.

'Well, if you're a friend of the owner, then sleep on. Sorry to have troubled you, sir.'

That the policeman departed without asking for identification troubled Willy.

'He's fucking well spotted me! I wonder if 'e recognised me? Na, I don't think the pigs 'round here are worried about me. I bet he spotted me!'

Willy finally convinced himself that he was in danger. He looked out of the window as he dressed. The copper was standing by Gwendoline's car noting the registration number.

'The fat woman's car! Where's the key?'

A vision of Gwendoline attached firmly to the tree, head slumped to one side, raced through Willy's mind. Where was she exactly? He took the gun from his 'protection' bag, and left to search the woods. She was easy to find. Not far from The Womb. She was hugging the tree in a final loving embrace. The inertia of her bulk moving at such speed had forced the broken branch to which she was attached go right through her, and its broken-off end protruded from her back.

Macabre, thought Willy, seeing beauty in the violent death. He searched through the pockets of her jacket, and became aware of the comfortable roundness beneath the clothing. 'You and I could have got along very well, my dear.'

*

Woodhead was more than a little disturbed by the presence of the red Mini Metro when he arrived to pick up Willy Grindle. He crept cautiously along the overgrown path that led to The Womb. Its door creaked open and shut in the wind.

'My God!'

Woodhead's cursory inspection of The Womb was all he needed to deduce that a violent struggle had taken place. The gaping hole in the plywood wall. The contents of The Womb in disarray at his feet. Where the hell was Willy Grindle, and who did the abandoned car belong to? Certainly, it belonged to no one he knew. The briefcase that contained Willy's money stood curiously upright and unopened by Woodhead's old typewriter. The author fumbled with its catch dials and frantically opened it. The money was still there! Woodhead was puzzled: if the money was there, then why wasn't Willy? Something serious must have happened to him. He took the briefcase back to his car and locked it in the boot. All that remained was for Woodhead to burn The Womb, and any evidence of his recent visits and Willy's stay there. He walked back to the wrecked caravan and liberally sprinkled its interior with petrol. He lit a cigarette, drew on it until the tip glowed, then threw it on to the soaked carpet. As soon as his old home burst into flames, he drove away as fast as he could.

★

The explosions nearby shocked Willy into panic.

'The fucking Bill.' He stumbled back to The Womb. More explosions. 'Bill? Shit no. My bloody hand grenades – and my fucking money all up in smoke. Shit.' Gwendoline's Mini started first time and Willy set off, not knowing where to go but knowing full well that he should not be where he was.

★

Woodhead had slept better than he had for many weeks. He stood in Cynthia's dressing gown, and looked out of the window of his bedroom in the Flute's hospitality suite. How could he have so much good fortune. He looked down at the briefcase he had rescued from The Womb:

'Seven hundred thousand lovely quid. Beinegger: dead. Cynthia: dead. Willy fucking Grindle: dead.'

Willy had waged a tough gun battle against the special armed police group that had tracked him down in the New Forest. But the morning paper gave all the praise to the police heroes.

Such good fortune.

Chapter Sixteen

'Is this you, or is it not you, Mr Kahn?'

The tiny Dickey Liverton-Smith MP, Dean of Manchester University, raised the small head on his long neck to gain height over the lofty Kahn sat uncomfortably on an inquisitional stool before him.

Kahn knew what the Fates held in store for him. Being objective, he could see that his behaviour had been nothing less than outrageous – but completely understandable in the circumstances. He had been beaten ruthlessly by thugs. He had been led blindly into a pimp's trap. How could he have possibly known – he was very drunk at the time – that Mandy would demand money? She simply looked like a nice, understanding girl. Kahn looked through half-closed eyes at the newspaper picture held up in front of him.

'Yes, that certainly is me,' he admitted.

'Mr Kahn, this is a national newspaper, and this picture has become rather famous – as far as I'm concerned, infamous. It was also shown on TV. Can you imagine what this does for the name of this fine University. It's a scandal!' exaggerated Liverton-Smith.

The picture before Kahn brought a smile to his face. There he was, standing – dangerously, he could see that now – on the parapet of the Iron Bridge over the Manchester Ship Canal, holding himself proudly and openly before all, directing a horizontally sinusoidal stream of urine down upon the party gathered on the deck of the boat, and raising an obscenely gesturing finger in the air.

This was a super press picture. Captured for posterity and for ever traceable in the archives of the *Daily Telegraph*. He had peed over the Dean, his daughter and her not-so-pristine new husband, and had topped up a large number of champagne glasses, some of them already raised in honour of the wedded couple.

The hateful Dickey Liverton-Smith was about to deliver an appropriate sentence based on the considered judgement of the Dean and his cohort team of senior professors. Kahn hated them all.

'This is no light matter for me, Kahn, but you must understand that such behaviour cannot be tolerated in one of the prime educational institutions of this country. Mr Kahn, your contract has been terminated on the grounds of your bringing Manchester University into disrepute. This is effective thirty days from today; that is, a month's notice. Goodbye.'

*

Life on the dole opened up a new reality for Benjamin Kahn – the worst kind of reality. As Kahn peered out of his bedsit window watching large snowflakes accumulate on the rooftop opposite, he recalled his day of judgement four months previously. He swept the devastating, albeit amusing, episode from his mind and sat down by a low and very rickety coffee table to study *Hoard*. The cold weather did little to lift his spirits as he hunched over the open book. He was shivering violently despite being dressed in three pairs of trousers, two jackets and a Parker he'd stolen from Oxfam. He would have worn more, but it was difficult to move his arms and legs as it was. Although life had become a Dickensian nightmare for the outcast scholar, he was not defeated easily by depressing circumstances. On the contrary, the hardships he now endured added to his sense of heroic determination. As if to illustrate this point to himself, he lit a candle and warmed his freezing fingers by the meagre flame. He knew he was close to the solution of Woodhead's puzzle. Just a little longer and he'd be there; he felt it strongly. Two hours later, after adding another eight pages to his already bulging file of treasure hunting notes, he was not so confident. Despair always clawed at him around tea-time; it was the prospect of eating baked beans and cornflakes again.

'Baked beans and cornflakes,' he muttered irritably, 'baked beans and cornflakes.' He stood up and paced about the room. 'Baked beans and cornflakes. What would you like to go with the claret, sir? We do an excellent baked beans and cornflakes. Perhaps you'd like to sample a few before you make up your mind?'

Kahn stopped at the window and looked out. The snow was several inches deep. He became aware of his own reflection in the window.

'You're talking to yourself again, Benjamin. That's a bad sign. What you need is some fresh air.'

He studied the sunken features and ghostly mouth that moved in unison with his own. No, he'd had enough fresh air, damn it. What he really needed now was a decent meal. Suddenly, he was overtaken by an irresistible dizziness. The room spun wildly around him as he staggered towards his chair. Years of tinned spinach might have worked wonders for Popeye, but weeks of tinned beans had done very little for Kahn. It was a curious thought, and the last one he had before flattening the coffee table as he blacked out.

★

Kahn could have been dreaming the voices around him. They were distant and light.

'He's such a quiet gentleman,' observed Mrs Price, Kahn's landlady.

Two ambulancemen nodded politely as they strapped Kahn on to a stretcher.

'That's how I knew something was wrong, you see. There was this terrible crash, and he was shouting and moaning. Oh, it was awful.'

'There's no need to worry, Missis,' said ambulance man number one. 'We'll take care of him now.'

'It's a good job you called us when you did,' added number two grimly. 'Looks like the poor sod's got scurvy to me.'

'*Hoard*,' moaned Kahn, '*Hoard*... on the table.'

'You just relax, mate,' said number one, 'we've got a nice warm bed waiting for you at the General.'

'I don't want to... relax... want *Hoard*.'

'He's delirious,' said Mrs Price, 'poor soul.'

'*Hoard*,' the jobless intellectual persisted, 'on the table... my treasure.'

Number two picked up the book, and stuffed it under the stretcher blankets with Kahn.

'Happy now?'

'Yes,' he smiled pathetically. 'Thank you.'

*

On the odd occasions in the past that Kahn had spent any length of time in hospital, his main bone of contention had been the poor quality of the food. But his first breakfast in Manchester General, a huge traditional fry-up, was the tastiest meal he had eaten for a very long time. Impoverished living had heightened his sense of taste; he savoured every mouthful, and then asked for more.

On the fourth day of his National Health sabbatical, Kahn was visited by an extremely attractive young woman who introduced herself as Doctor Hatt.

'But you can call me Alison,' she said with a smile that melted Kahn's frosty veneer and, momentarily, his interest in *Hoard*.

'Professor Benjamin Kahn. But you can call me Benjamin.'

Doctor Hatt had a splendid bedside manner, and Kahn rather wished it was an in-bed-with-him one.

'You're rather young to be a doctor, aren't you, Alison?' the professor continued, doing his best to be charming.

'I am?'

Doctor Hatt, pulled a note pad from her handbag and clicked a pen.

'You've been very poorly, Benjamin. I'd like you to think of me as one big ear. How do you feel about that?'

'I'm not sure I know what you mean.'

'You can say whatever you want. That's what I mean. Say whatever you want, and I'll listen.'

She pulled the curtain around Kahn's bed, and sat down again.

'There you are, Benjamin; now we're alone.'

'What's the note pad for?'

'Does it bother you?'

'Of course not, I just wondered what it was for.'

'It helps me remember.'

'Oh, I see… remember what?

'The conversations I have with people. It's a hobby of mine, actually.'

She smiled again, the same disarming smile that had worked so well at the beginning of their conversation.

'Please carry on.'

'Thank you, Benji. You don't mind if I call you that, do you? Benjamin seems so formal, and I'd like to think we could be friends.'

'I'd like that too.'

'Good. Now, remember what I said. I want you to think of me as one big ear.'

Kahn sat in silence for a few minutes, drinking in the exotic perfume and company of the voluptuous Miss Hatt.

'I expect you're wondering about my book,' he said finally, holding up his copy of *Hoard*.

'Why do you suppose that, Benji?'

'Everyone asks me about it.'

He stroked the cover protectively.

'It must be a very interesting book.'

'I think so.'

'Do you read it much?'

'Most of the time. People think I'm a bit unhinged, but I'm as sane as the next man.'

Doctor Hatt had discovered from hard professional experience that being as sane as the next man was not a commendable condition for anyone to be in. She made a note of Kahn's comparison.

'Why should people think you're crazy for reading a book? Has someone told you this to your face?'

'No, no one's said it to my face; but I can sense their hostility.'

He snarled as he spoke the words, and hugged *Hoard* close to his chest.

'They're all fools, idiots; they don't know anything about what I'm doing. They're just jealous because I'm cleverer than they are. It doesn't bother me, though. Great men have always been persecuted. I'm not the first and I dare say I'll not be the last.'

Doctor Hatt made a few more notes. The poor man was obviously right round the bend.

'This book of yours, Benji. I'm interested. What's it about?'

'Buried treasure. It's called *Hoard*. Actually, I don't normally talk about it, but I feel that I can trust you. You're different from the others.'

'Thank you, I'm flattered. Please go on.'

'It's a treasure hunt. It's got clues in it that lead to a buried treasure worth two million quid, and...' Kahn winked at Doctor Hatt and whispered the rest of the sentence: 'I'm within a hair's breadth of solving the bastard.'

'I think I've heard of this book before Benji. What's the author's name again?'

'Hollis Woodhead,' said Kahn bitterly.

'Oh yes, that's right. Hollis Woodhead.'

'I don't think I want to talk about this anymore,' said Kahn, suddenly whisking his copy of *Hoard* under the blankets. 'You seem to know an awful lot about *Hoard*, Doctor Hatt.'

'I'm sorry, Benji, I didn't mean to offend you. Let's talk about something else. What about your mother?'

'What about my mother?'

'You put her down as your next of kin.'

'Did I? I must have been out of my mind.'

Doctor Hatt raised an ironic eyebrow.

'You don't get on with her very well then?'

'She's a lunatic.'

'Why do you say that?'

'Because she is. Look, Alison, or whatever your name is, I don't want to answer any more of your ridiculous questions. Please go away.'

Kahn pulled the covers over his head to make it doubly clear that the interview was over.

'All right, Benji, I'm going. Perhaps I can call back when you're feeling a little better.'

There was an agitated thrashing from beneath the blankets.

'Don't call me Benji. I don't like it.'

Doctor Hatt swished back the curtains, and walked out of the ward for a consultation with Doctor Pecker, who had asked her to make an assessment of Kahn's unusual behaviour. Kahn peeped over the blankets to make sure she'd gone, and got back to the serious business of treasure hunting.

★

'What do you think Doctor Hatt? Was I right?'

'There's no doubt about it Doctor Pecker. Our Professor Kahn requires extensive therapy.'

Doctor Pecker nodded his head in agreement.

'I'm no expert, but that's exactly how it seemed to me... over quite a long time too, I would've thought.'

'Very probably, Doctor. I'm pleased you called me in. The man presents an interesting challenge from a psychiatric point of view.'

'What's your diagnosis, Doctor Hatt?'

'It's hard to know where to begin, really.'

'Just your initial impressions.'

'Well, I'd say he is an obsessive, sexually-frustrated and paranoid megalomaniac, with an enormous Oedipus complex. Quite possibly schizophrenic; but it's really a bit early to be absolutely sure about that.'

'Poor fellow.'

'I'm going to visit his mother. Perhaps she'll agree to having him put on a section for a while. It's the only way he can be helped. He certainly wouldn't volunteer for treatment in his present condition.'

'Oh dear.'

Doctor Hatt was right; Kahn would not have volunteered for treatment, and if he'd known about the visit to his mother by the crusading psychiatrist, he would have demonstrated in a way that would, no doubt, have lent even more weight to Doctor Hatt's initial diagnosis.

Chapter Seventeen

There was a dominant aura about the old woman who answered Doctor Hatt's knock on the front door of number thirty-two Ardwick Road, Manchester, that the psychiatrist found most appealing.

'Are you Mrs Kahn?' she asked, peering down at the pensioner's wrinkled features.

'If you mean, *was I foolish enough to marry an idiot with that name*? then I suppose I must be. At least that's what everyone's called me ever since. Can't say that I like it very much, though. What do you want?'

'It's about your son, Mrs Kahn.'

'Oh... him.'

'There's no need to worry. He's perfectly all right physically.'

'That's a pity. Who are you?'

'I'm his doctor, Mrs Kahn – Doctor Alison Hatt.'

'I thought you were about to tell me he'd got you pregnant, or something. Mind you, you look a bit too sensible to get mixed up with the likes of him. What does he need a doctor for, anyway? You just said he was all right.'

'I'm not really that sort of a doctor. I'm his psychiatrist.'

'I can't tell you how pleased I am to hear that my dear. He's needed one of those for years. Why don't you come in and have a cup of tea.'

'That would be very nice.'

'What did you say?'

'I said that would be very nice.'

202

It was quite obvious to Doctor Hatt, from her initial exchange with Kahn's mother, that she would have little difficulty in securing the woman's signature on the documents she had brought with her. The Professor was a most interesting case, and, whether he was interested or not, she would soon have the legal right to try out some wonderful new drugs on him.

★

Kahn spent a troubled last night in Manchester General. He slept from lights-out until breakfast, but dreamt the same dream over and over again in glorious Technicolor. Objects and characters from Woodhead's illustrations hung on golden-letter chains from the roof of a garishly decorated merry-go-round that spun faster and faster the more he wished it would slow down. The lights of the nightmare ride provided the only illumination. There was no shape or form outside it; only a black and terrifying void. Kahn could see himself in the wildly rotating machine, clinging for all he was worth to the central pole. Faster and faster and faster the merry-go-round would go, until, one by one, its prisoners freed themselves from their alphabetical bonds, and flew into the darkness. Then the letter chains began to hum as they cut through the air of the professor's imagination. It was only a whisper, but Kahn could always hear what they hummed:

'Words not things, words not things, words not things...'

'What do you mean?' he'd ask.

There was never a reply. Only the same whispered message again and again:

'Words not things, words not things, words not things...'

Then the vision would change, and he would see himself in a forest thick with fir trees. Suddenly, he would be in a clearing filled with sunlight; and in the centre of the clearing, Dr Alison Hatt would always stand, completely naked, and pointing with a huge syringe at a stone monument. She would never say anything; all she ever did was smile and point at the monument. Then, finally, the missing parts of the merry-go-round would fly over the tree tops and re-hitch themselves to the chains they had left at the start, and the terrifying sequence would begin all over again.

He spent the morning sat up in bed considering what on earth the whispering letters had been trying to tell him. He was certain that the message had something to do with the solution of the *Hoard* puzzle.

'Words not things,' he mumbled to himself, 'words not things.'

'What did you say, Benji?'

Kahn focused on the face of Dr Hatt.

'Oh, it's you,' he said. 'One Big Ear.' The young woman allowed herself a wry smile. 'I was just day-dreaming. What do you want?'

'Well actually, Benji, I'm your new doctor.'

'And?'

'I've decided to move you out of this hospital and into more agreeable surroundings.'

'And where exactly might these new surroundings be?'

'That's a surprise. I'm sure you'll like it there, though. We've got an ambulance waiting for you downstairs.'

'Short notice, isn't it, I'm still in my pyjamas.'

'Never mind about that,' said the psychiatrist, handing Kahn his dressing gown. 'Just put this on and follow me.'

'But I don't understand. What about my clothes?'

'They're ironed and pressed, and in the ambulance waiting for their owner. Come on, Benji.'

Kahn scowled, and got out of bed. Doctor Hatt helped him into the dressing gown, and he stepped into his National Health slippers. They walked out of Ward B2 side by side. The professor had the *Hoard* book and a folder full of notes in one hand, a pink plastic toiletry bag in the other, and several pencils wedged in his turban. Two tall and very heavily built men in white jackets acknowledged the doctor as she and Kahn reached the automatic doors.

'It's all right, gentlemen,' she said cheerfully. 'Professor Kahn doesn't need any help.'

In Kahn's mind the two ambulance attendants were disappointed gorillas – and he said as much.

'I'm sorry I don't live up to your expectations. Perhaps you'd like me to break a leg or two, or maybe catch yellow fever or something. There's just no pleasing some people is there?'

One of the gorillas curled his mouth in a mock grin that Kahn viewed as a threat to his well-being. Kahn read his mind: 'I'll bludgeon you to death later with a length of lead piping,' it said to him. It made Kahn feel uncomfortable.

After an hour of sitting silent, he made an effort to include himself in the banter that passed between the two gorillas and Doctor Hatt.

'Is that bloody siren absolutely necessary? It's beginning to get on my nerves.'

'Cedric refuses to drive unless he can have the siren on, Benji. He finds it very therapeutic. Do try to be a bit more tolerant. We're nearly there.'

'What do you mean?' asked Kahn with a sneer. 'Very therapeutic? He sounds like a bleeding nutcase to me.'

'Well, he is one of my patients, it's true, but he's making terrific progress. By the way, Benji, we don't approve of bad language at Cloxton Grange. We don't want to make any waves and upset the other patients now, do we?'

The professor stared at the woman dementedly.

'Cloxton Grange!' he squawked. 'Cloxton Grange! That's a fucking booby hatch! You wicked little bitch!' The gorillas leaned forward ready to pounce. 'Stop the ambulance!' demanded Kahn, 'this is kidnap!'

'No it isn't, Benji; you're on a section. I saw your mother yesterday. We had a heart-to-heart about you, and then she signed all the papers.'

'This is outrageous. I'm sane... completely normal... you can't... this isn't happening to me... I want to see my lawyer!' Kahn snarled and leapt at the doors.

'Grab him!' ordered the doctor.

The muscular male nurses had Kahn wrapped in a straightjacket in a matter of seconds. He made no attempt to struggle. There didn't seem to be any point. He would have to use all his wits to get out of the situation he was in, and rule number one would have to be cooperation. He would have to show them how sane he was, even if he went mad doing it. The gorillas returned Kahn to his seat, and solemnly sat down on either side of him.

'I'm sorry about that, Alison,' said Kahn, trying the new approach. 'It was the shock. My behaviour was entirely inappropriate, I realise that now. Honestly I do.'

'That's quite all right, Benji; I accept your apology, and I think it's very noble of you to make one. We'll let you out of the jacket when we get to Cloxton.'

'Thank you, Alison, thank you very much.'

'We're here to help you, Benji; remember that, and everything will be fine. Whatever we do, we do for your good because we care about you, and we want you to get better.'

'I know, and I want you to know that I truly appreciate your concern.'

'That's the spirit, Benji; I have the feeling we're going to get on famously.'

'I have that feeling too,' said Kahn.

He found it was hard work pretending to be reasonable in a straightjacket when, with every molecule in his body, he wished he could slowly strangle his travelling companions and cut them into little pieces. If he'd had the chance, he would have left the cuckoo in the driver's seat until last. Oh, yes, he would've shown that bastard exactly why unnecessary noise was bad for a person's health.

Chapter Eighteen

At first, Axelburger had looked upon the *Hoard* puzzle as a purely practical problem. Lola, his favourite 'wife', had made it clear in no uncertain terms that she wanted the *Hoard* treasure; and as he had at his disposal the technology and people necessary to do the job, he'd been happy to do his best for the woman. The episode with the Dobermans had changed all that. It was now a highly personal matter. He made it clear to Bracebridge that no expense was to be spared in the pursuit of Woodhead's gold. He also gave his butler the unenviable task of overseeing the project and supervising those scientists seconded from the laboratory to carry out the *Hoard* analysis.

'I want to see all the receipts, Bracebridge; every one of them. I want daily reports on progress as well.'

'Yes, my lord.'

'Right, take me over there now. I want to see what they're doing.'

'Yes, my lord.'

Bracebridge kicked the brake on Axelburger's wheelchair, and pushed the American along a dimly lit passageway. Its dark blue walls were adorned with oil paintings depicting gruesome battle scenes from the most memorable of violent international disagreements over oil and the acquisition of other people's lands.

'Hey! Go easy, Bracebridge, this is a wheelchair, not a goddamn lawnmower.'

'Sorry, my lord.'

'You will be in a minute. Okay, where have you put the boffins?'

'In the library, my lord. It seemed like the best place to me. Aside from the obvious research advantages to be gained from your excellent book collection, the room is entirely soundproofed.'

'How the hell is that gonna help?'

'To be perfectly frank, my lord, some of the men were a little nervous about coming to Charlbury Hall after what happened at the laboratory the other day. I thought the peace and quiet might improve their performance.'

'Yeah… good thinking.'

When they reached the library, the butler swung one of the two large oak doors open, and wheeled his disabled master inside.

'Good morning, gentlemen,' said Bracebridge, 'Mr Axelburger has—'

'All right, Bracebridge, I'm not dumb, you know.'

Axelburger surveyed the treasure-hunting scientists with a look of approval, and cleared his throat.

'Okay, men,' he said. 'I guess Bracebridge has told you already just how important the success of this project is to me; so I'm not gonna use phrases like: "a need to find alternative forms of employment", or anything gross like that.'

Someone dropped a pen at the far end of the room, and broke into a nervous cough.

'All I wanna do,' he continued, 'is impress upon you boffins the serious nature of the investigation you're carrying out for me. Now, remember, whichever one of you comes up with the answer to this book is gonna be one hell of a wealthy guy. And I mean – overnight.'

Axelburger's dangled carrot caught the undivided attention of the men. He raised a hand to silence their murmurings, and signalled Bracebridge to wheel him further into the room.

'Now, if you don't mind, gentlemen, I'd like to have a look at what you're doing.'

When Axelburger left the library, he was none the wiser. He was confused by the different approaches attempted by the team members. There was no convincing, cohesive argument from any of them. He could feel his blood pressure rise with anger at the stupidity of one whose approach was to cut the pictures from *Hoard* into strips and reassemble them randomly until the clues showed.

'Do you think they know what they're doing, Bracebridge?' asked the American as the butler wheeled him back to his study. 'It all looked like a lot of hogwash to me.'

'I have no idea, my lord,' said Bracebridge, not wishing to commit himself one way or the other. 'I suppose we'll have to wait and see what they come up with.'

'Yeah, well they'd better not be too long about it, or heads are definitely gonna fucking role.'

'Yes, my lord.'

'Okay, Bracebridge,' said Axelburger as they neared his study. 'I'll wheel myself from here. You can take care of the kids. I want you to go supervise them on the firing range.'

'But my lord, one of them nearly killed me the last time I—'

'Well, you shouldn't have shouted at the boy.'

'He was pointing a loaded machine gun at me.'

'He was only playing with you, man. If you hadn't tried to grab the barrel everything would've been all right. Now for heavens sake, Bracebridge, try to show a bit of backbone. I want you there on the double.'

'What about the reports you wanted on the *Hoard* investigation, my lord?'

'I've changed my mind... okay?'

Axelburger disappeared into his study, and left the butler to contemplate the terrifying nature of his assignment. The walk down to the bunker was a lonely one, and from the faint but unmistakable sound of rapid gunfire he could hear he deduced that the Axelburger brood had tired of waiting for him.

'Oh, my God,' he moaned as he leaned against the wall outside, a cold sweat breaking on his forehead. 'I just can't go through with it. I just can't.'

At that moment, as if to contradict him, the heavy metal door of the bunker slid open on automatic, and a furious young face looked him up and down. It was Irwin IX, the youngest member of the brood at five years of age, and one of the butler's offspring.

'Fuck it, Bracebridge,' said the child, waving a First World War Webley service revolver at his father indignantly. 'You're ten minutes late. Dad's gonna be real pissed when we tell him.'

Bracebridge wondered at how curious the huge revolver looked in Irwin IX's tiny hands. It was a great comfort to know that the little swine didn't have the strength in his fingers to pull the trigger.

'I'm afraid I don't feel very well, Master Irwin. I think I—'

'Bracebridge?' Axelburger's voice boomed over the loudspeaker system. 'Change of plan. One of the boffins has come up with a theory. Thinks he knows where the treasure's buried. I want you up here right away.'

The butler breathed a sigh of relief and looked down at Irwin IX. The five year old was looking up at Bracebridge with sheer devilry in his eyes, and both hands on the trigger. Bracebridge disarmed the mite, and twisted one of its tiny ears.

'If you ever try to do that again, Master Irwin,' said the butler, releasing his grip, 'I shall talk to the werewolves about you, and one of them will pay you a visit when you're in bed. You know what werewolves are, don't you, Master Irwin?'

The boy nodded and tears filled his eyes. He'd seen plenty of werewolves on videos and he wasn't at all happy about having one in his bedroom. Bracebridge smiled and walked off, leaving Irwin IX standing in a puddle.

*

When the butler entered Axelburger's study, the American was enthusiastically pumping the hand of a young man in a bright, colourful T-shirt and jeans.

'You know, Smith, you might be the youngest member of my *Hoard* team but you've certainly got the best idea so far,' enthused Axelburger. 'From what you've just shown me,' he said, beaming at the would-be genius, 'I'd say we've bagged it. No question about that at all, we've got it in the bag.'

'It was an interesting puzzle, Mr Axelburger,' said Smith, doing his utmost to appear both clever and modest. 'I'm pleased to have been involved in such an exciting project.'

'Involved? Don't be ridiculous man. You've done it single handed. I can see you going a long way in this company; you've got what it takes, young fellow.'

'Thank you, Mr Axelburger.'

Axelburger looked up and saw Bracebridge hovering by the door.

'Ah, Bracebridge, come over here, I want you to take a look at this. Tell me what you think.'

'Yes, my lord.'

'Go on, Smith, show Bracebridge what you've just shown me.'

Bracebridge walked over to Axelburger's desk, and stood to one side of his master while Smith, after a deep breath and a self-important cough, launched into his explanation of the *Hoard* puzzle.

'Well,' he began, barely able to contain himself, 'I'd been working for some time on the possibility that the pictures might actually yield a written message if they were dissected in a uniform manner and then re-assembled like a jigsaw. What I needed to know first of all, therefore, was the method Woodhead had used to break the pictures up. After a thorough examination of the text, I found the necessary clue.'

'Fucking unbelievable,' broke in Axelburger, nodding his head in admiration.

'Yes, my lord,' said Bracebridge, who most certainly thought that it was.

'Anyway,' continued the scientist, turning to what he considered to be the appropriate portion of text, 'here it is.'

As he read from the book, the American happily chewed on an unlit cigar, and Bracebridge studied the ceiling.

'Inch by terrible inch,' recited Smith, 'Sir Lexicon scaled the rocky face of Square Mountain. What this means is actually very straight forward.'

'Let me guess,' said the butler, 'it means you cut the pictures into inch squares.'

'As a matter of fact, it does,' sniffed Smith, a little offended by the sarcasm he detected in Bracebridge's contribution.

'Shut up, Bracebridge,' snapped Axelburger, 'and listen.'

'Yes, my lord.'

'Carry on, Smith.'

'After I'd cut the pictures up in this manner, I then set about reorganising them. I discovered that the fifteen pictures when re-assembled correctly each yielded a letter.

Take a took at the first one I solved.' Smith handed the evidence to Bracebridge. 'What letter do you see?'

'I'm afraid I can't see one,' said the butler. 'Perhaps you'd be good enough to show me.'

'Goddammit, Bracebridge!' Axelburger fumed. 'Are you blind?'

'No, my lord, I—'

'*R* Bracebridge; you're supposed to see the letter *R*.'

Smith traced the elusive member of the alphabet with his index finger.

'I'm sorry, my lord, but it doesn't look like the letter *R* to me.'

'Well, it does to me, dammit. Tell him the rest of it, Smith, he might come to his senses.'

Smith put his hands on his hips and looked at Bracebridge with irritation and disbelief that Bracebridge could not see what he and Axelburger could see so clearly.

'Take it from me, Mr Bracebridge,' he said sharply, 'that is most certainly an *R*.'

'I'm sure you're right, Mr Smith,' said the butler, deciding that it was more prudent under the circumstances to agree with the idiot. 'What about the other pictures?'

The scientist went through the remaining fourteen in quick succession.

'*E,D,R,U,T,H,C,O,R,N,W,A,L,L*; you see, Mr Bracebridge? They spell *Redruth, Cornwall*. That's where the treasure is buried.'

'I see,' said the butler. 'And where exactly in Redruth, Cornwall is the treasure buried?'

'That brings me to the next part of the solution. Pictures six and seven in their original state actually show the marker and compass direction from the marker. The marker is the Celtic cross in picture six and the stone compass in picture seven has the south west point broken off. There is only one Celtic cross in Redruth, and the treasure is buried south west of it. What I couldn't work out for some time was exactly how far south west.'

'Surprise me.'

'Well, it's quite simple really: feet.'

'Feet?'

'As feet are a human measurement, I decided to isolate the number of actual human feet pictured in the book. Apart from Sir Lexicon, all the other characters portrayed are either leprechauns or animals. Sir Lexicon's feet are not visible in all of the pictures. In fact, if you count them you will count only ten.'

'So, you're saying that the treasure lies ten feet to the south west of this cross in Redruth?'

'Exactly.'

'Well, Bracebridge?' asked Axelburger, 'What do you think?'

Bracebridge didn't believe a word of it.

'It seems plausible enough, my lord.'

'Okay, then, let's get moving!'

'Will we be requiring the helicopter, my lord?'

'You've got to be kidding, Bracebridge, we'd stick out like a sore thumb.'

'The limousine?'

'No, far too conspicuous. Hey, wait a minute, what kind of car do you drive, Smith?'

'A Ford Escort, Mr Axelburger.'

'Perfect, Bracebridge and I will take that. You take the rest of the day off. One of the maids can drive you home. We'll rustle up a pretty one for you.'

'Thank you, sir.'

'Bracebridge, get me my crutches.'

'Are you sure about this, my lord? With your injuries a long journey in such a small car may prove to be rather uncomfortable.'

'Hang it all, Bracebridge, where's your sense of adventure? Get my crutches, and then go find the gardener. What we need is a shovel and a ten foot tape measure. We'll get a compass on the way.'

'Yes, my lord.'

'If I might be so bold, Mr Axelburger,' simpered Smith, 'you may find a map of the area useful too.' He handed his Ordnance Survey map of Cornwall to the American. 'You'll notice I've marked the cross in ink.'

'Good thinking, Smith.'

*

An hour later, Axelburger and Bracebridge were roaring along a motorway in Smith's rusty Ford Escort.

'Fuck it, Bracebridge, can't you go any faster?'

'I'm afraid not, my lord, we're doing seventy as it is; any more and the engine will probably blow itself to pieces.'

'What if someone gets there before us?' shouted Axelburger.

'I would have thought that most unlikely, my lord.'

'Why so?'

'I can't imagine there are many people thinking along the same lines as our Mr Smith. His theory seemed extremely complicated to me.'

'Yeah, you're right, Bracebridge; it takes some kind of brain to come up with an answer like that.'

'Yes, my lord,' said the butler, pursing his lips, 'it certainly does.'

*

The two adventurers reached Redruth in the evening. The glow of twilight was giving way to the myriad stars that filled the cloudless, dark blue sky. It was cold and silent.

The only evidence of life were the lights in the town below them. As they rounded Rumbolt's Hill, Axelburger sighted the cross silhouetted against the last light of the day.

'There it is, Bracebridge!' he shouted triumphantly. 'Over there on the hill! Pull over, man, let's take a look.'

'Yes, my lord.'

Bracebridge drew the car to a halt, and peered out at the religious monument that dominated the top of the hill.

'It looks sort of mysterious, Bracebridge... don't you think it looks mysterious?'

'It looks very high up, my lord. Might I suggest we have something to eat before we do anything else? It could turn out to be a difficult climb.'

'Where do you suggest we go?'

'That looks like a pub just a bit further on,' said the butler. 'Let's try and get a bite there.'

'Okay, Bracebridge, let's do it.'

'Yes, my lord.'

'You'd better cut out the "my lord" routine, though; otherwise they'll think we're a couple of faggots.'

*

When Bracebridge walked out of The Mermaid his hunger for food and alcohol might have been satisfied, but he was feeling a lot less than enthusiastic about hunting for treasure. The same could not be said for Axelburger. Like a latter day Long John Silver, the American leant on his crutches and stared wildly at the Celtic cross. He gave no consideration to his inadequate mobility; he was just anxious to start climbing.

'Okay, Bracebridge,' he said as they got into the car, 'I'll do all the stuff with the compass. All you've got to do is dig.'

'Yes, my lord.'

'Right, then, let's move out.'

They drove along the road until eventually the hill loomed large over them from behind a barbed wire fence.

'Okay, Bracebridge, park here and get the shovel out of the trunk. We'll do the rest on foot.'

'I'm sure there must be an easier route, my lord. This side of the hill looks rather rugged to me.'

'Just do like I say, Bracebridge, we climb from here.'

'Yes, my lord.'

Bracebridge had studied the map thoroughly in the pub, and knew well that there was a footpath less than a mile from where they were that led up from the road directly to the cross; but, as Axelburger had been in such an infuriatingly adventurous mood all day, he felt the least he could do was accommodate him. Bracebridge pulled on his Wellington boots and armed himself with the shovel. The American heaved himself out of the car and shone the torch up the hill. He could not see the cross from where he stood, just the formidable slope and the large, rounded boulders that covered it. Tough heather lay in the deep crevasses between the boulders. Bracebridge was keen to see how the injured Axelburger would cope with such a hostile climb. He shut the car boot and walked over to Axelburger who stood peering unhappily along the thin beam of light from the torch.

'Shall I go first, my lord?' said the butler, throwing the shovel over the fence.

'Yeah, you'd better, take the torch too. I'll follow you.'

'Yes, my lord.'

The butler leapt nimbly over the first hurdle, much to Axelburger's disgust, and took the American's crutches from him while he scrambled under the barbed wire. Axelburger got to his feet breathlessly after a desperate struggle to free his jacket from the rusty teeth that snagged it on his way through.

'Thanks a fucking million, Bracebridge,' he scowled, grabbing his wooden stabilisers from the butler, 'you're a real help.'

'My lord?'

'Never mind, just get going.'

'Yes, my lord.'

Bracebridge began the long ascent, skipping effortlessly from boulder to boulder as though he had been doing it all his life. Half way up the hill he stopped to check on his master's progress, sweeping the rocky slope beneath him with torchlight. The American had vanished.

'Are you all right, my lord?' he shouted, cupping his ear against the wind.

'Never mind how I am,' rasped Axelburger, suddenly coming into view on all fours, 'stop shining that fucking torch in my face, that's all.'

'Yes, my lord.'

Axelburger ground his teeth in the darkness as Bracebridge resumed his effortless skipping. He'd rarely hated the butler as much as he did at that moment; the man was so irritatingly agile and versatile it made the arms dealer want to spit. He would have done too, if his mouth hadn't been so dry. By the time he reached the summit, his throat was raw from heavy gasping, and his hands and knees were caked in flattened rabbit droppings. Bracebridge was leaning on his shovel by the cross, contemplating a silent, seated figure, whose orange robes flapped and billowed in the wind. The American's arrival broke his concentration.

'A difficult climb, my lord?'

Axelburger barely heard him. He unthreaded his arms from the crutches he'd carried and lay on his back desperately drawing oxygen into his starving lungs.

'Shut the fuck up, Bracebridge,' he croaked, hardly able to stop himself from vomiting, 'just shut it.'

'Yes, my lord.'

Eventually the American hauled himself to his feet and hobbled over to the butler.

'Who's the orange asshole, Bracebridge?'

'I've no idea, my lord.'

'What the hell's he doing here?'

'I haven't asked him, my lord, but I'd say he was in some sort of meditative trance. He looks like a Buddhist to me.'

'Oh yeah,' said Axelburger, pulling a compass and tape measure from his pocket. 'Well, I don't give a hoot what the little commie faggot does, just as long as he stays the hell out of my way.'

'Yes, my lord.'

'Let's get on with it, then.'

Axelburger angrily fiddled with the compass, and was about to take a reading when he noticed the footpath that wound its way up to the cross from the other side of the hill.

'You moron, Bracebridge, can't you read a map? I nearly kill myself getting up here and all the time there's a path, a godamm path!'

'There are many paths,' interjected the Buddhist in a rich Birmingham accent, 'and each one will beautify the spirit. Those who choose to tread them will be at one with the Godhead and at peace with the universe.'

'Keep out of this, buddy,' rumbled the American, 'or you're not gonna be at peace with anything.'

'I'm sorry, my lord,' said Bracebridge, 'but I did say there might be an easier route. I'm afraid you were very insistent that we should climb from where we did.'

Axelburger gave the butler a disgusted took.

'Oh I was, was I?'

'Yes, my lord.'

'No man is lord over another,' intoned the Buddhist, ignoring the American's threat, 'we are all equal and equally important in the great circle of life.'

220

'I've had enough of you, pal,' said Axelburger, pulling a gun on the interfering mystic, 'now move your ass off this hill, or I'll blow you away!'

'Don't shoot! Don't shoot!' squawked the man, speedily disentangling himself from the lotus position and racing down the hill.

The treasure hunters watched his frenzied departure with interest.

'What an asshole,' said Axelburger.

'Indeed, my lord,' said Bracebridge, who loathed pretentiousness wherever he saw it, and for once had to agree with his employer's assessment.

'Okay, Bracebridge, let's get this gold.'

The butler held one end of the tape measure to the cross while Axelburger pulled up the slack and swung round until he was exactly south west and ten feet from it. He double-checked his bearing from the cross then marked the spot with the crutch he carried under his left arm.

'Okay, Bracebridge, get digging.'

The butler brought the shovel down with a sharp stab and hit rock at one inch.

'The ground seems rather hard here, my lord.

'Quit winging and dig.'

Bracebridge continued his attempts but to no effect. Each stab of the shovel gave the same unmistakable sound of metal on rock.

'I'm afraid this is quite impossible, my lord; everywhere I try to dig there's rock just under the surface.'

'Dig with your hands, man; Woodhead must have covered the treasure with a boulder. Get to the edges then we can lever it out.'

'Yes, my lord.' Bracebridge ripped away at the turf until, twenty minutes later, he had uncovered a huge dome of solid rock.

'I'm sorry, my lord,' he said finally, 'but I'm afraid it looks very much like Smith was mistaken.'

'Mistaken! Mistaken! I'll give the bastard mistaken!' ranted Axelburger, his face hot with rage. 'I'll kill the little swine when I get my hands round his frigging neck!'

Chapter Nineteen

Benjamin Kahn lay on a table in a spacious corridor at Cloxton Grange mental hospital, studying the male psychiatric nurse who stood over him. The man's large head and sloping shoulders reminded the scholar of a character from the board game *Cluedo*.

'Professor Plumb in the library with a dagger,' said Kahn as the nurse handed him a glass of water and his pill ration for the day.

'What was that?'

'Okay, if it wasn't Miss Scarlet in the drawing room with a candlestick, I'm giving up.'

'Just take your medication, will you, I'm busy.'

'Yes, of course you are,' said Kahn bitterly.

He popped the small pink pellets into his mouth and washed them down with a little water. He quite liked the pink ones; they weren't as incapacitating as some of the other colours he'd been obliged to take, and they made the *Hoard*less days more bearable. Alison Hatt had confiscated his treasure book on the grounds that it encouraged Kahn in his unhealthy obsessiveness. It had been the hardest part of the doctor's therapy game plan to swallow, much harder than the hypnotherapy or the pills, even the red and green ones, but it hadn't stopped him from thinking about the two million pounds prize. Although he was careful to give no indication of his continued interest in *Hoard*, he had not let a day go by without conducting some sort of research on the treasure hunt, albeit entirely from memory.

Like a surreal waiter, the nurse sauntered off with the pill trolley in search of another victim, and Kahn got down from the table to stretch his legs. He had honed his cooperation with the medical staff to a fine art since his arrival at Cloxton Grange. As long as he remained obedient, ostensibly at least, and took the medication prescribed for him by the good doctor, the staff left him alone. All he had to worry about was getting his name on the drugs list as early in the morning as possible, he was then free to do more or less what he wanted for the rest of the day. It was late spring.

Warm sunlight invaded the austere Victorian hospital through large windows that Kahn passed as he shuffled along the corridor in search of peace and quiet. The weather was sunny and pleasant, so he took a stroll in the hospital grounds. The fresh air lifted his spirits considerably. It was often too cold to venture out as, like all patients admitted against their will, he was allowed to wear only pyjamas and a dressing gown. He decided to walk to the perimeter fence and take a look at the world outside. By the time he reached the fence, he was high on his day's pill allocation. Somewhere, thought Kahn, on the other side of the fence, Woodhead had buried the *Hoard* treasure. He sat at the foot of a wild cherry tree and closed his eyes. The sweet smell of blossom filled his nostrils, bird-song filled the air and the warm sun felt good upon his face.

'What more could a man want?' he mumbled. 'Two million quid – that's what!'

*

Standing at her office window, Doctor Hatt thoughtfully chewed on a Biro and watched Kahn's progress across the grass. He hadn't worn his turban for several days. It was an encouraging behavioural change, and quite in keeping with his apparent lack of interest in treasure hunting. He had given up the religious habit of a lifetime and thereby symbolically rejected the very foundation of his cultural identity. In comparison, the *Hoard* compulsion was nothing more than a blip and must have ended weeks before. The drugs had done their work; the man was completely empty; his ego crushed. It was now time for her to rebuild the vanquished intellectual and turn him into the useful citizen he had never been. Alison Hatt was a player of mind games, a dedicated member of a psychiatric profession that offered enormous fortunes to those from its ranks with the right attitude. Once her book was published, her credibility as a psychiatrist would be beyond question. Kahn was a perfect case-study, and she was pleased now that she had chosen it as the central theme to the book. Stuff working for the NHS she mused, private practice was where it was at; plenty of rich neurotics with more money than sense.

She put down the nibbled pen and refocused on Kahn as he sat beneath a tree near the perimeter fence. He'd been confined to the hospital for long enough; what he needed now was a bit of healthy interaction with society. He would have to be supervised, of course, but it would be most interesting to observe his behaviour in an open environment. She had planned a trip to Blackpool for a few of her more promising cases, why not take Kahn along as well? Yes, she thought, why not? It would do him a lot of good. She returned to chewing the pen, and buzzed for an orderly.

'Did you call for me, Dr Hatt?'

At the door stood a thick-set, casually dressed orderly.

'Yes, Fred, come in, please. I'd like you to get Professor Kahn for me. He's over there by the fence.' She pointed at Kahn and handed the orderly a note. 'Just give him this,' she said, 'then you can walk him back. He's probably a bit stoned.'

'Right.'

*

Fred crept up on Kahn and vigorously shook the Indian's shoulders. He didn't like intellectuals; they were far too clever for their own good, and that was why there were always so many of them at Cloxton Grange.

'Hey, Kahn, wake up! Doctor Hatt wants to see you.'

'That might very well be true,' said Kahn angrily, 'but it doesn't give you the right to give me a bloody heart attack!'

'I don't know what you're talking about.'

'No, of course you don't.'

Fred handed Kahn the note from Alison Hatt.

'Come on Prof, I ain't got all day.'

'*Dear Benji,*' scoffed the scholar, reading the note aloud as he got to his feet, '*since your arrival at Cloxton, there has been a gradual but marked improvement in your condition.* Well that's nice to know,' he said, his voice thick with irony, 'there wasn't anything wrong with me in the first place.' He read the rest of the note as if he had a bad taste in his mouth. '*I would like to discuss this with you personally. Please be good enough to come to my office with Fred. Regards, Alison.*'

'Can we go now?'

'If the great analyst herself requires my humble presence, I suppose it would be imprudent for me to do otherwise. I mean, God might strike me down with forked lightning, or something.'

*

Alison Hatt dismissed Fred and beckoned Kahn into her office with a smile. A remarkable smile the Indian thought; he had discovered it to be as deadly as it was disarming. She offered him a chair in the centre of the room and sat at her desk facing him.

'How are you feeling, Benji?'

'Very well, thank you, Alison. In fact I'm feeling altogether better actually.'

'We are making encouraging progress, Benji, but I'm not sure we're out of the woods just yet.'

Kahn suppressed the urge to scowl and crossed his legs. 'Really?'

'What we need to work on now, Benji, is building your confidence. I'd like to see you mixing with the other patients more than you are at the moment. I'm sure you would be the first to admit that you're not the most gregarious person at Cloxton Grange. I'd like to see you making more of an effort in that direction; it would be good for you.'

'What do you suggest I do?'

'I've organised a trip for a few patients, I'd like you to come as well.'

'Where to?'

'Blackpool. Have you ever been there? It's just a day out really but I think you're ready for it.'

'Thank you,' said Kahn, with an obvious lack of enthusiasm, 'I'd like that very much.'

'We'll be leaving on Friday. It'll have to be an early start, I'm afraid – seven in the morning.'

'Great,' said Kahn, with a trace of sarcasm 'I can't wait.'

'In the meantime, Benji, try to open up a little bit more. Why don't you play ping-pong this afternoon?'

'I don't like ping-pong, Alison.'

'Try it anyway, it'll do you good.'

He disagreed with the doctor's assessment of ping-pong, but felt there was little point in voicing his opinion. He played the wretched game all afternoon.

★

Kahn endured three more days of in-hospital social inter-course before the Blackpool adventure, and when the big day arrived, he actually looked forward to the trip. He was the last of Cloxton's happy band of holidaymakers to climb aboard the minibus and, unhappily, the first to be noticed by Basil, a mute homosexual whose mania drove him to openly lewd demonstrations of his inclination. Basil was a singularly morbid case in Kahn's view, and one who should be avoided at all costs. It was extremely unnerving to be the object of another man's desire, particularly when the other man would have looked more at home in the belfry of Notre Dame.

Apart from Kahn and his love-struck admirer, two other inmates and two orderlies occupied the rear van space. The intrepid Doctor Hatt established a symbolic superiority by sitting in the front with the driver. As they pulled away from Cloxton Grange, Kahn had the feeling that the journey was going to be unpleasant. Although he under-stood problems of mental health – or mental ill-heath – his experience of the afflicted was that they were, at the very least, unpredictable and, at the worst, bizarre, and violent and generally he found it hard to cope with such people.

Throughout the journey, Basil kept touching Kahn's legs, sitting tightly close to him and smiling his 'come on' smile. Kahn felt tremendous relief when the tower came into view. At least half the rotten journey was over. The group alighted in a car park overlooking the beach. It was still early enough for the promenade to be quite deserted, apart from the occasional jogger, and a stiff breeze from the sea added to the ghostliness of the place. While the other patients chattered to one another excitedly, Basil expressed his appreciation by exposing himself to an orderly. Kahn leaned against a railing and stared at the horizon. There was an untameable wildness about the sea that made him envious. It had no feeling or ambition, it simply was and no one ever argued with it. His own feelings and ambitions, in contrast, had been subjected to every sort of argument under the sun for as long as he could remember. It was bloody outrageous. The ultra-reasonable voice of Alison Hatt broke his concentration.

'Benji, would you come over here, please, we're going to have a team conference.'

'How thrilling, Alison,' said Kahn, 'what about?'

'About how best to spend our day here, of course.'

Kahn reluctantly joined the others and Doctor Hatt clapped her hands to gain the attention of her assembled cast.

'The first thing I want you all to remember is that we're here to enjoy ourselves. And by the way, Basil, I don't think it was very nice of you to pull your trousers down just now. If you do it again you can spend the rest of the day wearing a jacket in the van.' Basil whimpered apologetic noises. 'Good, as I was saying, we're here to enjoy ourselves. You've all read the brochures, so you'll know there are plenty of exciting things to do. Now, I'm going to give each of you fifteen pounds. You can spend it as you see fit, but be careful because it's got to last you the whole day.'

The mention of money brought more excited chatter, and Basil pulled his trousers down again. The orderlies wrapped him in a straightjacket and dragged him into the van for a shot of thorazine, and Doctor Hatt continued unperturbed.

'Well, I don't know about you lot, but I'm hungry. I think the first thing we ought to do is find a café somewhere.'

'That sounds like an excellent idea,' said Kahn, whose spirits had risen somewhat since Basil's departure.

'Well done, Benji,' said the doctor, 'that was a very positive verbal contribution.'

'Thank you, Alison.'

*

They ate breakfast together in a promenade café that recalled to Kahn's memory the Albatross Café in Manchester and his less miserable days. The 'team' then set about exploring Blackpool. Kahn found himself falling into the 'Blackpool spirit', doing things he'd always hated others doing: eating ice cream, hot dogs and pickled whelks, playing the one-arm bandits and the computer games in the amusement arcade, ogling the bikini-clad women on the beach. All the while, Alison Hatt scribbled notes in a little black book.

'Okay, gather round everyone. It's just coming up to four o'clock, and time to go,' shouted Dr Hatt.

'What about Edward Pier, Alison?' said Kahn. 'I've never been on a pier before.'

He fell silent, suddenly embarrassed by his impulsive outburst.

'Why, Benji!' exclaimed Doctor Hatt, 'That was excellent. You voiced a personal desire under contrary pressure. I'm very pleased with you. Of course we can.' She looked at her watch: 'Okay, it's four o'clock now, one more hour. Let's get a tram, shall we?'

*

The garish mixture of novelty shops and seafood stalls on Edward Pier were something of a disappointment to Kahn, and he felt embarrassed that he had suggested the team should explore it. Towards the far end of the pier, a crowd of tourists had encircled two buskers. The trombone and trumpet played a colourful medley from Gershwin and Fats Waller and, as a diversion, Dr Hatt encouraged her retinue to mingle with the audience. Kahn wasn't in the mood for music. He stood next to the psychiatrist, impatient to be somewhere else.

As he looked away he noticed a familiar picture in a shop window. Surely not, he thought. His heart quickened. It was! There, not twenty feet from where he stood was a copy of Woodhead's *Hoard*! He crept carefully and unnoticed from Alison Hatt, and made towards the shop, barely able to contain his excitement. He heard the duo strike up with a lively and loud rendition of 'Ain't Misbehavin''. Feeling certain that his absence would soon be noticed, he whisked the second-hand book from the window and dashed to the counter, frightening the elderly woman who stood behind it.

'How much?' he demanded in a desperate, husky voice.

'Five pounds, dear.'

Kahn fumbled in his trouser pocket for the money.

'I'll take it,' he said, slapping a crinkled note into her outstretched palm. He stuffed the book inside his pullover and walked briskly out of the shop. The danger was over; even if Doctor Hatt had noticed his brief truancy, it was hardly likely to make him the subject of a strip search. As it was, no one had missed him. The last few bars of 'Ain't Misbehavin'' bubbled away as he slipped back into the crowd and tapped his doctor on the shoulder. She smiled.

'Great music, Benji, don't you think?'

'Marvellous, Alison, Fats Waller was never better.'

'Well done, Benji, well done.'

Chapter Twenty

Time ticked into early June, casting its hungry shadow ever closer to the end of the *Hoard* competition and the shattering of a million glorious dreams. Treasure hunters everywhere were becoming restless. They were not alone. Hollis Woodhead was feeling the strain himself. For several weeks, journalists from every tabloid in the country, bastions of fair play to a man, had hounded him for extra clues to satisfy a raging public demand. Television and radio producers pleaded for similar information, but the author of *Hoard* would not give way. They'd get their clue, he thought, as he sat in the Flute hospitality suite, gazing out of a window at his red Morgan, but not until he was good and ready and there wasn't enough time left for it to affect his claim on the prize money. Stuff appeasing the dubious morality of the media, he wasn't going to go soft right at the very end and have some wet-behind-the-ears intellectual run off with his hard earned cash. Who did they think they were dealing with? A registered charity?

*

The months following Irwin Axelburger's unpleasant treasure hunting experience in Cornwall, had shown his band of code-breaking scientists to be outrageously consistent in their ability to produce red herrings. As frustrating as these false trails were, Axelburger would not admit defeat, particularly not to Bracebridge whose tongue-in-cheek attitude to the *Hoard* project was a source of extreme irritation. *Hoard* was an obsession to Axelburger. The more hurt *Hoard* did to him, the more resources from his vast organisation he applied to its resolution. Even if he'd known the extent of Woodhead's corruption he would not have stooped to bribe him into disclosing the whereabouts of the treasure. His quest for treasure had become a matter of personal credibility; he was determined to triumph in the power struggle he perceived existed between himself and his butler.

His main problem was his inability to explain the logic behind his treasure hunting activities, and Bracebridge knew it. Instead of firing the investigation team, he put them back to work in the laboratory. He might have found the temptation to commit murder irresistible had they continued their analysis of *Hoard* at Charlbury Hall. He brushed the latest lab report from his desk with a hairy forearm, and drew heavily on a fat cigar until the smouldering end glowed in the dim light of his study.

'Two fucking weeks, Bracebridge!'

'My lord?'

'You know what I'm talking about, two more weeks and that bastard Woodhead's gonna be digging up the treasure.'

'Most unfortunate, my lord. However he would appear to be within his rights; the book states very clearly what would happen if the treasure wasn't found within the year.'

'You think I don't know that?' The butler remained silent. 'If I didn't know that, Bracebridge, then why the hell did I just say he'd be digging it up in two weeks?'

'I was simply trying to explain—'

'You're always simply trying to explain, aren't you, Bracebridge? If you want to simply explain anything, then why not start by simply explaining to me how the smartest people in my lab can spend month after month coming up with nothing better than the kind of horse shit you've just put on my desk.'

Axelburger puffed on his cigar and glared contempt-uously at the scattered papers.

'Perhaps the puzzle's too difficult, my lord.'

'Well, it's obviously too difficult for them, isn't it? Okay, Bracebridge, I've had enough, get the helicopter ready.'

'May I ask where we're going, my lord?'

'We're gonna pay the lab a visit, I'm gonna fire the bof-fins, every last one of the swines. From now on I'll be doing the research stuff myself.'

The butler bit his lower lip to conceal amusement.

*

Following the Blackpool trip, Doctor Hatt had noticed a remarkable improvement in Benjamin Kahn's behaviour. Previously insular and difficult, he had become outgoing, and positively helpful. It was a remarkable transformation and one that the psychiatrist wasn't altogether sure she believed. But there it was, Kahn had changed, and much sooner than she'd imagined possible. It was a frustrating development; completely at odds with the treatment she'd had in mind for him. There was nothing for it, if her work with the man was to mean anything at all she'd have to lift some of the restrictions he was under. She leaned against a wall in the recreation room, and watched the scholar as he engaged in a frantic ping-pong rally with one of the male nurses. Whatever had caused this radical character alteration? She didn't have the slightest idea, but it undoubtedly deserved a reward. She'd give him some responsibilities; let him out on his own for a couple of hours each day. He could visit the nearby village, perhaps run a few errands for the hospital staff.

*

Media speculation about the possibility of an extra clue from Hollis Woodhead ended in the last week of June. With only one week left before the end of the competition, the cunning ex-hippie walked into a press conference in a London hotel and gave the assembled newspaper men what they'd been dying to hear. As he sat down, a firing squad of cameras clicked and flashed and hundreds of ferocious voices competed for his attention.

'Gentlemen,' said Woodhead, raising a hand and appealing for silence, 'gentlemen, please.' He scanned the sea of expectant faces before him with a wry smile. Eventually, a hush fell over the place. 'I've decided to reveal an extra clue to the location of the treasure, but before I do, I want to make it clear that I shall not be answering any questions after its announcement.' Woodhead calmly looked at his watch and waited for the sound of mumbled disappointment to die down. 'All I'm prepared to say about the clue is that it's fair, and if anyone is on the right track, it will help them.' He cleared his throat. 'Here it is: you must follow the inscription on the leprechaun's tomb. Thank you, gentlemen, that's your lot.'

Woodhead didn't wait for the inevitable mass protest, he was out of the hotel and into a hired, chauffeur-driven car before his audience knew what was happening. The conference had gone according to plan, all he had to do was lay low for a week and he'd be adding another two million pounds to the seven hundred thousand Willy Grindle had so generously abandoned in the New Forest. He sat back comfortable and smug in the rear of the limousine.

'You rotten bastard, Woodhead! I'm going to kill you,' shouted a crazed man from the rear of the pressing crowd of journalists.

A shot rang out and the missile hit Woodhead at the side of the head. After a scuffle, the perpetrator, was on his back under a pile of have-a-go pressmen. Woodhead slumped forward.

'Have I killed him? Have I killed him?' screamed the captive through a tangle of arms and legs.

Woodhead stirred, and then sat up slowly, eventually raising his head upright. Blood poured through the fingers he held to his head. He looked at his bloodied hand and fainted.

'Oh my God, oh my God, he's still alive! Oh no! No, no, no! I've been trying to kill the bastard for years! And he's still alive.'

*

Woodhead stirred and rolled his bandaged head from side to side. The smell and whiteness of hospital.

'He's coming round. Hello, Mr Woodhead. Hello. Can you hear me, sir? It's okay, Mr Woodhead, you're not in danger. The shot just skimmed your temple.'

'What shot? Oh God, what happened?'

'Good evening, Mr Woodhead, Detective Sergeant Rollins. Would you happen to know this man?'

Rollins pushed a photo of the assailant before Woodhead's nose.

'Wally Waters. That's Wally Waters, my old drummer. So, it's Wally who's been trying to kill me. He came close to my head down in Dorset.'

'Why would he try to kill you, sir?'

'Ooo, my head! I can think of at least three good reasons, but I don't think I'll be sharing them with anyone.'

'Let him sleep now.'

*

Benjamin Kahn was probably the only *Hoard* fanatic in Great Britain who didn't hear about Hollis Woodhead's dramatic disclosure to the press, and the excitement that followed; but even if he had, it would have made very little difference to him. As Woodhead sat up in bed the morning after announcing the extra clue, gloating over a big *Hoard* story and a large photograph of himself, an extremely elated ex-professor of comparative religion and eastern philosophy walked out of Cloxton Grange Mental Hospital on a three-hour recreational pass. He followed a meandering lane to the village of Lower Buzzdale, a pleasant oasis of shops, whitewashed houses and, more importantly for Kahn, a modest library, just one and a half miles to the east of Cloxton Grange. Large water droplets from trees on either side of the lane splashed the tarmac, reminding him of the heavy rain he'd heard the night before. There had been lightning too; quick flashes that brightened his room, momentarily rendering redundant the pen-torch he'd been using to scan the pages of *Hoard*. He would never forget that night; it was the night he had solved the puzzle.

He sat on a bench with his copy of *Hoard*, and considered the remarkable achievement, tears of unspeakable joy streaming down his face. With only a few days to spare, and against almost insurmountable odds, he'd done it! The inscription on the leprechaun's tomb in the last of Woodhead's fifteen illustrations had intrigued the Indian scholar for some time. Interestingly, it had very little to do with leprechauns. It was, in fact, the second half of the inscription on William Shakespeare's tomb. Stranger still, it was written in contemporary English and divided into two parallel rows of thirty letters, with the last letter of the first row shifted to the beginning of the second row, and the last letter of the second row a seemingly inexplicable X:

BLE S S T HEMANWHOSP A R E S T HESESTONE

SANDCURSED B E H EWHOMOVESMYBONESX

In addition to Woodhead's obvious interest in symmetry, Kahn had noticed that the letters were coloured in columns according to the rainbow sequence: The first column (B and S) red, the second orange, the third yellow, the fourth green, the fifth blue, the sixth indigo, and the seventh violet, the sequence repeating itself throughout the remaining letter columns. As another busy salvo of lightning illuminated his room, Kahn had seen, as if inspired by the natural display of electrical power, a correlation between the inscription on the leprechaun's tomb and the trail of coloured letters that cascaded from the saddlebag of Sir Lexicon's horse in every picture.

There were fifteen paintings in *Hoard*; exactly half the number of coloured letter columns on the tomb inscription. He had excitedly turned to the first picture certain that there would be only one red letter and one orange letter. He'd been right! One red letter (H) and one orange letter (O)! Two letter columns for every picture! The inscription was a colour key for a thirty letter message! He'd tried the next picture; again only two letters (A and R)! Then the next (D and L)! *HOARD*! The next word began with an L. The remaining letters had come thick and fast. With the lightning storm raging overhead Kahn had read the message aloud in a quivering voice.

'*HOARD LIES BURIED AT MACDUFF'S CROSS.*'

He had worked out the compass direction and measurement away from the cross several weeks before, the ten feet south west so accurately resolved by Axelburger's man, Smith.

'Are you all right?'

'What?'

'Are you all right?'

Kahn came out of his trance and focused on a young man who stood in front of the bench looking at him.

'I'm fine, just fine, thank you.'

'No, you're not, you've been crying.'

'I haven't been crying. If you really want to know, I've got hay fever.'

'No you haven't, you're upset about something, aren't you? I can tell.'

'I'm not upset about anything.'

'Yes you are.'

'I'm telling you, I'm not.'

'Why don't you come back to my place? We could have a couple of cocktails, get to know one another better.'

'I can't believe this. Look, I don't want a couple of cocktails, and I don't want to get to know you at all. Fuck off and leave me alone!'

'Charming, I must say!'

'Why must you say anything to me?'

'Men! You're all the same!'

Kahn raised his eyebrows at the rapidly departing figure in disbelief. He just hoped that the rest of the walk to Lower Buzzdale was less eventful. The village library was housed in a converted Methodist Chapel opposite the post office, and as he stood at the threshold, adrenaline coursing through his veins, it occurred to him that the religious history of the building was most appropriate. He was, after all, the most brilliant and dedicated of his treasure hunting brethren; the High Priest of Hollis Woodhead's *Hoard*. He had suffered terrible indignities in its name, and the god of money was about to reward him. He took a deep breath and walked inside. An old woman sat at a desk, staring icily at a snoring tramp. Kahn took her to be the librarian.

'Excuse me,' he said, 'I wonder if you could tell me where you keep your Ordnance Survey maps?'

The woman peered at him over her spectacles and then nodded in the tramp's direction.

'He's always here, you know.'

'Pardon me?' said Kahn.

'That dreadful man; he's always here. He never reads anything, probably can't read. He just sits there and snores. I hate him. What do you want anyway?'

'Your Ordnance Survey maps; I'd like to see them.'

'Over there,' snapped the woman, pointing through the tramp, 'in the very-clearly-labelled map section.'

'Thank you so very much,' said Kahn, ignoring her severe tongue.

'Just make sure you put them back in the right order when you've finished.'

Kahn hurried over to the maps, his heart thumping with the excitement of the chase. He flicked through the pages of the Ordnance Survey Gazetteer, quietly chanting the name of Macduff under his breath. The chant stopped as he touched the name in print. There it was, in black ink for anyone to see: Macduff's Cross! The good news for Kahn was that the Gazetteer listed only one cross of that name in Great Britain; the bad news, as Kahn discovered when he looked up the grid reference on the map, was that Hollis Woodhead had chosen to bury his treasure in the wilds of Langwell Forest, twenty miles or so to the south of Thurso, a small town on the northern coast of Scotland.

Prudently, Kahn had made financial provision for the possibility of a long journey by saving his small weekly allowance. Over the months he'd managed to accrue one hundred and fifty pounds. He also had an extra twenty pounds which had been entrusted to him that day by the hospital staff for various odds and ends they wanted in the village. He pocketed the Ordnance Survey map and walked out of the library thinking of Scottish bound trains and

Manchester's Piccadilly Station. Sadly, Lower Buzzdale hadn't figured in British Rail's plans.

He went into the village pub to find a bus timetable; he had to get to Manchester quickly. The Lower Buzzdale transport system consisted of a twice-daily bus to Manchester that ran irregularly, he discovered from the landlord.

'The next one arrives outside the pub this afternoon at two-thirty, and usually goes at three-thirty.'

The publican explained that it all depended on whether the driver was drunk enough to face the rest of his route. According to him, the man's marriage had taken a monumental turn for the worse.

Kahn sat down in an alcove with his copy of *Hoard* and a pint of bitter. The bus wouldn't be leaving for an hour and a half, so he filled in the time checking through his solution with the book. The warm glow of satisfaction he felt as he pored over Woodhead's colourful illustrations, dreaming of the fame and fortune that would soon be his, evaporated when he caught sight of familiar faces at the bar. Doctor Alison Hatt had decided to treat Basil to a Coca Cola. He needed a little treat to lift his spirits after solitary confinement. The psychiatrist and her beastly Coca Cola slurping patient were accompanied by two orderlies. Kahn walked quickly to the toilet and locked himself in a cubicle, hoping that Basil had not spotted him before he rushed through the door, but Basil had.

'What's wrong, Basil?' asked Doctor Hatt. 'Don't you like Coca Cola?' Basil pointed at the gentlemen's toilet. 'Do you want to go to the toilet?' Basil nodded his head vigorously. 'All right, Basil, off you go, then.'

Basil soon found Kahn's stall. He pulled himself up it and peered over the top.

'Get out of here!' Kahn growled through closed teeth. 'If you don't go right now, I'll tell Alison, and she'll have you locked away again!'

Basil grinned and disappeared from view. For a moment Kahn thought his blackmail tactic had worked, but Basil was impervious to appeal and argument. He slipped a hand under the door and grabbed Kahn's crumpled trousers. The scholar was pulled from his throne and dragged slowly across the tiled floor. He could think of only one thing: violent murder. For a moment the thought was strangely calming. He freed himself from his trousers, leapt out of the cubicle in a roaring rage, and attacked Basil's throat.

'Sounds like Basil's lost control again,' said Doctor Hatt. 'I think we'd better check it out.' She turned to the land-lord, and smiled. 'I'm sorry about this, he's one of my patients.' The landlord cast a worried expression at the door of the gentlemen's toilet.

'I don't care if he's the King of Siam, lady, just get him out of here before he causes any damage.'

Kahn, trouserless and hot with malice, was strangling the life out of Basil as the psychiatrist and her two assistants walked into the toilet.

'Benjamin Kahn!' she shouted, 'put Basil down this instant!'

Kahn growled loudly, and applied more pressure to his victim's throat. Basil's face turned blue.

'Okay, boys, break them up. I'll go and get a jacket.'

A few minutes later, straight-jacketed and howling with hysterical laughter, Kahn was dragged out of the pub and bundled unceremoniously into the back of the Cloxton Grange ambulance.

'I'm very angry with you, Benji,' said Doctor Hatt, her arms folded in disapproval. 'I think you'll be having some hypnotherapy with me later today.'

To be undone at the very last by such a cruel twist of fate was simply too much for the poor man to bear. While Kahn was driven back to the hospital, Basil sat in the pub, flicking through the pages of *Hoard*.

'You can keep it if you like, Basil,' said Doctor Hatt, pouring him another Coca Cola, 'Benjamin won't be needing it anymore.'

Basil smiled. He liked pretty pictures.

Chapter Twenty-One

Bracebridge knocked on the door of the library at Charlbury Hall with a copy of every newspaper containing
information on Hollis Woodhead's extra clue. His American master had spent the best part of a week ensconced in
the room attempting to solve the *Hoard* puzzle.

'Who the fuck is it this time?' Axelburger shouted irritably.

'It's me, my lord.'

The butler heard heavy footsteps and the sound of a key
turning in the lock. The door opened and Axelburger
stood, swaying unsteadily in the corridor. He was unshaven
and bleary-eyed with fatigue.

'How goes the investigation, my lord?'

Axelburger snarled and snatched the bundle of newspapers from his butler.

'Just get me some coffee, asshole.'

'Yes, my lord.'

Axelburger sat miserably at his desk, and turned to the
first *Hoard* article. To his great surprise, it made extremely
interesting reading. For that matter, so did all the other
pieces on Woodhead's extra clue. Like *Hoard* punters
throughout Great Britain, he had just learnt, by dint of
thorough journalism rather than any personal research or
knowledge, that the inscription on the leprechaun's tomb
was really the second half of William Shakespeare's epitaph.
He'd also learnt from the same source that Shakespeare was
buried in the charming market town of Stratford-upon-

Avon, in Warwickshire. When his sardonic butler came back with the coffee, Axelburger was a changed man.

'Listen to this, Bracebridge!' gasped the American, frantically brandishing a copy of the *Sun*.

'I've seen it already, my lord.'

'Well? What do you think?'

'I thought it most intriguing.'

'Okay, Bracebridge, take the limo into town. I want all the info you can get on Stratford-upon-Avon. You'd better get some stuff on this Shakespeare guy as well.'

'Yes, my lord.'

'One more thing.'

'My lord?'

'I want the whirly-bird ready at a moment's notice.'

The butler hovered for a moment without replying.

'My lord?'

'Yeah?'

'Do you really think it likely that Mr Woodhead's treasure is buried there? Forgive me for saying so, but it does seem rather obvious. Couldn't the inscription have some bearing on the puzzle? I was reading an article in the *Guardian* and—'

'Shut the fuck up, Bracebridge.'

'Yes, my lord.'

*

Barrington Farnworth played nervously with his mayoral chain as he sat in an upstairs room at Stratford-upon-Avon Town Hall, presiding over a hastily convened meeting of the District Council. He was about to come to the boil.

'Who the bloody hell does this Hollis Woodhead think he is? Implicating our town in his silly little game! The man ought to be strung up!' He looked to Councillor Grimes for inspiration. 'Are you sure there's no way of getting the bastard to say it's not here, Eric?'

'We've been trying to reach him all week. He's gone into hiding. Nobody has a clue where he is.'

'Well, that's bloody marvellous, isn't it? We'll be lucky if anything's left standing by the time this thing is over.'

'I don't think it's as bad as all that, Barrington.'

'Oh, don't you, Eric, don't you? Have you seen the state of the Bancroft Gardens? Woodhead's terminating the competition at midnight tonight. We'll have a riot on our hands by then, you mark my words.' The mayor drummed his fingers on the large oak table around which the council sat. 'How many of the swines have your boys arrested so far, Jack?'

Chief Inspector Jack Nately took a long hard draw on a cigarette before replying. He looked haggard; it had been a tough week for Stratford CID.

'Fifty-eight so far, Mayor, but I'd say that was just the tip of the iceberg. Trouble is, it's hard to tell them apart from genuine tourists during the day. There isn't a lot we can do either. Just confiscate their shovels and book them, that's all. We look more like a Spear and Jackson warehouse than a nick at the moment. It makes no difference, though, they're at it again as soon as they leave the station. We've caught some of them digging with their bare hands.'

'I'm not interested in the legal technicalities, Jack, I'm not interested in their infernal burrowing habits either. This is wanton vandalism, for God's sake! I want to know what you're going to do about it!'

'There's only one thing we can do. Wait for the rein-forcements the Chief is sending us, and dig in.'

'This is not the time for puns, Jack.'

'None intended, Mayor.'

★

It wasn't until the last day of the treasure hunt that Irwin Axelburger III felt comfortable about committing himself to activity in the field. No impetuous foolery for him, he thought, as he rang the buzzer for his butler. Oh no; he'd chased after too many mare's nests already. Curiously enough, he'd considered the fireplace in the back bar of Stratford's Garrick Inn earlier in the week, but put the idea to one side while he examined other possibilities. Now, though, he was sure. The more he'd thought about the unusual fireplace that he had seen in the Stratford brochures, the more it had captured his imagination. It was no coincidence that the fire's copper flue was cone-shaped; it could have been the mother of the golden cones Woodhead had buried. And then there was the Garrick itself. The Stratford High Street pub had apparently been named after an actor. That Shakespeare fellow had been some sort of an actor. The pub was very old too, perhaps the oldest in the town. This meant it was historical, and a bit weird. He was on his feet before Bracebridge could open the library door.

'You rang, my lord?'

'Start the chopper up, Bracebridge, we're going to Stratford. I know where that fucker Woodhead put the gold.'

'Yes, my lord.'

'I'll be with you in quarter of an hour. I'm gonna get a few things from the bunker just in case we run into any opposition when we get there.'

Bracebridge busied himself with helicopter safety checks, while Axelburger went about the serious business of arming himself to the teeth. The American was on the helipad fifteen minutes later dressed in battle fatigues. He had a couple of high-tech time bombs on his belt, an automatic machine gun in one hand and a backpack filled with hand grenades in the other.

'What do you think, Bracebridge? Am I ready to rock and roll or what?'

'Most impressive, my lord.'

'Yeah I know. I've got enough pineapples here to start World War Three.'

'Shall we go, my lord?' said the butler, with the look of a man who wanted to be anywhere but where he was.

'Yeah, let's move out, Bracebridge.'

The helicopter took off, and flew, like an angry dragonfly, into the Oxfordshire countryside. Bracebridge heaved a frustrated sigh. He'd had just about all he could take of Irwin Axelburger III. Although the butler hadn't visited Stratford for many years, he remembered it with affection. It appalled him to think that such a beautiful town could be visited by such a colossal cretin. There ought to be a law, he thought.

'To tell you the truth, Bracebridge, I just can't fucking wait to get there,' said Axelburger, augmenting the butler's feelings of resentment. 'I just can't fucking wait. Give me an ETA, man.'

'Seven thirty, my lord.'

'Sounds good to me.'

The American lit a cigar and broke into a discordant rendition of 'The Star Spangled Banner'.

Bracebridge's estimate was accurate. At seven thirty they were hovering at five hundred feet over the town centre. The sun was low on the western horizon, lending a golden glow to the chaotic view beneath them. From the air, Stratford looked like a mini-Armageddon. Hundreds of irate treasure hunters were taking out their frustration on the tarmac and each other with picks and shovels. Sirens wailed; abandoned cars, some in flames, blocked the streets for as far as Axelburger and Bracebridge could see, and pitched battles raged between bands of uniformed policeman and everyone else. A police helicopter came alongside and the pilot boomed a message over the loud speaker.

'This airspace has been declared restricted. Please leave the area at once!'

'It's okay, son,' the American shouted back, 'I'm with the CIA.'

This implausible excuse seemed to satisfy the occupant of the other craft, who flew off. The poor man was prepared to believe just about anything after what he had witnessed that day. Axelburger turned to his butler in amazement.

'Hey, Bracebridge, this is far out! Ain't you excited?'

'I suppose that's one way of putting it, my lord,' said Bracebridge bitterly.

'Good job I brought the hardware with me, eh? I'll teach these limey bastards a thing or two about war!'

'Where would you like me to drop you, my lord?'

Axelburger mused over his map.

'Okay… we're just about… here… and I wanna be… just about… there. Right, drop me in the next street, Bracebridge. That's High Street. Get as close to the Garrick as you can. I'll get the rope ladder ready.'

Bracebridge took the helicopter into a controlled descent, and hovered at fifty feet over the High Street.

'Okay, Bracebridge, I'm gonna let the ladder go. Maintain your position while I'm gone.'

'Yes, my lord.'

As Axelburger turned to open the door, the butler took providence in both hands and twisted the time dial on one of the bombs attached to the American's belt. He just couldn't help himself. Axelburger grabbed his grenade-filled backpack and the machine gun, saluted Bracebridge in a military fashion and got on to the ladder.

'You're an okay guy, Bracebridge. You hang in there, you hear?'

The butler smiled.

'Thank you, my lord. You hang in there too.'

When the American touched down into the crowd, he had less than three minutes left on his belt. Unaware of his impending obliteration, he let off a volley of machine gun fire and ran for the pub. The Garrick was closed, but that wasn't about stop Axelburger in his tracks. He blew the lock away with the rest of the magazine and kicked the smouldering door ajar. It was dark inside; the only illumination came from a soft light above the bar optics. He crept into the lounge and went over to inspect the cone-shaped copper flue.

'Who the hell are you?' demanded the landlady, looking him straight in the eye.

Axelburger was always uncomfortable in the company of forthright females; they made him feel like he was back at school.

'Relax, ma'am, I'm with American intelligence.'

'I don't give a damn who you're with, you big bully, it doesn't give you the right to come barging into my home with a gun. There isn't any treasure buried here, this is a listed building in case you didn't know.'

'I'm getting a bit tired of you lady.'

'You're breaking my heart.'

'Look, I'm in the middle of something real important at the moment, understand? All I want to do is check the fireplace, and I'll be on my way.'

'Oh, I see. Now you're going to tell me you're from the gas board.'

Axelburger swore under his breath.

'I don't believe this. Listen, lady, I'm not telling you anything. Just stand out of the way or I'll—'

Bracebridge watched the explosion from a hundred feet above the roof tops. He'd had no idea what two time bombs and a backpack full of hand grenades might do if they exploded simultaneously, but he'd guessed they'd do a sight more than blacken the walls of the pub. The roof appeared to implode and the first floor front of the building disintegrated into high speed lumps of wood and lethal shards of glass that killed several passing treasure hunters and shattered all the windows in the buildings opposite. The butler turned the nose of the helicopter to the south, and cast a delighted last look at the smoking remains of the Garrick, he wondered at how easy it had been to eliminate Irwin III. Over the years, he had considered a number of complex assassination plots, many of them suggested by Axelburger's own exasperated 'wives'; but in the end, all it had taken was a simple twist of a dial. He could hardly wait to get back to Charlbury Hall. There were three stunningly beautiful women living in the Oxfordshire manor house who would be only too willing to demonstrate their appreciation.

*

By nine o'clock in the evening, Chief Inspector Nately was standing in the doorway of Stratford's Holy Trinity Church, praying for midnight and the cessation of hostilities he hoped that hour would bring. He lit his sixtieth cigarette of the day with a trembling hand and looked out at the sea of blue uniforms and riot shields in front of him. The spectacle was comforting; for the first time in several hours he actually felt safe. Given the nature of Hollis Woodhead's clue, it had seemed logical to concentrate manpower around the riverside resting place of the town's most famous son. Mayhem and murder, structural damage to buildings and roads, that was one thing. The desecration of William Shakespeare's tomb by rampaging treasure hunters, the exhumation of the immortal Bard by a frenzied mob of pick-wielding hooligans, quite another.

The town's international reputation was on the line and, what was more, so was Nately's job.

According to the intelligence reports he had been receiving at five minute intervals on his cordless telephone, the treasure hunters appeared to be 'resting'. It was not a word that Nately felt comfortable with; it carried the worrying implication of future activity. The policeman's instincts were not unfounded. Just after ten, heads started to pop up around the church walls, and by half past, the graveyard was crammed with *Hoard* fanatics, their digging implements glinting ominously under the waxing moon. A terrible truce of silence fell over the law and the lawless, but to Nately, and every one of his men, the intention of the lawless was clear.

'They're gonna go for it, Jack,' muttered Detective Constable Yates, 'I can see it in their faces. What are we going to do? There are fucking thousands of them!'

Nately wiped his forehead and lit another cigarette.

'Calm down, Colin. In situations like this, it's essential to keep a cool head. What's called for here is reason. Pass me that megaphone, lad.'

'Whatever you say, Jack, but they don't look very reasonable to me. Why don't we just let them get on with it? It's only a silly little grave after all.'

Nately gave DC Yates a reproachful look, and raised the megaphone to his mouth.

'My name is Chief Inspector Nately of Stratford CID,' he bellowed, 'and I want you all to listen very carefully to what I'm about to say.' The police shuffled closer together, and the mob remained silent. 'I know what you're thinking,' he said. 'I'm sure I'd be thinking exactly the same thing if I was after the treasure, but you must believe me when I tell you that it isn't even buried in this town, let alone Shakespeare's grave. We've just managed to contact

Mr Woodhead and he's given us his personal assurance that this is the case.'

The mob responded with a chorus of 'liar!' and moved forward, every eye fixed on the church door. Nately started to panic.

'You've got to listen to me!' he screamed, backing up against the door. 'It is not buried in this church!'

'Perhaps Shakespeare isn't either!' someone shouted.

'There's only one way to find out!' shouted another. 'Are we going to find out or aren't we?'

The crowd let up a terrifying roar and rushed forward. Sensibly, the police threw their shields and clubs to the ground and leapt out of the way. Nately stayed in the doorway, feverishly reciting the Riot Act into his megaphone. It was a touching demonstration of dedication to duty for which the Chief Inspector would later receive a posthumous OBE. The iron railings immediately in front of the church entrance were ripped from their brick sockets by the frenzied mob in scenes reminiscent of the storming of the Winter Palace. The door itself was a mere trifle in comparison, and the church quickly filled with treasure hunters fighting to get at the Swan of Avon.

'Brothers!' yelled the vicar as he stood by the grave, holding a large golden crucifix. 'We are all God's children. I appeal to you in the name of Christ to stop this carnage now!'

There was no mercy. No respite. 'To the grave!'

The vicar persisted:

'Remember the curse! Remember the curse!'

Another angry chorus echoed on the stone walls of The Holy Trinity:

'Bugger the curse!'

The steeple bell rang out the first stroke of midnight as the first pick struck the grave. Sparks flew as the famous stone slab and its inscription cracked and chipped under the onslaught. The heavy clang of metal on stone lent a busy counterpoint to the even spread of the midnight chimes: BONG! Clang! Clink! Clink! Clink! Clink! Clang! BONG!

The last stroke of midnight and the slab gave way – and those responsible for the sacrilege fought tooth and nail for the right to force the investigation further.

'It's fucking empty!'

Apart from the shattered fragments of its once revered cover, the Bard's grave was as bare as a badger's arse.

Chapter Twenty-Two

As news of the centuries-old fraud spread through Stratford, Hollis Woodhead walked nonchalantly along a moonlit footpath in the centre of Langwell Forest, northern Scotland, unaware of the chaos for which he was currently being roundly blamed. It was a warm night and strangely peaceful amongst the regiments of Scotch pine trees. Macduff's Cross lay some fifty yards ahead of him on the flat top of a modest, tree-covered hill. He shifted his shovel from the left shoulder to the right, and walked in darkness along the last uphill leg of the journey. His innards were filled with excitement and anticipation.

'No one has written to claim the prize! No solutions! No claims! Yeehaa! Yeehaa!' he screamed into the darkness. He kissed the tip of the fingers on his free hand and threw his arm towards the heavens. 'I am fucking-well rich. Rich as assholes!'

The 1st of July. A whole year had passed since the launch of *Hoard* and the start of '*Hoard* madness'. Woodhead's mind wandered back over a year in which he had played dangerously many times with death. He had assisted in the disposal – he could not accept the word *murder* – of two humans. He had saved humanity from the strain of living with the dreadful Cynthia by organising her demise, and he had directly killed a mad scientist who was determined to put an end to the world.

'A service to mankind – in both cases,' he whispered.

He had lost his appetite for right-wing politics, not that he was ever an activist or anything like that.

'Those beautiful Asian girls. Wow! What an experience that evening was!'

A pang of sadness hit him when he thought of Ernest Clamp. He would never see him again – as far as he knew. It was all too much for Woodhead to comprehend in the peace of this Scottish woodland. The strain had been immense. But that was over now. When he reached the moss-covered cross, he shined the light from his torch at his compass. More as an academic exercise than a necessary action, he took the compass bearing and measured the distance from the cross and marked the point of inter-section. He sunk the blade edge of his spade into the earth. It was soft!

'Oh my God! Oh my God! Somebody's been here!'

In panic, he ripped at the earth with his bare hands. 'It's gone! The casket's gone!'

Unable to believe the terrible truth, he continued to dig, tears welling in his eyes. Suddenly, bright halogen lights flashed on.

'Hello, Mr Woodhead, I'm Doctor Alison Hatt, finder of *Hoard*. I found your treasure hunt absolutely hypnotic. Let me introduce you to the press.'